1991

To Gavin—

This book should be one of every young man's introductions to literature. Mr Compton, Mr Clemens. Mr Clemens...

Love,
Chuck

THE BOOKLOVERS LIBRARY

TOM SAWYER

BY

MARK TWAIN

THE ADVENTURES OF
TOM SAWYER

CHAPTER I

" Tom ! "

No answer.

" Tom ! "

No answer.

" What's gone with that boy, I wonder ? You Tom ! "

The old lady pulled her spectacles down and looked over them, about the room ; then she put them up and looked out under them. She seldom or never looked *through* them for so small a thing as a boy, for they were her state pair, the pride of her heart, and were built for " style " not service ; she could have seen through a pair of stove lids as well. She looked perplexed a moment and said, not fiercely, but still loud enough for the furniture to hear, " Well, I lay if I get hold of you, I'll——"

She did not finish, for by this time she was bending down and punching under the bed with the broom—and so she needed breath to punctuate the punches with. She resurrected nothing but the cat.

" I never did see the beat of that boy ! "

She went to the open door and stood in it, and looked out among the tomato vines and " jimpson " weeds that constituted the garden. No Tom. So she lifted up her voice, at an angle calculated for distance, and shouted,

" Y-o-u-u *Tom !* "

There was a slight noise behind her, and she turned just in time to seize a small boy by the slack of his roundabout and arrest his flight. " There ! I might 'a thought of that closet. What you been doing in there ? "

" Nothing."

" Nothing ! Look at your hands, and look at your mouth. What *is* that truck ? "

" *I* don't know, aunt."

" Well, *I* know. It's jam, that's what it is. Forty times I've said if you didn't let that jam alone I'd skin you. Hand me that switch."

The switch hovered in the air. The peril was desperate.

" My ! Look behind you, aunt ! "

The old lady whirled around and snatched her skirts out of danger, and the lad fled, on the instant, scrambled up the high board fence, and disappeared over it. His aunt Polly stood surprised a moment, and then broke into a gentle laugh.

" Hang the boy ! can't I never learn anything ? Ain't he played me tricks enough like that for me to be looking out for him by this time ? But old fools is the biggest fool there is. Can't learn any old dog new tricks, as the saying is. But, my goodness, he never plays them alike two days, and how is a body to know what's coming ? He 'pears to know just how long he can torment me before I get my dander up, and he knows if he can make out to put me off for a minute, or make me laugh, it's all down again, and I can't hit him a lick. I ain't doing my duty by that boy, and that's the Lord's truth, goodness knows. Spare the rod and spile the child, as the good book says. I'm a-laying up sin and suffering for us both, *I* know. He's full of the old scratch, but laws-a-me! he's my own dead sister's boy, poor thing, and I ain't got the heart to lash him, somehow. Every time I let him off my conscience does hurt me so; and every time I hit him my old heart most breaks. Well-a-well, man that is born of a woman is of few days and full of trouble, as the Scripture says, and I reckon it's so. He'll play hookey this evening,* and I'll just be obliged to make him work to-morrow, to punish him. It's mighty hard to make him work Saturdays, when all the boys is having a holiday, but he hates work more than he hates anything else, and I've got to do some of my duty by him, or I'll be the ruination of the child."

Tom did play hookey, and he had a very good time. He got back home barely in season to help Jim, the small coloured boy, saw next day's wood, and split the kindlings before supper—at least he was there in time to tell his adventures to Jim, while Jim did three fourths of the work. Tom's younger brother (or rather half-brother), Sid, was already through with his part of the work (picking up chips), for he was a quiet boy, and had no adventurous, troublesome ways. While Tom was eating his supper and stealing sugar as opportunity offered, Aunt Polly asked him questions that were full of guile, and very deep—for she wanted to trap him

* South-western for " afternoon."

into damaging revealments. Like many other simple-hearted souls, it was her pet vanity to believe she was endowed with a talent for dark and mysterious diplomacy, and she loved to contemplate her most transparent devices as marvels of low cunning. Said she, " Tom, it was middling warm in school, warn't it ? "

" Yes, 'm."

" Powerful warm, warn't it ? "

" Yes, 'm."

" Didn't you want to go in a-swimming, Tom ? "

A bit of a scare shot through Tom—a touch of uncomfortable suspicion. He searched Aunt Polly's face, but it told him nothing. So he said :

" No, 'm——well, not very much."

The old lady reached out her hand and felt Tom's shirt, and said :

" But you ain't too warm now, though."

And it flattered her to reflect that she had discovered that the shirt was dry without anybody knowing that that was what she had in her mind. But in spite of her Tom knew where the wind lay now. So he forestalled what might be the next move.

" Some of us pumped on our heads—mine's damp yet. See ? "

Aunt Polly was vexed to think she had overlooked that bit of circumstantial evidence and missed a trick. Then she had a new inspiration :

" Tom, you didn't have to undo your shirt collar where I sewed it to pump on your head, did you ? Unbutton your jacket ! "

The trouble vanished out of Tom's face. He opened his jacket. His shirt collar was securely sewed.

" Bother ! Well, go 'long with you. I made sure you'd played hookey and been a-swimming. But I forgive ye, Tom, I reckon you're a kind of a singed cat, as the saying is—better'n you look. *This* time."

She was half sorry her sagacity had miscarried, and half glad that Tom had stumbled into obedient conduct for once.

But Sidney said :

" Well, now, if I didn't think you sewed his collar with white thread, but it's black."

" Why, I did sew it with white ! Tom ! "

But Tom did not wait for the rest. As he went out of the door, he said,

" Siddy, I'll lick you for that."

In a safe place Tom examined two large needles which were thrust into the lappels of his jacket— and had thread bound about them—one needle carried white thread and the other black. He said :

" She'd never noticed if it hadn't been for Sid. Confound it, sometimes she sews it with white and sometimes she sews it with black. I wish to gee-miny she'd stick to one or t'other—*I* can't keep the run of 'em. But I bet you I'll lam Sid for that. If I don't, blame my cats."

He was not the model boy of the village. He knew the model boy very well, though, and loathed him.

Within two minutes, or even less, he had forgotten all his troubles. Not because his troubles were one whit less heavy and bitter to him than a man's are to a man, but because a new and powerful in-terest bore them down and drove them out of his mind for the time ; just as men's misfortunes are forgotten in the excitement of new enterprises.

This new interest was a valued novelty in whistling, which he had just acquired from a negro, and he was suffering to practise it undisturbed. It consisted in a peculiar bird-like turn, a sort of liquid warble, produced by touching the tongue to the roof of the mouth at short intervals in the midst of the music. The reader probably remembers how to do it if he has ever been a boy. Diligence and attention soon gave him the knack of it, and he strode down the street with his mouth full of harmony and his soul full of gratitude. He felt much as an astronomer feels who has discovered a new planet. No doubt as far as strong, deep, unalloyed pleasure is concerned, the advantage was with the boy, not the astronomer.

The summer evenings were long. It was not dark yet. Presently Tom checked his whistle. A stranger was before him ; a boy a shade larger than himself. A new-comer of any age or either sex was an impressive curiosity in the poor little village of St Petersburg. This boy was well dressed, too—well dressed on a weekday. This was simply astounding. His cap was a dainty thing, his close-buttoned blue cloth roundabout was new and natty, and so were his pantaloons. He had shoes on, and yet it was only Friday. He even wore a neck-tie, a bright bit of ribbon. He had a citified air about him that ate into Tom's vitals. The more Tom stared at the splendid marvel, the higher he turned up his nose at his finery, and the shabbier and shabbier his own outfit seemed to him to grow. Neither boy spoke. If one moved the other moved—but only sidewise, in a circle They kept face to face and eye to eye all the time. Finally, Tom said :

" I can lick you ! "

" I'd like to see you try it."

" Well, I can do it."

" No, you can't either."

" Yes, I can."

" No, you can't."

" I can."

" You can't."

" Can."

" Can't."

An uncomfortable pause.   Then Tom said :

" What's your name ? "

" Tisn't any of your business, maybe."

" Well, I 'low I'll *make* it my business."

" Well, why don't you ? "

" If you say much I will."

" Much—much—much !   There, now."

" Oh, you think you're mighty smart, *don't* you ? I could lick you with one hand tied behind me, if I wanted to."

" Well, why don't you *do* it ?   You *say* you can do it."

" Well, I *will*, if you fool with me."

" Oh yes, I've seen whole families in the same fix."

" Smarty ! you think you're *some* now, *don't* you ? "

" Oh, what a hat ! "

" You can lump that hat if you don't like it. I dare you to knock it off ; and anybody that'll take a dare will suck eggs."

" You're a liar ! "

" You're another."

" You're a fighting liar, and darn't take it up."

" Aw—take a walk ! "

" Say—if you give me much more of your sass, I'll take and bounce a rock off'n your head."

" Oh, of *course* you will."

" Well, I *will*."

" Well, why don't you *do* it, then ? What do you keep *saying* you will, for ? Why don't you *do* it ? It's because you're afraid."

" I *ain't* afraid."

" You are."

" I ain't."

" You are."

Another pause, and more eyeing and sidling around each other. Presently they were shoulder to shoulder. Tom said :

" Get away from here ! "

" Get away yourself ! "

" I won't."

" *I* won't, either."

So they stood, each with a foot placed at an angle as a brace, and both shoving with might and main, and glowering at each other with hate. But neither could get an advantage. After struggling till both were hot and flushed, each relaxed his strain with watchful caution, and Tom said :

" You're a coward and a pup. I'll tell my big brother on you, and he can lam you with his little finger, and I'll make him do it, too."

" What do I care for your big brother ? I've got a brother that's bigger than he is ; and, what's more, he can throw him over that fence, too." (Both brothers were imaginary.)

" That's a lie."

" *Your* saying so don't make it so."

Tom drew a line in the dust with his big toe, and said :

" I dare you to step over that, and I'll lick you till you can't stand up. Anybody that'll take a dare will steal a sheep."

The new boy stepped over promptly, and said :

" Now you said you'd do it, now let's see you do it."

" Don't you crowd me, now ; you'd better look out."

" Well, you *said* you'd do it—why don't you do it ? "

" By jingoes, for two cents I *will* do it."

The new boy took two broad coppers out of his pocket, and held them out with derision.

Tom struck them to the ground.

In a instant both boys were rolling and tumbling in the dirt, gripped together like cats ; and for the space of a minute they tugged and tore at each other's hair and clothes, punched and scratched each other's noses, and covered themselves with dust and glory. Presently the confusion took form, and through the fog of battle Tom appeared, seated astride the new boy, and pounding him with his fists.

" Holler 'nuff ! " said he.

The boy only struggled to free himself. He was crying, mainly from rage.

" Holler 'nuff ! " and the pounding went on.

At last the stranger got out a smothered " 'nuff ! " and Tom let him up, and said, " Now that'll learn you. Better look out who you're fooling with next time."

The new boy went off brushing the dust from his clothes, sobbing, snuffling, and occasionally looking back and shaking his head, and threatening what he would do to Tom the " next time he caught him out." To which Tom responded with jeers, and started off in high feather ; and as soon as his back was turned the new boy snatched up a stone, threw it. and hit him between the shoulders, and then turned tail and ran like an antelope. Tom chased the traitor home, and thus found out where he lived. He then held a position at the gate for some time, daring the enemy to come outside ; but the enemy only made faces at him through the window, and declined. At last the enemy's mother appeared, and called Tom a bad, vicious, vulgar child, and ordered him away. So he went away, but he said he " 'lowed " to " lag " for that boy.

He got home pretty late that night, and when he climbed cautiously in at the window he uncovered an ambuscade in the person of his aunt ; and when she saw the state his clothes were in, her resolution to turn his Saturday holiday into captivity at hard labour became adamantine in its firmness.

CHAPTER II

SATURDAY morning was come and all the summer world was bright and fresh, and brimming with life. There was a song in every heart ; and if the heart was young the music issued at the lips. There was cheer in every face, and a spring in every step. The locust trees were in bloom, and the fragrance of the blossoms filled the air.

Cardiff Hill, beyond the village and above it, was green with vegetation, and it lay just far enough away to seem a Delectable Land, dreamy, reposeful, and inviting.

Tom appeared on the side-walk with a bucket of whitewash and a long-handled brush. He surveyed the fence, and the gladness went out of nature, and a deep melancholy settled down upon his spirit. Thirty yards of broad fence nine feet high ! It seemed to him that life was hollow, and existence but a burden. Sighing he dipped his brush and passed it along the topmost plank ; repeated the operation ; did it again ; compared the insignificant whitewashed streak with the far-reaching continent of unwhitewashed fence, and sat down on a tree-box discouraged. Jim came skipping out at the gate with a tin pail, and singing " Buffalo Gals." Bringing water from the town pump had always been hateful work in Tom's eyes before, but now it did not strike him so. He remembered that there was company at the pump. White, mulatto, and negro boys and girls were always there waiting their turns, resting, trading playthings, quarrelling, fighting, skylarking. And he remembered that although the pump was only a hundred and fifty yards off, Jim never got back with a bucket of water under an hour; and even then somebody generally had to go after him. Tom said:

" Say, Jim; I'll fetch the water if you'll whitewash some."

Jim shook his head, and said:

" Can't, Ma'rs Tom. Ole missis she tole me I got to go an' git dis water an' not stop foolin' 'roun wid anybody. She say she spec' Ma'rs Tom gwyne to ax me to whitewash, an' so she tole me go 'long an' 'tend to my own business—she 'lowed *she'd* 'tend to de whitewashin'.' "

" Oh, never you mind what she said, Jim. That's the way she always talks. Gimme the bucket—I won't be gone only a minute. *She* won't ever know."

" Oh, I dasn't, Ma'rs Tom. Ole missis she'd take an' tar de head off'n me. 'Deed she would."

" *She!* she never licks anybody—whacks 'em over the head with her thimble, and who cares for that, I'd like to know? She talks awful, but talk don't hurt—anyways, it don't if she don't cry. Jim, I'll give you a marble. I'll give you a white alley!"

Jim began to waver.

" White alley, Jim; and it's a bully tow."

" My; dat's a mighty gay marvel, *I* tell you. But, Ma'rs Tom, I's powerful 'fraid ole missis."

But Jim was only human—this attraction was too much for him. He put down his pail, took the white alley. In another minute he was flying down the street with his pail and a tingling rear,

Tom was whitewashing with vigour, and Aunt Polly was retiring from the field with a slipper in her hand and triumph in her eye.

But Tom's energy did not last. He began to think of the fun he had planned for this day, and his sorrows multiplied. Soon the free boys would come tripping along on all sorts of delicious expeditions, and they would make a world of fun of him for having to work —the very thought of it burnt him like fire. He got out his worldly wealth and examined it—bits of toys, marbles, and trash; enough to buy an exchange of work maybe, but not enough to buy so much as half-an-hour of pure freedom. So he returned his straitened means to his pocket, and gave up the idea of trying to buy the boys. At this dark and hopeless moment an inspiration burst upon him. Nothing less than a great, magnificent inspiration. He took up his brush and went tranquilly to work. Ben Rogers hove in sight presently; the very boy of all boys whose ridicule he had been dreading. Ben's gait was the hop, skip, and jump —proof enough that his heart was light and his anticipations high. He was eating an apple, and giving a long, melodious whoop at intervals, followed by a deep-toned ding dong dong, dong dong dong, for he was personating a steamboat. As he drew near he slackened speed, took the middle of the street, leaned far over to starboard, and rounded-to ponderously, and with laborious pomp and circumstance, for he was personating the *Big Missouri*, and considered himself to be drawing nine feet of water. He was boat, and captain, and engine-bells combined, so he had to imagine himself standing on his own hurricane-deck giving the orders and executing them.

"Stop her, sir! Ling-a-ling-ling." The headway ran almost out, and he drew up slowly toward the side-walk. "Ship up to back! Ling-a-ling-ling!" His arms straightened and stiffened down his sides. "Set her back on the stabboard! Ling-a-ling-ling! Chow! ch-chow-wow-chow!" his right hand meantime describing stately circles, for it was representing a forty-foot wheel. "Let her go back on the labboard! Ling-a-ling-ling! Chow-ch-chow-chow!" The left hand began to describe circles.

"Stop the stabboard! Ling-a-ling-ling! Stop the labboard! Come ahead on the stabboard! Stop her! Let your outside turn over slow! Ling-a-ling-ling! Chow-ow-ow! Get out that head-line! Lively, now! Come—out with your spring line— what're you about there? Take a turn round that stump with the bight of it! Stand by that stage now—let her go! Done with the engines, sir! Ling-a-ling-ling!"

"Sht! s'sht! sht!" (Trying the gauge-cocks.)

Tom went on whitewashing—paid no attention to the steamer. Ben stared a moment, and then said:

"Hi-yi! You're up a stump, ain't you!"

No answer. Tom surveyed his last touch with the eye of an artist; then he gave his brush another gentle sweep, and surveyed the result as before. Ben ranged up alongside of him. Tom's mouth watered for the apple, but he stuck to his work. Ben said:

"Hello, old chap! you got to work, hey?"

"Why, it's you, Ben! I warn't noticing."

"Say, I'm going in a-swimming, I am. Don't you wish you could? But of course you'd druther work, wouldn't you? 'Course you would!"

Tom contemplated the boy a bit, and said:

"What do you call work?"

"Why, ain't that work?"

Tom resumed his whitewashing, and answered carelessly:

"Well, maybe it is, and maybe it ain't. All I know is, it suits Tom Sawyer."

"Oh, come now, you don't mean to let on that you like it?"

The brush continued to move.

"Like it? Well, I don't see why I oughtn't to like it. Does a boy get a chance to whitewash a fence every day?"

That put the thing in a new light. Ben stopped nibbling his apple. Tom swept his brush daintily back and forth—stepped back to note the effect—added a touch here and there—criticised the effect again, Ben watching every move, and getting more and more interested, more and more absorbed. Presently he said:

"Say, Tom, let me whitewash a little."

Tom considered; was about to consent; but he altered his mind: "No, no; I reckon it wouldn't hardly do, Ben. You see, Aunt Polly's awful particular about this fence—right here on the street, you know—but if it was the back fence I wouldn't mind, and she wouldn't. Yes, she's awful particular about this fence; it's got to be done very careful; I reckon there ain't one boy in a thousand, maybe two thousand, that can do it the way it's got to be done."

"No—is that so? Oh, come now; lemme just try, only just a little. I'd let you, if you was me, Tom."

"Ben, I'd like to, honest injun; but Aunt Polly—

well, Jim wanted to do it, but she wouldn't let him. Sid wanted to do it, but she wouldn't let Sid. Now, don't you see how I am fixed? If you was to tackle this fence, and anything was to happen to it——"

"Oh, shucks; I'll be just as careful. Now lemme try. Say—I'll give you the core of my apple."

"Well, here. No, Ben; now don't; I'm afeard——"

"I'll give you all of it!"

Tom gave up the brush with reluctance in his face, but alacrity in his heart. And while the late steamer *Big Missouri* worked and sweated in the sun, the retired artist sat on a barrel in the shade close by, dangled his legs, munched his apple, and planned the slaughter of more innocents. There was no lack of material; boys happened along every little while; they came to jeer, but remained to whitewash. By the time Ben was fagged out, Tom had traded the next chance to Billy Fisher for a kite in good repair; and when he played out, Johnny Miller bought in for a dead rat and a string to swing it with; and so on, and so on, hour after hour. And when the middle of the afternoon came, from being a poor poverty-stricken boy in the morning, Tom was literally rolling in wealth. He had, besides the things I have mentioned, twelve marbles, part of a jew's harp, a piece of blue bottle-glass to look through, a spool-cannon, a key that wouldn't unlock anything, a fragment of chalk, a glass stopper of a decanter, a tin soldier, a couple of tadpoles, six fire-crackers, a kitten with only one eye, a brass door-knob, a dog-collar—but no dog —the handle of a knife, four pieces of orange-peel, and a dilapidated old window-sash. He had had a nice, good, idle time all the while—plenty of company— and the fence had three coats of whitewash on it!

If he hadn't run out of whitewash, he would have bankrupted every boy in the village.

Tom said to himself that it was not such a hollow world after all. He had discovered a great law of human action, without knowing it, namely, that, in order to make a man or a boy covet a thing, it is only necessary to make the thing difficult to attain. If he had been a great and wise philosopher, like the writer of this book, he would now have comprehended that work consists of whatever a body is obliged to do, and that play consists of whatever a body is not obliged to do. And this would help him to understand why constructing artificial flowers, or performing on a tread-mill, is work, whilst rolling nine-pins or climbing Mont Blanc is only amusement. There are wealthy gentlemen in England who drive four-horse passenger-coaches twenty or thirty miles on a daily line, in the summer, because the privilege costs them considerable money; but if they were offered wages for the service, that would turn it into work, and then they would resign.

CHAPTER III

TOM presented himself before Aunt Polly, who was sitting by an open window in a pleasant rearward apartment which was bedroom, breakfast-room, dining-room, and library combined. The balmy summer air, the restful quiet, the odour of the flowers, and the drowsing murmur of the bees, had had their effect, and she was nodding over her knitting—for she had no company but the cat, and it was asleep in her lap. Her spectacles were propped up on her grey head for safety. She had thought that of course Tom had deserted long ago, and she wondered to see him place himself in her power again in this intrepid way. He said:

"Mayn't I go and play now, aunt?"

"What, a'ready? How much have you done?"

"It's all done, aunt."

"Tom, don't lie to me. I can't bear it."

"I ain't, aunt; it *is* all done."

Aunt Polly placed small trust in such evidence. She went out to see for herself; and she would have been content to find twenty per cent. of Tom's statement true. When she found the entire fence whitewashed, and not only whitewashed but elaborately coated and recoated, and even a streak added to the ground, her astonishment was almost unspeakable. She said:

"Well, I never! There's no getting around it: you *can* work when you're a mind to, Tom." And then she diluted the compliment by adding, " But it's powerful seldom you're a mind to, I'm bound to say. Well, go 'long and play ; but mind you get back some time in a week, or I'll tan you."

She was so overcome by the splendour of his achievement that she took him into the closet and selected a choice apple, and delivered it to him, along with an improving lecture upon the added value and flavour a treat took to itself when it came without sin through virtuous effort. And while she closed with a happy Scriptural flourish, he " hooked " a doughnut.

Then he skipped out, and saw Sid just starting up the outside stairway that led to the back rooms on the second floor. Clods were handy, and the air was full of them in a twinkling. They raged around Sid like a hailstorm ; and before Aunt Polly could collect her surprised faculties and rally to the rescue, six or seven clods had taken personal effect, and Tom was over the fence and gone. There was a gate, but as a general thing he was too crowded for time to make use of it. His soul was at peace, now that he had settled with Sid for calling attention to his black thread and getting him into trouble.

Tom skirted the block and came around into a muddy alley that led by the back of his aunt's cow stable. He presently got safely beyond the reach of capture and punishment, and wended towards the public square of the village, where two " military " companies of boys had met for conflict, according to previous appointment. Tom was general of one of these armies, Joe Harper (a bosom friend) general of the other. These two great commanders did not condescend to fight in person—that being better suited to the smaller fry—but sat together on an eminence and conducted the field operations by orders delivered through aides-de-camp. Tom's army won a great victory, after a long and hard-fought battle. Then the dead were counted, prisoners exchanged, the terms of the next disagreement agreed upon, and the day for the necessary battle appointed ; after which the armies fell into line and marched away, and Tom turned homeward alone.

As he was passing by the house where Jeff Thatcher lived, he saw a new girl in the garden—a lovely little blue-eyed creature with yellow hair plaited into two long tails, white summer frock, and embroidered pantalettes. The fresh-crowned hero fell without firing a shot. A certain Amy Lawrence vanished out of his heart, and left not even a memory of herself behind. He had thought he loved her to distraction ; he had regarded his passion as adoration ; and behold it was only a poor little evanescent partiality. He had been months winning her, she had confessed hardly a week ago ; he had been the happiest and the proudest boy in the world only seven short days, and here, in one instant of time, she had gone out of his heart like a casual stranger whose visit is done.

He worshipped this new angel with furtive eye, till he saw that she had discovered him ; then he pretended he did not know she was present, and began to " show off " in all sorts of absurd boyish ways in order to win her admiration. He kept up this grotesque foolishness for some little time ; but by-and-by, while he was in the midst of some danger-ous gymnastic performances, he glanced aside, and saw that the little girl was wending towards the house. Tom came up to the fence, and leaned on it, grieving, and hoping she would tarry yet a while longer. She halted a moment on the steps, and then moved to-wards the door. Tom heaved a great sigh as she put her foot on the threshold, but his face lit up, right away, for she tossed a pansy over the fence a moment before she disappeared. The boy ran around and stopped within a foot or two of the flower, and then shaded his eyes with his hand, and began to look down street as if he had discovered something of interest going on in that direction. Presently he picked up a straw and began trying to balance it on his nose, with his head tilted far back ; and as he moved from side to side in his efforts he edged nearer and nearer towards the pansy ; finally his bare foot rested upon it, his pliant toes closed upon it, and he hopped away with his treasure, and disappeared around the corner. But only for a minute —only while he could button the flower inside his jacket, next his heart, or next his stomach possibly, for he was not much posted in anatomy and not hypercritical anyway.

He returned now and hung about the fence till nightfall, " showing off " as before ; but the girl never exhibited herself again, though Tom comforted himself a little with the hope that she had been near some window meantime, and been aware of his attentions. Finally, he went home reluctantly with his poor head full of visions.

All through supper his spirits were so high that his aunt wondered " what had got into the child." He took a good scolding about clodding Sid, and did not seem to mind it in the least. He tried to steal sugar under his aunt's very nose, and got his knuckles rapped for it. He said :

" Aunt, you don't whack Sid when he takes it."

" Well, Sid don't torment a body the way you do. You'd be always into that sugar if I warn't watching you."

Presently she stepped into the kitchen, and Sid, happy in his immunity, reached for the sugar-bowl, a sort of glorying over Tom which was well-nigh unbearable. But Sid's fingers slipped, and the bowl dropped and broke. Tom was in ecstasies—in such ecstasies that he even controlled his tongue and was silent. He said to himself that he would not speak a word, even when his aunt came in, but would sit perfectly still till she asked who did the mischief; and then he would tell, and there would be nothing so good in the world as to see that pet model " catch it." He was so brimful of exultation that he could hardly hold himself when the old lady came back and stood above the wreck discharging lightnings of wrath from over her spectacles. He said to himself, " Now it's coming ! " And the next instant he was sprawling on the floor ! The potent palm was uplifted to strike again, when Tom cried out :

" Hold on, now, what're you belting *me* for ? Sid broke it ! "

Aunt Polly paused perplexed, and Tom looked for healing pity. But when she got her tongue again she only said :

" Umph ! Well, you didn't get a lick amiss, I reckon. You'd been into some other owdacious mischief when I wasn't around, like enough."

Then her conscience reproached her, and she yearned to say something kind and loving ; but she judged that this would be construed into a confession that she had been in the wrong, and discipline forbade that. So she kept silence, and went about her affairs with a troubled heart. Tom sulked in a corner, and exalted his woes. He knew that in her heart his aunt was on her knees to him, and he was morosely gratified by the consciousness of it. He would hang out no signals, he would take notice of none. He knew that a yearning glance fell upon him, now and then, through a film of tears, but he refused recognition of it. He pictured himself lying sick unto death and his aunt bending over him, beseeching one little forgiving word, but he would turn his face to the wall, and die with that word unsaid. Ah, how would she feel then? And he pictured himself brought home from the river, dead, with his curls all wet, and his poor hands still for ever, and his sore heart at rest. How she would throw herself upon him, and how her tears would fall like rain, and her lips pray God to give her back her boy, and she would never, never, abuse him any more! But he would lie there cold and white and make no sign—a poor little sufferer whose griefs were at an end. He so worked upon his feelings with the pathos of these dreams that he had to keep swallowing—he was so like to choke; and his eyes swam in a blur of water, which overflowed when he winked, and ran down and trickled from the end of his nose. And such a luxury to him was this petting of his sorrows, that he could not bear to have any worldly cheeriness or any grating delight intrude upon it; it was too sacred for such contact; and so presently, when his cousin Mary danced in, all alive with the joy of seeing home again after an age-long visit of one week to the country, he got up and moved in clouds and darkness out at one door as she brought song and sunshine in at the other. He wandered far away from the accustomed haunts of boys, and sought desolate places that were in harmony with his spirit. A log raft in the river invited him, and he seated himself on its outer edge, and contemplated the dreary vastness of the stream, wishing the while that he could only be drowned all at once and unconsciously, without undergoing the uncomfortable routine devised by nature. Then he thought of his flower. He got it out, rumpled and wilted, and it mightily increased his dismal felicity. He wondered if *she* would pity him if she knew? Would she cry, and wish that she had a right to put her arms around his neck and comfort him? Or would she turn coldly away like all the hollow world? This picture brought such an agony of pleasurable suffering that he worked it over and over again in his mind and set it up in new and varied lights till he wore it threadbare. At last he rose up sighing and departed in the darkness. About half-past nine or ten o'clock he came along the deserted street to where the adored unknown lived; he paused a moment, no sound fell upon his listening ear; a candle was casting a dull glow upon the curtain of a second-story window. Was the sacred presence there? He climbed the fence, threaded his stealthy way through the plants, till he stood under that window; he looked up at it long, and with emotion; then he laid him down on the ground under it, disposing himself upon his back, with his hands clasped upon his breast, and holding his poor wilted flower. And thus he would die— out in the cold world with no shelter over his homeless head, no friendly hand to wipe the death-damps from his brow, no loving face to bend pityingly over him when the great agony came. And thus *she* would see him when she looked out upon the glad morning—and oh, would she drop one tear upon his poor lifeless form, would she heave one little sigh to see a bright young life so rudely blighted, so untimely cut down?

The window went up; a maid-servant's discordant

voice profaned the holy calm, and a deluge of water drenched the prone martyr's remains !

The strangling hero sprang up with a relieving snort ; there was a whiz as of a missile in the air, mingled with the murmur of a curse, a sound as of shivering glass followed, and a small vague form went over the fence and shot away in the gloom.

Not long after, as Tom, all undressed for bed, was surveying his drenched garments by the light of a tallow dip, Sid woke up ; but if he had any dim idea of making "references to allusions," he thought better of it, and held his peace—for there was danger in Tom's eye. Tom turned in without the added vexation of prayers, and Sid made mental note of the omission.

CHAPTER IV

THE sun rose upon a tranquil world, and beamed down upon the peaceful village like a benediction. Breakfast over, Aunt Polly had family worship ; it began with a prayer built from the ground up of solid courses of scriptural quotations wedded together with a thin mortar of originality ; and from the summit of this she delivered a grim chapter of the Mosaic Law, as from Sinai.

Then Tom girded up his loins, so to speak, and went to work to " get his verses." Sid had learned his lesson days before. Tom bent all his energies to the memorising of five verses ; and he chose part of the Sermon on the Mount, because he could find no verses that were shorter.

At the end of half-an-hour Tom had a vague general idea of his lesson, but no more, for his mind was traversing the whole field of human thought, and his hands were busy with distracting recreations. Mary took his book to hear him recite, and he tried to find his way through the fog.

" Blessed are the—a—a—"

" Poor—"

" Yes—poor ; blessed are the poor—a—a—"

" In spirit—"

" In spirit ; blessed are the poor in spirit, for they —they—"

" Theirs—"

28

" For theirs. Blessed are the poor in spirit, for theirs—is the kingdom of heaven. Blessed are they that mourn, for they—they—"

" Sh—"

" For they—a—"

" S-H-A—"

" For they S-H—. Oh, I don't know what it is !

" Shall ! "

" Oh, shall ! for they shall—for they shall—a—a —shall mourn—a—a—blessed are they that shall— they that—a—they that shall mourn, for they shall —a—shall what ? Why don't you tell me, Mary ? What do you want to be so mean for ? "

" Oh, Tom, you poor thick-headed thing, I'm not teasing you. I wouldn't do that. You must go and learn it again. Don't you be discouraged, Tom, you'll manage it—and if you do, I'll give you some-thing ever so nice ! There, now, that's a good boy."

" All right ! What is it, Mary ? tell me what it is."

" Never you mind, Tom. You know if I say it's nice, it is nice."

" You bet you that's so, Mary. All right, I'll tackle it again."

And he did " tackle it again " ; and under the double pressure of curiosity and prospective gain, he did it with such spirit that he accomplished a shining success.

Mary gave him a bran-new " Barlow " knife, worth twelve and a half cents ; and the convulsion of delight that swept his system shook him to his foundations. True, the knife would not cut anything, but it was a " sure-enough " Barlow, and there was inconceivable grandeur in that—though where the western boys ever got the idea that such a weapon could possibly be counterfeited to its injury, is an imposing mystery, and will always remain so, perhaps. Tom contrived to scarify the cupboard with it and was arranging to begin on the bureau, when he was called off to dress for Sunday-school.

Mary gave him a tin basin of water and a piece of soap, and he went outside the door and set the basin on a little bench there ; then he dipped the soap in the water and laid it down ; turned up his sleeves ; poured out the water on the ground gently, and then entered the kitchen, and began to wipe his face diligently on the towel behind the door. But Mary removed the towel and said :

" Now ain't you ashamed, Tom ? You mustn't be so bad. Water won't hurt you."

Tom was a trifle disconcerted. The basin was re-filled, and this time he stood over it a little while, gathering resolution ; took in a big breath and began. When he entered the kitchen presently, with both eyes shut, and groping for the towel with his hands, an honourable testimony of suds and water was dripping from his face. But when he emerged from the towel, he was not yet satisfactory ; for the clean territory stopped short at his chin and his jaws like a mask ; below and beyond this line there was a dark expanse of unirrigated soil that spread downward in front and backward around his neck. Mary took him in hand, and when she was done with him he was a man and a brother, without distinction of colour, and his saturated hair was neatly brushed, and its short curls wrought into a dainty and symmetrical general effect. (He privately smoothed out the curls, with labour and difficulty, and plastered his hair close down to his head ; for he held curls to be effeminate, and his own filled his life with bitterness.)

Then Mary got out a suit of his clothing that had been used only on Sundays during two years—they were simply called his " other clothes "—and so by that we know the size of his wardrobe. The girl " put him to rights " after he had dressed himself ; she buttoned his neat roundabout up to his chin, turned his vast shirt-collar down over his shoulders, brushed him off and crowned him with his speckled straw hat. He now looked exceedingly improved and uncomfortable ; and he was fully as uncomfortable as he looked ; for there was a restraint about whole clothes and cleanliness that galled him. He hoped that Mary would forget his shoes, but the hope was blighted ; she coated them thoroughly with tallow, as was the custom, and brought them out. He lost his temper and said he was always being made to do everything he didn't want to do. But Mary said persuasively :

" Please, Tom—that's a good boy."

So he got into his shoes, snarling. Mary was soon ready, and the three children set out for Sunday-school, a place that Tom hated with his whole heart ; but Sid and Mary were fond of it.

Sabbath-school hours were from nine to half-past ten ; and then church service. Two of the children always remained for the sermon voluntarily ; and the other always remained, too—for stronger reasons. The church's high-backed uncushioned pews would seat about three hundred persons ; the edifice was but a small, plain affair, with a sort of pine-board tree-box on top of it for a steeple. At the door Tom dropped back a step and accosted a Sunday-dressed comrade :

" Say, Bill, got a yaller ticket ? "

" Yes."

" What'll you take for her ? "

" What'll you give ? "

" Piece of lickrish and a fish-hook."

" Less see 'em."

Tom exhibited. They were satisfactory, and the property changed hands. Then Tom traded a couple of white alleys for three red tickets, and some small trifle or other for a couple of blue ones. He waylaid other boys as they came, and went on buying tickets of various colours ten or fifteen minutes longer. He entered the church, now, with a swarm of clean and noisy boys and girls, proceeded to his seat and started a quarrel with the first boy that came handy. The teacher, a grave, elderly man, interfered; then turned his back a moment, and Tom pulled a boy's hair in the next bench, and was absorbed in his book when the boy turned around ; stuck a pin in another boy, presently, in order to hear him say " Ouch ! " and got a new reprimand from his teacher. Tom's whole class were of a pattern—restless, noisy, and troublesome. When they came to recite their lessons, not one of them knew his verses perfectly, but had to be prompted all along. However, they worried through, and each got his reward in small blue tickets, each with a passage of Scripture on it ; each blue ticket was pay for two verses of the recitation. Ten blue tickets equalled a red one, and could be exchanged for it ; ten red tickets equalled a yellow one ; for ten yellow tickets the Superintendent gave a very plainly bound Bible (worth forty cents in those easy times) to the pupil. How many of my readers would have the industry and the application to memorise two thousand verses, even for a Doré Bible ? And yet Mary had acquired two Bibles in this way ; it was the patient work of two years : and a boy of German parentage had won four or five. He once recited three thousand verses without stopping ; but the strain upon his mental faculties was too great, and he was little better than an idiot from that day forth—a grievous misfortune for the school, for on great occasions before company, the Superintendent (as Tom expressed it) had always made this boy come out and "spread himself." Only the older pupils managed to keep their tickets and stick to their tedious work long enough to get a Bible, and so the delivery of one of these prizes was a rare and noteworthy circumstance ; the successful pupil was so great and conspicuous for that day that on the spot every scholar's breast was fired with a fresh ambition that often lasted a couple of weeks. It is possible that Tom's mental stomach had never really hungered for one of those prizes, but unquestionably his entire being had for many a day longed for the glory and the éclat that came with it.

In due course the Superintendent stood up in front of the pulpit, with a closed hymn-book in his hand and his forefinger inserted between its leaves, and commanded attention. When a Sunday-school superintendent makes his customary little speech, a hymn-book in the hand is as necessary as is the inevitable sheet of music in the hand of a singer who stands forward on the platform and sings a solo at a concert—though why is a mystery ; for neither the hymn-book nor the sheet of music is even referred to by the sufferer. This superintendent was a slim creature of thirty-five, with a sandy goatee, and short sandy hair ; he wore a stiff standing-collar whose upper edge almost reached his ears, and whose sharp points curved forward abreast the the corners of his mouth—a fence that compelled a

straight lookout ahead, and a turning of the whole
body when a side view was required. His chin was
propped on a spreading cravat, which was as broad
and as long as a bank-note, and had fringed ends ;
his boot toes were turned sharply up, in the fashion
of the day, like sleigh-runners—an effect patiently
and laboriously produced by the young men by sitting with their toes pressed against a wall for hours
together. Mr. Walters was very earnest of mien,
and very sincere and honest at heart ; and he held
sacred things and places in such reverence, and so
separated them from worldly matters, that unconsciously to himself his Sunday-school voice had
acquired a peculiar intonation which was wholly
absent on week-days. He began after this fashion :
" Now, children, I want you all to sit up just as
straight and pretty as you can, and give me all your
attention for a minute or two. There, that is it.
That is the way good little boys and girls should
do. I see one little girl who is looking out of the
window—I am afraid she thinks I am out there
somewhere—perhaps up in one of the trees making
a speech to the little birds. [Applausive titter.]
I want to tell you how good it makes me feel to
see so many bright, clean little faces assembled in a
place like this, learning to do right and be good."

And so forth, and so on. It is not necessary to set
down the rest of the oration. It was of a pattern
which does not vary, and so it is familiar to us all.

The latter third of the speech was marred by the
resumption of fights and other recreations among
certain of the bad boys, and by fidgetings and
whisperings that extended far and wide, washing
even to the bases of isolated and incorruptible rocks
like Sid and Mary. But now every sound ceased

suddenly with the subsidence of Mr. Walter's voice, and the conclusion of the speech was received with a burst of silent gratitude.

A good part of the whispering had been occasioned by an event which was more or less rare—the entrance of visitors; Lawyer Thatcher, accompanied by a very feeble and aged man, a fine, portly, middle-aged gentleman with iron-grey hair, and a dignified lady who was doubtless the latter's wife. The lady was leading a child. Tom had been restless and full of chafings and repinings, conscience-smitten, too,—he could not meet Amy Lawrence's eye, he could not brook her loving gaze. But when he saw this small new-comer his soul was all ablaze with bliss in a moment. The next moment he was "showing off" with all his might—cuffing boys, pulling hair, making faces, in a word, using every art that seemed likely to fascinate a girl, and win her applause. His exultation had but one alloy—the memory of his humiliation in this angel's garden; and that record in sand was fast washing out under the waves of happiness that were sweeping over it now. The visitors were given the highest seat of honour, and as soon as Mr. Walters' speech was finished, he introduced them to the school. The middle-aged man turned out to be a prodigious personage; no less an one than the county judge—altogether the most august creation these children had ever looked upon; and they wondered what kind of material he was made of; and they half wanted to hear him roar, and were half afraid he might, too. He was from Constantinople, twelve miles away—so he had travelled and seen the world—these very eyes had looked upon the County Court House, which was

said to have a tin roof. The awe which these
reflections inspired was attested by the impressive
silence and the ranks of staring eyes. This was the
great Judge Thatcher, brother of their own lawyer.
Jeff Thatcher immediately went forward to be
familiar with the great man and be envied by the
school. It would have been music to his soul to
hear the whisperings.

"Look at him, Jim! he's a going up there. Say
look! he's a going to shake hands with him; he *is*
a shaking hands with him. By jinks, don't you
wish you was Jeff?"

Mr. Walters fell to "showing off" with all sorts
of official bustlings and activities, giving orders,
delivering judgments, discharging directions here,
there, and everywhere that he could find a target.
The librarian "showed off," running hither and
thither with his arms full of books and making a
deal of the splutter and fuss that insect authority
delights in. The young lady teachers "showed off"
—bending sweetly over pupils that were lately being
boxed, lifting pretty warning fingers at bad little
boys and patting good ones lovingly. The young
gentleman teachers "showed off" with small scold-
ings and other little displays of authority and fine
attention to discipline; and most of the teachers,
of both sexes, found business up at the library by
the pulpit; and it was business that frequently had
to be done over again two or three times (with much
seeming vexation). The little girls "showed off"
in various ways, and the little boys "showed off"
with such diligence that the air was thick with
paper wads and the murmur of scufflings. And
above it all the great man sat and beamed a majestic
judicial smile upon all the house, and warmed him

self in the sun of his own grandeur, for he was " showing off " too. There was only one thing wanting
to make Mr. Walters' ecstasy complete, and that
was a chance to deliver a Bible-prize and exhibit
a prodigy. Several pupils had a few yellow tickets,
but none had enough—he had been around among
the star pupils inquiring. He would have given
worlds, now, to have that German lad back again
with a sound mind.

And now at this moment, when hope was dead,
Tom Sawyer came forward with nine yellow tickets,
nine red tickets, and ten blue ones, and demanded a
Bible ! This was a thunderbolt out of a clear sky.
Walters was not expecting an application from this
source for the next ten years. But there was no getting around it—here were the certified checks, and
they were good for their face. Tom was therefore
elevated to a place with the Judge and the other
elect, and the great news was announced from head-
quarters. It was the most stunning surprise of
the decade ; and so profound was the sensation that
it lifted the new hero up to the judicial one's altitude,
and the school had two marvels to gaze upon in
place of one. The boys were all eaten up with
envy ; but those that suffered the bitterest pangs
were those who perceived too late that they themselves had contributed to this hated splendour by
trading tickets to Tom for the wealth he had amassed
in selling whitewashing privileges. These despised
themselves, as being the dupes of a wily fraud, a
guileful snake in the grass.

The prize was delivered to Tom with as much
effusion as the Superintendent could pump up under
the circumstances ; but it lacked somewhat of the
true gush, for the poor fellow's instinct taught him

that there was a mystery here that could not well bear the light, perhaps ; it was simply preposterous that *this* boy had warehoused two thousand sheaves of Scriptural wisdom on his premises—a dozen would strain his capacity, without a doubt. Amy Lawrence was proud and glad, and she tried to make Tom see it in her face ; but he wouldn't look. She wondered ; then she was just a grain troubled ; next a dim suspicion came and went—came again ; she watched ; a furtive glance told her worlds— and then her heart broke, and she was jealous, and angry, and the tears came and she hated every- body ; Tom most of all. she thought.

Tom was introduced to the judge ; but his tongue was tied, his breath would hardly come, his heart quaked—partly because of the awful greatness of the man, but mainly because he was *her* parent. He would have liked to fall down and worship him, if it were in the dark. The Judge put his hand on Tom's head and called him a fine little man, and asked him what his name was. The boy stammered, gasped, and got it out.

"Tom."

"Oh no, not Tom—it is——"

"Thomas."

"Ah, that's it. I thought there was more to it, maybe. That's very well. But you've another one I dare say, and you'll tell it to me, won't you ? "

"Tell the gentleman your other name, Thomas," said Walters, "and say *sir*. You mustn't forget your manners."

"Thomas Sawyer—Sir."

"That's it ! that's a good boy. Fine boy. Fine, manly little fellow. Two thousand verses is a great many—very, very great many. And you never

can be sorry for the trouble you took to learn them ;
for knowledge is worth more than anything there
is in the world ; it's what makes great men and good
men ; you'll be a great man and a good man yourself
some day, Thomas, and then you'll look back and
say, It's all owing to the precious Sunday-school
privileges of my boyhood ; it's all owing to my dear
teachers that taught me to learn ; it's all owing to
the good Superintendent, who encouraged me and
watched over me, and gave me a beautiful Bible,
a splendid, elegant Bible, to keep and have it all
for my own, always ; it's all owing to right bringing
up ! That is what you will say, Thomas ; and you
wouldn't take any money for those two thousand
verses, then—no, indeed you wouldn't. And now
you wouldn't mind telling me and this lady some of
the things you've learned—no, I know you wouldn't
—for we are proud of little boys that learn. Now
no doubt you know the names of all the twelve disciples. Won't you tell us the names of the first
two that were appointed ? "

Tom was tugging at a button and looking sheepish.
He blushed, now, and his eyes fell. Mr. Walters'
heart sank within him. He said to himself, It is
not possible that the boy can answer the simplest
question—why *did* the Judge ask him ? Yet he
felt obliged to speak up and say :

" Answer the gentleman, Thomas—don't be
afraid."

Tom still hung fire.

" Now I know you'll tell *me*," said the lady.
" The names of the first two disciples were——"

" DAVID AND GOLIAH ! "

Let us draw the curtain of charity over the rest
of the scene.

CHAPTER V

ABOUT half-past ten the cracked bell of the small church began to ring, and presently the people began to gather for the morning sermon. The Sunday-school children distributed themselves about the house, and occupied pews with their parents, so as to be under supervision. Aunt Polly came, and Tom, and Sid, and Mary sat with her. Tom being placed next the aisle, in order that he might be as far away from the open window and the seductive outside summer scenes as possible. The crowd filed up the aisles ; the aged and needy postmaster, who had seen better days ; the mayor and his wife—for they had a mayor there, among other unnecessaries ; the justice of the peace ; the widow Douglas, fair, smart, and forty, a generous, good-hearted soul and well-to-do, her hill mansion the only palace in the town, and the most hospitable and much the most lavish in the matter of festivities that St. Petersburg could boast ; the bent and venerable mayor and Mrs. Ward ; Lawyer Riverson, the new notable from a distance ; next the belle of the village, followed by a troop of lawn-clad and ribbon-decked young heart-breakers ; then all the young clerks in town in a body—for they had stood in the vestibule sucking their cane-heads, a circling wall of oiled and simpering admirers, till the last girl had run their gauntlet ; and last of all came the model boy, Willie Mufferson, taking as heedful care of his mother as if she were cut glass. He always brought his mother to church, and was the pride of all the matrons. The boys all hated him, he was so good; and besides, he had been " thrown up to them " so much. His white handkerchief was hanging out of his pocket behind, as usual on Sundays—acciden- tally. Tom had no handkerchief and he looked upon boys who had as snobs. The congregation being fully assembled now, the bell rang once more, to warn laggards and stragglers, and then a solemn hush fell upon the church which was only broken by the tittering and whispering of the choir in the gallery. The choir always tittered and whispered all through service. There was once a church choir that was not ill-bred, but I have forgotten where it was, now. It was a great many years ago, and I can scarcely remember anything about it, but I think it was in some foreign country.

The minister gave out the hymn, and read it through with a relish, in a peculiar style which was much admired in that part of the country. His voice began on a medium key, and climbed steadily up till it reached a certain point, where it bore with strong emphasis upon the topmost word, and then plunged down as if from a spring-board.

Shall I be car-ri-ed toe the skies on flow'ry *beds*
of ease,

Whilst others fought toe win the prize, and sailed thro' *blood*-
y seas?

He was regarded as a wonderful reader. At church " sociables " he was always called upon to read poetry ; and when he was through, the ladies would lift up their hands and let them fall helplessly in their laps, and " wall " their eyes, and shake their heads, as much as to say, " Words cannot express it ; it is too beautiful, *too* beautiful for this mortal earth."

After the hymn had been sung, the Rev. Mr. Sprague turned himself into a bulletin board and read off " notices " of meetings and societies and things till it seemed that the list would stretch out to the crack of doom—a queer custom which is still kept up in America, even in cities, away here in this age of abundant newspapers. Often the less there is to justify a traditional custom, the harder it is to get rid of it.

And now, the minister prayed. A good, generous prayer it was, and went into details ; it pleaded for the Church, and the little children of the Church ; for the other churches of the village ; for the village itself ; for the county ; for the State ; for the State officers ; for the United States ; for the churches of the United States ; for Congress ; for the President ; for the officers of the Government ; for poor sailors, tossed by stormy seas ; for the oppressed millions groaning under the heel of European monarchies and Oriental despotisms ; for such as have the light and the good tidings, and yet have not eyes to see nor ears to hear withal ; for the heathen in the far islands of the sea ; and closed with a supplication that the words he was about to speak might find grace and favour, and be as seed sown in fertile ground, yielding in time a grateful harvest of good. Amen.

There was a rustling of dresses, and the standing congregation sat down. The boy whose history

this book relates did not enjoy the prayer, he only
endured it—if he even did that much. He was
restive all through it; he kept tally of the details
of the prayer, unconsciously—for he was not listening, but he knew the ground of old and the clergyman's regular route over it—and when a little trifle
of new matter was interlarded, his ear detected it
and his whole nature resented it; he considered
additions unfair, and scoundrelly. In the midst of
the prayer a fly had lit on the back of the pew in
front of him, and tortured his spirit by calmly rub-
bing its hands together; embracing its head with
its arms and polishing it so vigorously that it seemed
to almost part company with the body, and the
slender thread of a neck was exposed to view; scrap-
ing its wings with its hind legs and smoothing them
to its body as if they had been coat-tails; going
through its whole toilet as tranquilly as if it knew
it was perfectly safe. As indeed it was; for as sorely
as Tom's hands itched to grab for it they did not
dare—he believed his soul would be instantly de-
stroyed if he did such a thing while the prayer was
going on. But with the closing sentence his hand
began to curve and steal forward; and the instant
the "Amen" was out, the fly was a prisoner of war.
His aunt detected the act, and made him let it go.

The minister gave out his text and droned along
monotonously through an argument that was so
prosy that many a head by-and-by began to nod—
and yet it was an argument that dealt in limitless
fire and brimstone, and thinned the predestined elect
down to a company so small as to be hardly worth
the saving. Tom counted the pages of the sermon;
after church he always knew how many pages there
had been, but he seldom knew anything else about

the discourse. However, this time he was really
interested for a little while. The minister made a
grand and moving picture of the assembling together of the world's hosts at the millennium when
the lion and the lamb should lie down together and
a little child should lead them. But the pathos,
the lesson, the moral of the great spectacle were lost
upon the boy ; he only thought of the conspicuous-
ness of the principal character before the on-looking
nations ; his face lit up with the thought, and he
said to himself that he wished he could be that
child, if it was a tame lion.

Now he lapsed into suffering again as the dry
argument was resumed. Presently he bethought
himself of a treasure he had, and got it out. It was
a large black beetle with formidable jaws—a " pinch-
bug," he called it. It was in a percussion-cap box.
The first thing the beetle did was to take him by
the finger. A natural fillip followed, the beetle
went floundering into the aisle, and lit on its back,
and the hurt finger went into the boy's mouth.
The beetle lay there working its helpless legs, unable
to turn over. Tom eyed it, and longed for it, but it
was safe out of his reach. Other people, uninterested
in the sermon, found relief in the beetle, and they
eyed it too.

Presently a vagrant poodle dog came idling along,
sad at heart, lazy with the summer softness and the
quiet, weary of captivity, sighing for change. He
spied the beetle ; the drooping tail lifted and wagged.
He surveyed the prize ; walked around it ; smelt
of it from a safe distance ; walked around it again ;
grew bolder, and took a closer smell ; then lifted his
lip, and made a gingerly snatch at it, just missing
it ; made another, and another ; began to enjoy the

diversion; subsided to his stomach with the beetle between his paws, and continued his experiments; grew weary at last, and then indifferent and absent-minded. His head nodded, and little by little his chin descended and touched the enemy, who seized it. There was a sharp yelp, a flirt of the poodle's head, and the beetle fell a couple of yards away and lit on its back once more. The neighbouring spectators shook with a gentle inward joy, several faces went behind fans and handkerchiefs, and Tom was entirely happy. The dog looked foolish, and probably felt so; but there was resentment in his heart, too, and a craving for revenge. So he went to the beetle and began a wary attack on it again; jumping at it from every point of a circle, lighting with his forepaws within an inch of the creature, making even closer snatches at it with his teeth, and jerking his head till his ears flapped again. But he grew tired once more, after a while; tried to amuse himself with a fly, but found no relief; followed an ant around, with his nose close to the floor, and quickly wearied of that; yawned, sighed, forgot the beetle entirely, and sat down on it. Then there was a wild yelp of agony, and the poodle went sailing up the aisle; the yelps continued, and so did the dog; he crossed the house in front of the altar, he flew down the other aisle; he crossed before the doors; he clamoured up the home-stretch; his anguish grew with his progress, till presently he was but a woolly comet moving in its orbit with the gleam and the speed of light. At last the frantic sufferer sheered from its course and sprang into its master's lap: he flung it out of the window, and the voice of distress quickly thinned away and died in the distance.

By this time the whole church was red-faced and suffocating with suppressed laughter, and the sermon had come to a dead standstill. The discourse was resumed presently, but it went lame and halting, all possibility of impressiveness being at an end; for even the gravest sentiments were constantly being received with a smothered burst of unholy mirth, under cover of some remote pew-back, as if the poor parson had said a rarely facetious thing. It was a genuine relief to the whole congregation when the ordeal was over and the benediction pronounced.

Tom Sawyer went home quite cheerful, thinking to himself that there was some satisfaction about divine service when there was a bit of variety in it. He had but one marring thought; he was willing that the dog should play with his pinch-bug, but he did not think it was upright in him to carry it off.

CHAPTER VI

MONDAY morning found Tom Sawyer miserable.
Monday morning always found him so, because it
began another week's slow suffering in school. He
generally began that day with wishing he had had
no intervening holiday, it made the going into
captivity and fetters again so much more odious.

Tom lay thinking. Presently it occurred to him
that he wished he was sick ; then he could stay home
from school. Here was a vague possibility. He
canvassed his system. No ailment was found, and
he investigated again. This time he thought he
could detect colicky symptoms, and he began to
encourage them with considerable hope. But they
soon grew feeble and presently died wholly away.
He reflected further. Suddenly he discovered
something. One of his upper teeth was loose. This
was lucky ; he was about to begin to groan, as a
" starter," as he called it, when it occurred to him
that if he came into court with that argument his
aunt would pull it out, and that would hurt. So
he thought he would hold the tooth in reserve for
the present, and seek further. Nothing offered for
some little time, and then he remembered hearing
the doctor tell about a certain thing that laid up a
patient for two or three weeks and threatened to
make him lose a finger. So the boy eagerly drew

47

his sore toe from under the sheet and held it up for inspection. But now he did not know the necessary symptoms. However, it seemed well worth while to chance it, so he fell to groaning with considerable spirit.

But Sid slept on, unconscious.

Tom groaned louder, and fancied that he began to feel pain in the toe.

No result from Sid.

Tom was panting with his exertions by this time. He took a rest and then swelled himself up and fetched a succession of admirable groans.

Sid snored on.

Tom was aggravated. He said " Sid, Sid ! " and shook him. This course worked well, and Tom began to groan again. Sid yawned, stretched, then brought himself up on his elbow with a snort, and began to stare at Tom. Tom went on groaning. Sid said :

" Tom ! say Tom ! "

No response.

" Here, Tom ! Tom ! What is the matter, Tom ? " And he shook him, and looked in his face anxiously.

Tom moaned out :

" Oh, don't, Sid. Don't joggle me."

" Why, what's the matter, Tom ? I must call auntie."

" No, never mind. It'll be over by-and-by, maybe. Don't call anybody."

" But I must ! Don't groan so, Tom, it's awful. How long you been this way ? "

" Hours. Ouch ! Oh, don't stir so, Sid. You'll kill me."

" Tom, why didn't you wake me sooner ? Oh,

Tom, don't ! It makes my flesh crawl to hear you. Tom. what is the matter ? "

" I forgive you everything Sid. (Groan.) Everything you've ever done to me. When I'm gone——"

" Oh, Tom, you ain't dying, are you ? Don't, Tom. Oh, don't. Maybe——"

" I forgive everybody Sid. (Groan) Tell 'em so, Sid. And, Sid. you give my window-sash and my cat with one eye to that new girl that's come to town, and tell her——'

But Sid had snatched his clothes and gone. Tom was suffering in reality now, so handsomely was his imagination working, and so his groans had gathered quite a genuine tone.

Sid flew downstairs and said :

" Oh, Aunt Polly, come ! Tom's dying ! "

" Dying ! "

" Yes'm. Don't wait. come quick ! "

" Rubbage ! I don't believe it ! "

But she fled upstairs nevertheless, with Sid and Mary at her heels. And her face grew white, too, and her lips trembled. When she reached the bedside she gasped out :

" You Tom ! Tom, what's the matter with you ? "

" Oh, auntie, I'm ——"

" What's the matter with you—what *is* the matter with you, child ? "

" Oh, auntie, my sore toe's mortified ! "

The old lady sank down into a chair and laughed a little, then cried a little, then did both together. This restored her, and she said :

" Tom, what a turn you did give me. Now you shut up that nonsense and climb out of this."

The groans ceased, and the pain vanished from the toe. The boy felt a little foolish, and he said :

" Aunt Polly, it *seemed* mortified, and it hurt so I never minded my tooth at all."

" Your tooth, indeed! What's the matter with your tooth ? "

" One of them's loose, and it aches perfectly awful."

" There, there now, don't begin that groaning again. Open your mouth. Well, your tooth *is* loose, but you're not going to die about that. Mary, get me a silk thread, and a chunk of fire out of the kitchen."

Tom said :

" Oh, please, auntie, don't pull it out, it don't hurt any more. I wish I may never stir if it does. Please don't, auntie. *I* don't want to stay home from school."

" Oh, you don't, don't you ? So all this row was because you thought you'd get to stay home from school and go a-fishing ? Tom, Tom, I love you so, and you seem to try every way you can to break my old heart with your outrageousness."

By this time the dental instruments were ready. The old lady made one end of the silk thread fast to Tom's tooth with a loop and tied the other to the bedpost. Then she seized the chink of fire and suddenly thrust it almost into the boy's face. The tooth hung dangling by the bedpost, now.

But all trials bring their compensations. As Tom wended to school after breakfast, he was the envy of every boy he met because the gap in his upper row of teeth enabled him to expectorate in a new and admirable way. He gathered quite a following of lads interested in the exhibition ; and one that had cut his finger and had been a centre of fascination and homage up to this time, now found himself suddenly without an adherent, and shorn of his glory. His heart was heavy, and he said with a disdain which he did not feel, that it wasn't anything to spit like Tom Sawyer; but another boy said " Sour grapes ! " and he wandered away a dismantled hero.

Shortly Tom came upon the juvenile pariah of the village, Huckleberry Finn, son of the town drunkard. Huckleberry was cordially hated and dreaded by all the mothers of the town because he was idle, and lawless, and vulgar, and bad—and because all their children admired him so, and delighted in his forbidden society and wished they dared to be like him. Tom was like the rest of the respectable boys in that he envied Huckleberry his gaudy outcast condition, and was under strict orders not to play with him. So he played with him every time he got a chance. Huckleberry was always dressed in the cast-off clothes of full-grown men, and they were in perennial bloom and fluttering with rags. His hat was a vast ruin with a wide crescent lopped out of its brim ; his coat, when he wore one, hung nearly to his heels, and had the rearward buttons far down the back ; but one suspender supported his trousers ; the seat of the trousers bagged low and contained nothing ; the fringed legs dragged in the dirt when not rolled up. Huckleberry came and went at his own free will. He slept on doorsteps in fine weather, and in empty hogsheads in wet ; he did not have to go to school or to church, or call any being master, or obey anybody : he could go fishing or swimming when and where he chose, and stay as long as it suited him ; nobody forbade him to fight ; he could sit up as late as he pleased ; he was always the first boy that went barefoot in the spring and the last to resume leather in the fall ; he never had to wash, nor put on clean clothes ; he could swear wonderfully. In a word, everything that goes to make life precious, that boy had. So thought

every harassed, hampered, respectable boy in St.
Petersburg. Tom hailed the romantic outcast :

" Hello, Huckleberry ! "

" Hello yourself, and see how you like it."

" What's that you got ? "

" Dead cat."

" Lemme see him, Huck. My, he's pretty stiff.
Where'd you get him ? "

" Bought him off 'n a boy."

" What did you give ? "

" I give a blue ticket and a bladder that I got
at the slaughter-house."

" Where'd you get the blue ticket ? "

" Bought it off'n Ben Rogers two weeks ago for a
hoopstick."

" Say—what is dead cats good for, Huck ? "

" Good for ? Cure warts with."

" No ? Is that so ? I know something that's
better."

" I bet you don't. What is it ? "

" Why, spunk water."

" Spunk water ! I wouldn't give a dern for spunk
water."

" You wouldn't, wouldn't you ? D'you ever try
it ? "

" No, I hain't. But Bob Tanner did."

" Who told you so ? "

" Why, he told Jeff Thatcher, and Jeff told
Johnny Baker, and Johnny told Jim Hollis, and Jim
told Ben Rogers, and Ben told a nigger, and the
nigger told me. There, now ! "

" Well, what of it ? They'll all lie. Leastways
all but the nigger, I don't know *him*. But I never
see a nigger that *wouldn't* lie. Shucks ! Now you
tell me how Bob Tanner done it, Huck."

" Why, he took and dipped his hand in a rotten stump where the rain water was."

" In the daytime ? "

" Certainly."

" With his face to the stump ? "

" Yes. Least I reckon so."

" Did he *say* anything ? "

" I don't reckon he did ; I don't know."

" Aha ! Talk about trying to cure warts with spunk water such a blame fool way as that ! Why, that ain't a going to do any good. You got to go by yourself to the middle of the woods, where you know there's a spunk water stump, and just as it's midnight you back up against the stump and jam your hand in and say :—

> Barley-corn, barley-corn, injun-meal shorts,
> Spunk-water, spunk-water, swaller these warts.

and then walk away quick, eleven steps, with your eyes shut, and then turn around three times and walk home without speaking to anybody. Because if you speak the charm's busted."

" Well, that sounds like a good way ; but that ain't the way Bob Tanner done."

" No, sir, you can bet he didn't ; becuz he's the wartiest boy in this town ; and he wouldn't have a wart on him if he'd knowed how to work spunk water. I've took off thousands of warts off of my hands that way, Huck. I play with frogs so much that I've always got considerable many warts. Sometimes I take 'em off with a bean."

" Yes, bean's good. I've done that."

" Have you ? What's your way ? "

" You take and split the bean, and cut the wart so as to get some blood, and then you put the blood on one piece of the bean, and take and dig a hole and bury it 'bout midnight at the cross-roads in the dark of the moon, and then you burn up the rest of the bean. You see that piece that's got the blood on it will keep drawing and drawing, trying to fitch the other piece to it, and so that helps the blood to draw the wart, and pretty soon, off she comes."

"Yes, that's it, Huck—that's it; though, when you're burying it, if you say, ' Down bean, off wart ; come no more to bother me ! ' it's better. That's the way Joe Harper does, and he's ben nearly to Coonville, and most everywhere. But say—how do you cure 'em with dead cats ? "

"Why, you take your cat and go and get in the graveyard, long about midnight, where somebody that was wicked has been buried ; and when it's midnight a devil will come, or maybe two or three, but you can't see 'em, you can only hear something like the wind, or maybe hear 'em talk ; and when they're taking that feller away, you heave your cat after 'em and say, ' Devil follow corpse, cat follow devil, warts follow cat, *I'm* done with ye ! ' That'll fetch *any* wart."

"Sounds right. D'you ever try it, Huck ? "

"No, but old Mother Hopkins told me."

"Well, I reckon it's so, then, becuz they say she's a witch."

"*Say !* Why, Tom, I *know* she is. She witched pap. Pap says so his own self. He came along one day, and he see she was a witching him, so he took up a rock, and if she hadn't dodged he'd a got her. Well, that very night he rolled off'n a shed wher' he was a layin' drunk, and broke his arm."

"Why, that's awful. How did he know she was a witching him."

" Lord, pap can tell, easy. Pap says when they keep looking at you right stiddy, they're a witching you, specially if they mumble. Becuz when they mumble they're a saying the Lord's Prayer backards."

" Say, Hucky, when you going to try the cat ? "

" To-night. I reckon they'll come after old Hoss Williams to-night."

" But they buried him Saturday, Huck. Didn't they get him Saturday night ? "

" Why, how you talk ! How could their charms work till midnight ? and then it's Sunday. Devils don't slosh around much of a Sunday, I don't reckon."

" I never thought of that. That's so. Lemme go with you ? "

" Of course—if you ain't afeard."

" Afeard ! 'Taint likely. Will you meow ? "

" Yes, and you meow back if you get a chance. Last time you kep' me a meowing around till old Hays went to throwing rocks at me, and says, ' Dern that cat ! ' So I hove a brick through his window —but don't you tell."

" I won't. I couldn't meow that night becuz auntie was watching me ; but I'll meow this time. Say, Huck, what's that ? "

" Nothing but a tick."

" Where'd you get him ? "

" Out in the woods."

" What'll you take for him ? "

" I don't know. I don't want to sell him."

" All right. It's a mighty small tick, anyway."

" Oh, anybody can run a tick down that don't belong to them. I'm satisfied with it. It's a good enough tick for me."

" Sho, there's ticks a plenty. I could have a thousand of 'em if I wanted to."

"Well, why don't you? Becuz you know mighty well you can't. This is a pretty early tick, I reckon. It's the first one I've seen this year."

"Say, Huck, I'll give you my tooth for him."

"Less see it."

Tom got out a bit of paper and carefully unrolled it. Huckleberry viewed it wistfully. The temptation was very strong. At last he said :

"Is it genuwyne?"

Tom lifted his lip and showed the vacancy.

"Well, all right," said Huckleberry; "it's a trade."

Tom enclosed the tick in the percussion-cap box that had lately been the pinch-bug's prison, and the boys separated, each feeling wealthier than before.

When Tom reached the little isolated frame school-house, he strode in briskly, with the manner of one who had come with all honest speed. He hung his hat on a peg, and flung himself into his seat with business-like alacrity. The master, throned on high in his great splint-bottom arm-chair, was dozing, lulled by the drowsy hum of study. The interruption roused him :

"Thomas Sawyer!"

Tom knew that when his name was pronounced in full, it meant trouble.

"Sir!"

"Come up here. Now, sir, why are you late again, as usual?"

Tom was about to take refuge in a lie, when he saw two long tails of yellow hair hanging down a back that he recognised by the electric sympathy of love; and by that form was *the only vacant place* on the girls' side of the school-house. He instantly said :

"I STOPPED TO TALK WITH HUCKLEBERRY FINN!"

The master's pulse stood still, and he stared helplessly. The buzz of study ceased ; the pupils wondered if this foolhardy boy had lost his mind. The
master said :

" You—you did what ? "

" Stopped to talk with Huckleberry Finn."

There was no mistaking the words.

" Thomas Sawyer, this is the most astounding
confession I have ever listened to ; no mere ferule
will answer for this offence. Take off your jacket."

The master's arm performed until it was tired,
and the stock of switches notably diminished. Then
the order followed :

" Now, sir, go and sit with the *girls !* And let
this be a warning to you."

The titter that rippled around the room appeared
to abash the boy, but in reality that result was caused
rather more by his worshipful awe of his unknown
idol and the dread pleasure that lay in his high good-
fortune. He sat down upon the end of the pine
bench, and the girl hitched herself away from him
with a toss of the head. Nudges and winks and
whispers traversed the room, but Tom sat still, with
his arms upon the long, low desk before him, and
seemed to study his book. By-and-by attention
ceased from him, and the accustomed school murmur
rose upon the dull air once more. Presently the boy
began to steal furtive glances at the girl. She observed it, " made a mouth " at him, and gave him
the back of her head for the space of a minute.
When she cautiously faced around again, a peach
lay before her. She thrust it away ; Tom gently
put it back ; she thrust it away again, but with less
animosity. Tom patiently returned it to its place ;
then she let it remain. Tom scrawled on his slate,

" Please take it—I got more." The girl glanced at the words, but made no sign. Now the boy began to draw something on the slate, hiding his work with his left hand. For a time the girl refused to notice ; but her human curiosity presently began to manifest itself by hardly perceptible signs. The boy worked on, apparently unconscious. The girl made a sort of non-committal attempt to see, but the boy did not betray that he was aware of it. At last she gave in, and hesitatingly whispered :

" Let me see it."

Tom partly uncovered a dismal caricature of a house with two gable ends to it and a cork-screw of smoke issuing from the chimney. Then the girl's interest began to fasten itself upon the work, and she forgot everything else. When it was finished, she gazed a moment, then whispered :

" It's nice—make a man."

The artist erected a man in the front yard, that resembled a derrick. He could have stepped over the house ; but the girl was not hypercritical ; she was satisfied with the monster, and whispered :

" It's a beautiful man—now make me coming along."

Tom drew an hourglass, with a full moon and straw limbs to it, and armed the spreading fingers with a portentous fan. The girl said :

" It's ever so nice—I wish I could draw."

" It's easy," whispered Tom. " I'll learn you."

" Oh, will you ? When ? "

" At noon. Do you go home to dinner ? "

" I'll stay if you will."

" Good—that's a go."

" What's your name ? "

" Becky Thatcher."

"What's yours? Oh, I know. It's Thomas Sawyer."

"That's the name they lick me by. I'm Tom when I'm good. You call me Tom, will you?"

"Yes."

Now Tom began to scrawl something on the slate, hiding the words from the girl. But she was not backward this time. She begged to see. Tom said:

"Oh, it ain't anything."

"Yes, it is."

"No, it ain't; you don't want to see."

"Yes, I do, indeed I do. Please let me."

"You'll tell."

"No, I won't—deed and deed and double deed I won't."

"You won't tell anybody at all? Ever as long as you live?"

"No, I won't ever tell anybody. Now let me.

"Oh, *you* don't want to see!"

"Now that you treat me so I *will* see, Tom"— and she put her small hand on his, and a little scuffle ensued, Tom pretending to resist in earnest, but letting his hand slip by degrees till these words were revealed: "*I love you.*"

"Oh, you bad thing!" And she hit his hand a smart rap, but reddened and looked pleased nevertheless.

Just at this juncture the boy felt a slow fateful grip closing on his ear, and a steady lifting impulse. In that vice he was borne across the house and deposited in his own seat, under a peppering fire of giggles from the whole school. Then the master stood over him during a few awful moments, and finally moved away to his throne without saying a word. But although Tom's ear tingled, his heart was jubilant.

As the school quieted down, Tom made an honest effort to study, but the turmoil within him was too great. In turn he took his place in the reading class and made a botch of it, then in the geography class and turned lakes into mountains, mountains into rivers, and rivers into continents, till chaos was come again; then in the spelling class, and got " turned down " by a succession of mere baby words till he brought up at the foot and yielded up the pewter medal which he had worn with ostentation for months.

CHAPTER VII

THE harder Tom tried to fasten his mind on his book, the more his ideas wandered. So at last, with a sigh and a yawn, he gave it up. It seemed to him that the noon recess would never come. The air was utterly dead. There was not a breath stirring. It was the sleepiest of sleepy days. The drowsing murmur of the five-and-twenty studying scholars soothed the soul like the spell that is in the murmur of bees. Away off in the flaming sunshine Cardiff Hill lifted its soft green sides through a shimmering veil of heat tinted with the purple of distance ; a few birds floated on lazy wing high in the air ; no other living thing was visible but some cows, and they were asleep.

Tom's heart ached to be free, or else to have something of interest to do to pass the dreary time. His hand wandered into his pocket, and his face lit up with a glow of gratitude that was prayer, though he did not know it. Then furtively the percussion cap box came out. He released the tick, and put him on the long flat desk. The creature probably glowed with a gratitude that amounted to prayer, too, at this moment, but it was premature ; for when he started thankfully to travel off, Tom turned him aside with a pin, and made him take a new direction. Tom's bosom friend sat next him, suffering just as Tom had been, and now he was deeply and gratefully interested in this entertainment in an instant. This bosom friend was Joe Harper. The two boys were sworn friends all the week, and embattled enemies on Saturdays. Joe took a pin out of his lappel, and began to assist in exercising the prisoner. The sport grew in interest momently. Soon Tom said that they were interfering with each other, and neither getting the fullest benefit of the tick. So he put Joe's slate on the desk and drew a line down the middle of it from top to bottom.

"Now," said he, "as long as he is on your side you can stir him up and I'll let him alone: but if you let him get away and get on my side, you're to leave him alone as long as I can keep him from crossing over."

"All right, go ahead—start him up."

The tick escaped from Tom, presently, and crossed the equator. Joe harassed him awhile, and then he got away and crossed back again. This change of base occurred often. While one boy was worrying the tick with absorbing interest, the other would look on with interest as strong, the two heads bowed together over the slate and the two souls dead to all things else. At last luck seemed to settle and abide with Joe. The tick tried this, that, and the other course, and got as excited and as anxious as the boys themselves, but time and again, just as he would have victory in his very grasp, so to speak, and Tom's fingers would be twitching to begin, Joe's pin would deftly head him off and keep possession At last Tom could stand it no longer. The temptation was too strong. So he reached out and lent a hand with his pin. Joe was angry in a moment. Said he:

"Tom, you let him alone."

"I only just want to stir him up a little, Joe."

" No, sir, it ain't fair ; you just let him alone."

" Blame it, I ain't going to stir him much."

" Let him alone, I tell you ! "

" I won't ! "

" You shall—he's on my side of the line."

" Look here, Joe Harper, whose is that tick ? "

" *I* don't care whose tick he is—he's on my side of the line, and you shan't touch him."

" Well, I'll just bet I will, though. He's my tick, and I'll do what I blame please with him, or die ! "

A tremendous whack came down on Tom's shoulders, and its duplicate on Joe's ; and for the space of two minutes the dust continued to fly from the two jackets and the whole school to enjoy it. The boys had been too absorbed to notice the hush that had stolen upon the school a while before when the master came tip-toeing down the room and stood over them. He had contemplated a good part of the performance before he contributed his bit of variety to it. When school broke up at noon, Tom flew to Becky Thatcher, and whispered in her ear :

" Put on your bonnet and let on you're going home ; and when you get to the corner, give the rest of 'em the slip, and turn down through the lane and come back. I'll go the other way, and come it over 'em the same way."

So the one went off with one group of scholars, and the other with another. In a little while the two met at the bottom of the lane, and when they reached the school they had it all to themselves. Then they sat together, with a slate before them, and Tom gave Becky the pencil and held her hand in his, guiding it, and so created another surprising house. When the interest in art began to wane, the two fell to talking. Tom was swimming in bliss. He said :

" Do you love rats ? "

" No, I hate them ! "

" Well, I do too—live ones. But I mean dead ones, to swing around your head with a string."

" No, I don't care for rats much, anyway. What *I* like is chewing-gum ! "

" Oh, I should say so ! I wish I had some now ! "

" Do you ? I've got some. I'll let you chew it awhile, but you must give it back to me."

That was agreeable, so they chewed it turn about, and dangled their legs against the bench in excess of contentment.

" Was you ever at a circus ? " said Tom.

" Yes, and my Pa's going to take me again some-time, if I'm good."

" I been to the circus three or four times—lots of times. Church ain't shucks to a circus. There's things going on at a circus all the time. I'm going to be a clown in a circus when I grow up."

" Oh, are you ! That will be nice. They're so lovely all spotted up."

" Yes, that's so. And they get slathers of money —most a dollar a day, Ben Rogers says. Say, Becky, was you ever engaged ? "

" What's that ? "

" Why engaged to be married."

" No."

" Would you like to ? "

" I reckon so. I don't know. What is it like ? "

" Like ? Why it ain't like anything. You only just tell a boy you won't ever have anybody but him, ever, *ever*, and then you kiss, and that's all. Anybody can do it."

" Kiss ? What do you kiss for ? "

"Why that, you know, is to—well, they always do that."

"Everybody?"

"Why yes, everybody that's in love with each other. Do you remember what I wrote on the slate?"

"Ye—yes."

"What was it?"

"I shan't tell you."

"Shall I tell *you*?"

"Ye—yes—but some other time."

"No, now."

"No, not now—to-morrow."

"Oh no, *now*, please, Becky. I'll whisper it, I'll whisper it ever so easy."

Becky hesitating, Tom took silence for consent, and passed his arm about her waist and whispered the tale ever so softly, with his mouth close to her ear. And then he added:

"Now you whisper it to me—just the same."

She resisted for a while, and then said:

"You turn your face away, so you can't see, and then I will. But you mustn't ever tell anybody— *will* you, Tom? Now you won't—*will* you?"

"No, indeed indeed I won't. Now, Becky."

He turned his face away. She bent timidly around till her breath stirred his curls, and whispered, "I— love—you!"

Then she sprang away and ran around and around the desks and benches, with Tom after her, and took refuge in a corner at last, with her little white apron to her face. Tom clasped her about her neck and pleaded.

"Now, Becky, it's all over—all over but the kiss. Don't you be afraid of that—it ain't anything at all. Please, Becky."

And he tugged at the apron and the hands.

By-and-by she gave up and let her hands drop; her face, all glowing with the struggle, came up and submitted. Tom kissed the red lips and said:

"Now it's all done, Becky. And always after this, you know, you ain't ever to love anybody but me, and you ain't ever to marry anybody but me, never never and for ever. Will you?"

"No, I'll never love anybody but you, Tom, and I'll never marry anybody but you, and you ain't to ever marry anybody but me, either."

"Certainly. Of course. That's *part* of it. And always, coming to school, or when we're going home, you're to walk with me, when there ain't anybody looking—and you choose me and I choose you at parties, because that's the way you do when you're engaged."

"It's so nice. I never heard of it before."

"Oh, it's ever so jolly! Why me and Amy Lawrence——"

The big eyes told Tom his blunder, and he stopped confused.

"Oh, Tom! Then I ain't the first you've ever been engaged to!"

The child began to cry. Tom said:

"Oh, don't cry, Becky. I don't care for her any more."

"Yes, you do, Tom—you know you do."

Tom tried to put his arm about her neck, but she pushed him away and turned her face to the wall, and went on crying. Tom tried again, with soothing words in his mouth, and was repulsed again. Then his pride was up, and he strode away and went outside. He stood about, restless and uneasy, for a while, glancing at the door every now and then, hoping she would repent and come to find him. But she did not. Then he began to feel badly, and fear that he was in the wrong. It was a hard struggle with him to make new advances now, but he nerved himself to it and entered. She was still standing back there in the corner, sobbing with her face to the wall. Tom's heart smote him. He went to her and stood a moment, not knowing exactly how to proceed. Then he said, hesitatingly:

" Becky, I—I don't care for anybody but you."

No reply—but sobs.

" Becky," pleadingly.

" Becky, won't you say something ? " More sobs.

Tom got out his chiefest jewel, a brass knob from the top of an andiron, and passed it around her so that she could see it, and said :

" Please, Becky, won't you take it ? "

She struck it to the floor. Then Tom marched out of the house and over the hills and far away, to return to school no more that day. Presently Becky began to suspect. She ran to the door ; he was not in sight ; she flew around to the play-yard ; he was not there. Then she called ;

" Tom ! Come back, Tom ! "

She listened intently, but there was no answer. She had no companions but silence and loneliness. So she sat down to cry again and upbraid herself, and by this time the scholars began to gather again, and she had to hide her grief and still her broken heart, and take up the cross of a long dreary aching afternoon with none among the strangers about her to exchange sorrows with.

CHAPTER VIII

Tom dodged hither and thither through lanes until he was well out of the track of returning scholars, and then fell into a moody jog. He crossed a small " branch " two or three times, because of a prevailing juvenile superstition that to cross water baffled pursuit. Half-an-hour later he was disappearing behind the Douglas mansion on the summit of Cardiff Hill, and the schoolhouse was hardly distinguishable away off in the valley behind him. He entered a dense wood, picked his pathless way to the centre of it, and sat down on a mossy spot under a spreading oak. There was not even a zephyr stirring; the dead noonday heat had even stilled the songs of the birds; nature lay in a trance that was broken by no sound but the occasional far-off hammering of a woodpecker, and this seemed to render the pervading silence and sense of loneliness the more profound. The boy's soul was steeped in melancholy; his feelings were in happy accord with his surroundings. He sat long with his elbows on his knees and his chin in his hands, meditating. It seemed to him that life was but a trouble at best, and he more than half envied Jimmy Hodges, so lately released. It must be very peaceful, he thought, to lie and slumber and dream for ever and ever, with the wind whispering through the trees and caressing the grass and the flowers of the grave.

and nothing to bother and grieve about, ever any more. If he only had a clean Sunday-school record he could be willing to go, and be done with it all. Now as to this girl. What had he done? Nothing. He had meant the best in the world and been treated like a dog—like a very dog. She would be sorry some day, —maybe when it was too late. Ah, if he could only die *temporarily!*

But the elastic heart of youth cannot be kept compressed into one constrained shape long at a time. Tom presently began to drift insensibly back into the concerns of this life again. What if he turned his back, now, and disappeared mysteriously? What if he went away—ever so far away, into unknown countries beyond the seas—and never came back any more? How would she feel then? The idea of being a clown recurred to him now, only to fill him with disgust. For frivolity and jokes, and spotted tights, were an offence when they intruded themselves upon a spirit that was exalted into the vague, august realm of the romantic. No, he would be a soldier, and return after long years, all warworn and illustrious. No, better still, he would join the Indians and hunt buffaloes, and go on the war-path in the mountain ranges and the trackless great plains of the Far West, and away in the future, come back a great chief, bristling with feathers, hideous with paint, and prance into Sunday-school, some drowsy summer morning, with a blood-curdling war-whoop, and sear the eyeballs of all his companions with unappeasable envy. But no, there was something grander even than this. He would be a pirate! That was it! *Now* his future lay plain before him, and glowing with unimaginable splendour. How his name would fill the world, and make

people shudder ! How gloriously he would go
ploughing the dancing seas, in his long, low, black
racer, the *Spirit of the Storm*, with his grisly flag
flying at the fore ! And, at the zenith of his fame,
how he would suddenly appear at the old village
and stalk into church all brown and weather-beaten,
in his black velvet doublet and trunks, his great
jack-boots, his crimson sash, his belt bristling with
horse-pistols, his crime-rusted cutlass at his side,
his slouch hat with waving plumes, his black flag
unfurled with the skull and crossbones on it, and hear
with swelling ecstasy the whisperings : " It's Tom
Sawyer the Pirate ! the Black Avenger of the
Spanish Main ! "

Yes, it was settled ; his career was determined.
He would run away from home and enter upon it.
He would start the very next morning. Therefore
he must now begin to get ready. He would collect
his resources together. He went to a rotten log
near at hand, and began to dig under one end of it
with his Barlow knife. He soon struck wood that
sounded hollow. He put his hand there, and uttered
this incantation impressively :

" What hasn't come here, *come !* What's here,
stay here ! "

Then he scraped away the dirt and exposed a pine
shingle. He took it up and disclosed a shapely
little treasure-house whose bottom and sides were
of shingles. In it lay a marble. Tom's astonishment was boundless ! He scratched his head with a
perplexed air, and said :

" Well that beats anything ! "

Then he tossed the marble away pettishly, and
stood cogitating. The truth was, that a superstition of his had failed here, which he and all his

comrades had always looked upon as infallible.
If you buried a marble with certain necessary
incantations, and left it alone a fortnight, and then
opened the place with the incantation he had just
used, you would find that all the marbles you had
ever lost had gathered themselves together there,
meantime, no matter how widely they had been
separated. But now this thing had actually and
unquestionably failed. Tom's whole structure of
faith was shaken to its foundations. He had many
a time heard of this thing succeeding, but never
of its failing before. It did not occur to him that
he had tried it several times before, himself, but could
never find the hiding-place afterwards. He puzzled
over the matter some time, and finally decided that
some witch had interfered and broken the charm.
He thought he would satisfy himself on that point,
so he searched around till he found a small sandy
spot with a little funnel-shaped depression in it.
He laid himself down and put his mouth close to this
depression and called :

"Doodle-bug, doodle-bug, tell me what I want to know !
Doodle-bug, doodle-bug, tell me what I want to know ! "

The sand began to work, and presently a small
black bug appeared for a second, and then darted
under again in a fright.

" He dasn't tell ! So it *was* a witch that done it.
I just knowed it."

He well knew the futility of trying to contend
against witches, so he gave up. discouraged. But it
occurred to him that he might as well have the
marble he had just thrown away, and therefore he
went and made a patient search for it. But he could
not find it. Now he went back to his treasure-house,

and carefully placed himself just as he had been standing when he tossed the marble away ; then he took another marble from his pocket, and tossed it in the same way, saying :

" Brother, go find your brother ! "

He watched where it stopped, and went there and looked. But it must have fallen short or gone too far, so he tried twice more. The last repetition was successful. The two marbles lay within a foot of each other.

Just here the blast of a toy tin trumpet came faintly down the green aisles of the forest. Tom flung off his jacket and trousers, turned a suspender into a belt, raked away some brush behind the rotten log, disclosing a rude bow and arrow, a lath sword, and a tin trumpet, and in a moment had seized these things, and bounded away, barelegged, with fluttering shirt. He presently halted under a great elm, blew an answering blast, and then began to tip-toe and look warily out, this way and that. He said cautiously—to an imaginary company :

" Hold, my merry men ! Keep hid till I blow."

Now appeared Joe Harper, as airily clad and elaborately armed as Tom. Tom called :

" Hold ! Who comes here into Sherwood Forest without my pass ? "

" Guy of Guisborne wants no man's pass ! Who art thou that—that——"

" Dares to hold such language," said Tom, prompting, for they talked " by the book," from memory.

" Who art thou that dares to hold such language ?"

" I, indeed ! I am Robin Hood, as thy caitiff carcase soon shall know."

" Then art thou indeed that famous outlaw ?

Right gladly will I dispute with thee the passes of the merry wood. Have at thee!"

They took their lath swords, dumped their other traps on the ground, struck a fencing attitude, foot to foot, and began a grave, careful combat, "two up and two down." Presently Tom said:

"Now if you've got the hang, go it lively!"

"So they "went it lively," panting and perspiring with the work. By-and-by Tom shouted:

"Fall! fall! Why don't you fall?"

"I shan't! Why don't you fall yourself? You're getting the worst of it."

"Why, that ain't anything. *I* can't fall. That ain't the way it is in the book. The book says, 'Then with one back-handed stroke he slew poor Guy of Guisborne!' You're to turn around and let me hit you in the back."

There was no getting around the authorities, so Joe turned, received the whack, and fell.

"Now," said Joe, getting up, "you got to let me kill you. That's fair."

"Why, I can't do that. It ain't in the book."

"Well, it's blamed mean. That's all."

"Well, say Joe, you can be Friar Tuck, or Much the Miller's son, and lam me with a quarter-staff; or I'll be the Sheriff of Nottingham, and you be Robin Hood, a little while, and kill me."

This was satisfactory, and so these adventures were carried out. Then Tom became Robin Hood again, and was allowed by the treacherous nun to bleed his strength away through his neglected wound. And at last Joe, representing a whole tribe of weeping outlaws, dragged him sadly forth, gave his bow into his feeble hands, and Tom said, "Where this arrow falls, there bury poor Robin Hood under the greenwood tree." Then he shot the arrow, and fell back, and would have died ; but he lit on a nettle, and sprang up too gaily for a corpse.

The boys dressed themselves, hid their accoutrements, and went off grieving that there were no outlaws any more, and wondering what modern civilisation could claim to have done to compensate for their loss. They said they would rather be outlaws a year in Sherwood Forest than President of the United States for ever.

CHAPTER IX

At half-past nine that night, Tom and Sid were sent
to bed as usual. They said their prayers, and Sid
was soon asleep. Tom lay awake and waited in
restless impatience. When it seemed to him that
it must be nearly daylight, he heard the clock strike
ten! This was despair. He would have tossed and
fidgeted, as his nerves demanded, but he was afraid
he might wake Sid. So he lay still and stared up
into the dark. Everything was dismally still. By-
and-by, out of the stillness little scarcely perceptible
noises began to emphasise themselves. The ticking
of the clock began to bring itself into notice. Old
beams began to crack mysteriously. The stairs
creaked faintly. Evidently spirits were abroad.
A measured, muffled snore issued from Aunt Polly's
chamber. And now the tiresome chirping of a
cricket that no human ingenuity could locate,
began. Next the ghastly ticking of a death-watch
in the wall at the bed's head made Tom shudder—it
meant that somebody's days were numbered. Then
the howl of a far-off dog rose on the night air and
was answered by a fainter howl from a remoter
distance. Tom was in an agony. At last he was
satisfied that time had ceased and eternity begun;
he began to doze in spite of himself; the clock
chimed eleven, but he did not hear it. And then
there came, mingling with his half-formed dreams,

a most melancholy caterwauling. The raising of a
neighbouring window disturbed him. A cry of
" Scat ! you devil ! " and the crash of an empty
bottle against the back of his aunt's wood-shed
brought him wide awake, and a single minute later
he was dressed and out of the window and creeping
along the roof of the " ell " on all fours. He
" meow'd " with caution once or twice as he went ;
then jumped to the roof of the wood-shed, and thence
to the ground. Huckleberry Finn was there, with
his dead cat. The boys moved off and disappeared
in the gloom. At the end of half-an-hour they were
wading through the tall grass of the graveyard.

It was a graveyard of the old-fashioned western
kind. It was on a hill, about a mile and a half
from the village. It had a crazy board fence around
it, which leaned inward in places, and outward the
rest of the time, but stood upright nowhere. Grass
and weeds grew rank over the whole cemetery. All
the old graves were sunken in. There was not a
tombstone on the place, round-topped worm-eaten
boards staggered over the graves, leaning for support
and finding none. " Sacred to the memory of "
so-and-so had been painted on them once, but it
could no longer have been read, on the most of them,
now, even if there had been light.

A faint wind moaned through the trees, and Tom
feared it might be the spirits of the dead complaining
at being disturbed. The boys talked little, and only
under their breath, for the time and the place and the
pervading solemnity and silence oppressed their
spirits. They found the sharp new heap they were
seeking, and ensconced themselves within the protection of three great elms that grew in a bunch
within a few feet of the grave.

Then they waited in silence for what seemed a long time. The hooting of a distant owl was all the sound that troubled the dead stillness. Tom's reflections grew oppressive. He must force some talk. So he said in a whisper:

"Hucky, do you believe the dead people like it for us to be here?"

Huckleberry whispered:

"I wisht I knowed. It's awful solemn like, ain't it?"

"I bet it is."

There was a considerable pause, while the boys canvassed this matter inwardly. Then Tom whispered:

"Say, Hucky—do you reckon Hoss Williams hears us talking?"

"O' course he does. Least his spirit does."

Tom, after a pause:

"I wish I'd said *Mister* Williams. But I never meant any harm. Everybody calls him Hoss."

"A body can't be too particular how they talk 'bout these yer dead people, Tom."

This was a damper, and conversation died again. Presently Tom seized his comrade's arm and said:

"*Sh!*"

"What is it, Tom?" And the two clung together with beating hearts.

"*Sh!* There 'tis again! Didn't you hear it?"

"I——"

"There! Now you hear it!"

"Lord, Tom, they're coming! They're coming, sure. What'll we do?"

"I dono. Think they'll see us?"

"Oh, Tom, they can see in the dark same as cats. I wish I hadn't come."

" Oh, don't be afeard. I don't believe they'll bother us. We ain't doing any harm. If we keep perfectly still, maybe they won't notice us at all."

" I'll try to, Tom, but Lord, I'm all of a shiver."

" Listen ! "

The boys bent their heads together and scarcely breathed. A muffled sound of voices floated up from the far end of the graveyard.

" Look ! see there ! " whispered Tom. " What is it ? "

" It's devil-fire. Oh, Tom, this is awful."

Some vague figures approached through the gloom, swinging an old-fashioned tin lantern that freckled the ground with innumerable little spangles of light. Presently Huckleberry whispered with a shudder :

" It's the devils, sure enough. Three of 'em ! Lordy, Tom, we're goners ! Can you pray ? "

" I'll try, but don't you be afeard. They ain't going to hurt us. ' Now I lay me down to sleep, I——.' "

" Sh ! "

" What is it, Huck ? "

" They're *humans* ! One of 'em is, anyway. One of 'em's old Muff Potter's voice."

" No—'tain't so, is it ? "

" I bet I know it. Don't you stir nor budge. He ain't sharp enough to notice us. Drunk, same as usual, likely—blamed old rip ! "

" All right, I'll keep still. Now they're stuck. Can't find it. Here they come again. Now they're hot. Cold again. Hot again. Red hot ! They're pinted right, this time. Say, Huck, I know another o' them voices ; it's Injun Joe."

" That's so—that murderin' half-breed ! I'd

druther they was devils a dern sight. What kin they be up to ? "

The whispers died wholly out now, for the three men had reached the grave, and stood within a few feet of the boys' hiding-place.

" Here it is," said the third voice ; and the owner of it held the lantern up and revealed the face of young Dr. Robinson.

Potter and Injun Joe were carrying a handbarrow with a rope and a couple of shovels on it. They cast down their load and began to open the grave. The doctor put the lantern at the head of the grave, and came and sat down with his back against one of the elm-trees. He was so close the boys could have touched him.

" Hurry, men ! " he said in a low voice. " The moon might come out at any moment."

They growled a response and went on digging. For some time there was no noise but the grating sound of the spades discharging their freight of mould and gravel. It was very monotonous. Finally a spade struck upon the coffin with a dull, woody accent, and within another minute or two the men had hoisted it out on the ground. They prised off the lid with their shovels, got out the body and dumped it rudely on the ground. The moon drifted from behind the clouds and exposed the pallid face. The barrow was got ready and the corpse placed on it, covered with a blanket, and bound to its place with the rope. Potter took out a large spring-knife and cut off the dangling end of the rope, and then said :

" Now the cussed thing's ready, Sawbones, and you'll just out with another five, or here she stays."

" That's the talk ! " said Injun Joe.

"Look here; what does this mean?" said the doctor. "You required your pay in advance and I've paid you."

"Yes, and you done more than that," said Injun Joe, approaching the doctor, who was now standing. "Five year ago you drove me away from your father's kitchen one night when I come to ask for something to eat, and you said I wern't there for any good; and when I swore I'd get even with you if it took a hundred years, your father had me jailed for a vagrant. Did you think I'd forget? The Injun blood ain't in me for nothing. And now I've got you, and you got to *settle*, you know!"

He was threatening the doctor with his fist in his face by this time. The doctor struck out suddenly, and stretched the ruffian on the ground. Potter dropped his knife, and exclaimed:

"Here, now, don't you strike my pard!" and the next moment he had grappled with the doctor, and the two were struggling with might and main, trampling the grass, and tearing the ground with their heels. Injun Joe sprang to his feet, his eyes flaming with passion, snatched up Potter's knife, and went creeping, catlike, and stooping round and round about the combatants, seeking an opportunity. All at once the doctor flung himself free, seized the heavy headboard of Williams's grave and felled Potter to the earth with it; and in the same instant the half-breed saw his chance, and drove the knife to the hilt in the young man's breast. He reeled and fell partly upon Potter, flooding him with his blood, and in the same moment the clouds blotted out the dreadful spectacle, and the two frightened boys went speeding away in the dark.

Presently, when the moon emerged again, Injun

Joe was standing over the two forms, contemplating them. The doctor murmured inarticulately, gave a long gasp or two, and was still. The half-breed muttered :

" That score is settled, damn you."

Then he robbed the body. After which he put the fatal knife in Potter's open right hand, and sat down on the dismantled coffin. Three—four—five minutes passed, and then Potter began to stir and moan. His hand closed upon the knife, he raised it, glanced at it, and let it fall with a shudder. Then he sat up, pushing the body from him, and gazed at it and then around him confusedly. His eyes met Joe's.

" Lord, how is this, Joe ? " he said.

" It's a dirty business," said Joe, without moving.

" What did you do it for ? "

" I ! I never done it ! "

" Look here ! that kind of talk won't wash."

Potter trembled and grew white.

" I thought I'd got sober. I'd no business to drink to-night. But it's in my head yet—worse'n when we started here. I'm all in a muddle ; can't recollect anything of it hardly. Tell me, Joe— *honest, now, old feller*—did I do it, Joe ? I never meant to ; 'pon my soul and honour I never meant to, Joe. Tell me how it was, Joe. Oh, it's awful —and him so young and promising."

" Why, you two was scuffling, and he fetched you one with the headboard, and you fell flat ; and then up you come, all reeling and staggering like, and snatched the knife and jammed it into him just as he fetched you another awful clip, and here you've laid dead as a wedge till now."

" Oh, I didn't know what I was a doing. I wish

I may die this minute if I did. It was all on accounts of the whisky and the excitement, I reckon. I never used a weapon in my life before, Joe. I've fought, but never with weapons. They'll all say that. Joe, don't tell! Say you won't tell, Joe ; that's a good feller. I always liked you, Joe, and stood up for you too. Don't you remember? You won't tell, will you, Joe ? " And the poor creature dropped on his knees before the stolid murderer, and clasped his appealing hands.

" No, you've always been fair and square with me, Muff Potter, and I won't go back on you. There, now, that's as fair as a man can say."

" Oh, Joe, you're an angel. I'll bless you for this the longest day I live." And Potter began to cry.

" Come, now, that's enough of that. This ain't any time for blubbering. You be off yonder way and I'll go this. Move, now, and don't leave any tracks behind you."

Potter started on a trot that quickly increased to a run. The half-breed stood looking after him. He muttered :

" If he's as much stunned with the lick and fuddled with the rum as he had the look of being, he won't think of the knife till he's gone so far he'll be afraid to come back after it to such a place by himself—chicken-heart ! "

Two or three minutes later the murdered man, the blanketed corpse, the lidless coffin, and the open grave, were under no inspection but the moon's. The stillness was complete again, too.

CHAPTER X

THE two boys flew on and on towards the village, speechless with horror. They glanced backward over their shoulders from time to time apprehensively, as if they feared they might be followed. Every stump that started up in their path seemed a man and an enemy, and made them catch their breath, and as they sped by some outlying cottages that lay near the village, the barking of the aroused watch-dogs seemed to give wings to their feet.

" If we can only get to the old tannery before we break down ! " whispered Tom, in short catches between breaths. " I can't stand it much longer."

Huckleberry's hard pantings were his only reply, and the boys fixed their eyes on the goal of their hopes, and bent to their work to win it. They gained steadily on it, and at last, breast to breast, they burst through the open door, and fell, grateful and exhausted, in the sheltering shadows beyond. By-and-by their pulses slowed down, and Tom whispered : " Huckleberry, what do you reckon 'll come of this ? "

" If Dr. Robinson dies, I reckon hanging 'll come of it."

" Do you, though ? "

" Why, I know it, Tom."

Tom thought awhile ; then he said : " Who'll tell ? We ? "

" What are you talking about ? S'pose something happened and Injun Joe didn't hang, why he'd kill us some time or other, just as dead sure as we're a lying here."

" That's just what I was thinking to myself, Huck."

"If anybody tells, let Muff Potter do it, if he's fool enough. He's generally drunk enough."

Tom said nothing—went on thinking. Presently he whispered:

"Huck, Muff Potter don't know it. How can he tell?"

"What's the reason he don't know it?"

"Because he'd just got that whack when Injun Joe done it. D'you reckon he could see anything? D'you reckon he knowed anything?"

"By hokey, that's so, Tom!"

"And besides, look-a-here—maybe that whack done for him!"

"No! 'tain't likely, Tom. He had liquor in him; I could see that; and besides, he always has. Well, when Pap's full, you might take and belt him over the head with a church and you couldn't phase him. He says so his own self. So it's the same with Muff Potter, of course. But if a man was dead sober, I reckon, maybe that whack might fetch him; I dono."

After another reflective silence, Tom said:

"Hucky, you sure you can keep mum?"

"Tom, we got to keep mum. You know that. That Injun devil wouldn't make any more of drownding us than a couple of cats, if we was to squeak 'bout this and they didn't hang him. Now look-a-here, Tom, less take and swear to one another—that's what we got to do—swear to keep mum."

"I'm agreed Huck It's the best thing. Would you just hold hands and swear that we——"

"Oh no that wouldn't do for this. That's good enough for 'ittle rubbishy common things—specially with gals, cuz they go back on you any way, and blab if they get into a huff—but there orter be writing 'bout a big thing like this. And blood.''

Tom's whole being applauded this idea. It was deep, and dark, and awful; the hour, the circumstances, the surroundings, were in keeping with it. He picked up a clean pine shingle that lay in the moonlight, took a little fragment of "red keel" out of his pocket, got the moon on his work, and painfully scrawled these lines, emphasising each slow downstroke by clamping his tongue between his teeth, and letting up the pressure on the upstrokes :—

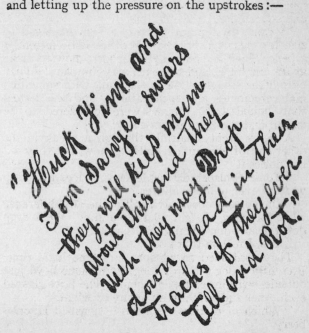

"Huck Finn and Tom Sawyer swears they will keep mum about this and they wish they may Drop down dead in their Tracks if they ever Tell and Rot."

Huckleberry was filled with admiration of Tom's facility in writing and the sublimity of his language. He at once took a pin from his lappel and was going to prick his flesh, but Tom said :

"Hold on ! Don't do that. A pin's brass. It might have verdigrease on it."

"What's verdigrease ? "

"It's pison. That's what it is. You just swaller some of it once—you'll see."

So Tom unwound the thread from one of his needles, and each boy pricked the ball of his thumb and squeezed out a drop of blood.

In time, after many squeezes, Tom managed to sign his initials, using the ball of his little finger for a pen. Then he showed Huckleberry how to make an H and an F, and the oath was complete. They buried the shingle close to the wall, with some dismal ceremonies and incantations, and the fetters that bound their tongues were considered to be locked and the key thrown away.

A figure crept stealthily through a break in the other end of the ruined building now, but they did not notice it

"Tom," whispered Huckleberry, "does this keep us from ever telling—always ? "

"Of course it does. It don't make any difference what happens, we got to keep mum. We'd drop down dead—don't you know that ? "

"Yes, I reckon that's so."

They continued to whisper for some little time. Presently a dog set up a long, lugubrious howl just outside—within ten feet of them. The boys clasped each other suddenly, in an agony of fright.

"Which of us does he mean ? " gasped Huckleberry.

" I dono—peep through the crack. Quick ! "

" No, you, Tom ! "

" I can't—I can't do it, Huck ! "

" Please, Tom. There 'tis again ! "

" Oh, Lordy, I'm thankful ! " whispered Tom. " I know his voice. It's Bull Harbison." *

" Oh, that's good—I tell you, Tom, I was most scared to death : I'd a bet anything it was a stray dog."

The dog howled again. The boys' hearts sank once more.

" Oh, my ! that ain't no Bull Harbison ! " whispered Huckleberry. " Do Tom ! "

Tom, quaking with fear, yielded, and put his eye to the crack. His whisper was hardly audible when he said :

" Oh, Huck, it's A STRAY DOG ! "

" Quick, Tom, quick ! Who does he mean ? "

" Huck, he must mean us both—we're right together."

" Oh, Tom, I reckon we're goners. I reckon there ain't no mistake 'bout where *I'll* go to. I been so wicked."

" Dad fetch it ! This comes of playing hookey and doing everything a feller's told *not* to do. I might a been good, like Sid, if I'd a' tried— but no, I wouldn't, of course. But if ever I get off this time, I lay I'll just *waller* in Sunday-schools ! "

And Tom began to snuffle a little.

" *You* bad ! " And Huckleberry began to snuffle, too. " Confound it, Tom Sawyer, you're just old

---

* If Mr. Harbison had owned a slave named Bull, Tom would have spoken of him as " Harbison's Bull ; " but a son or a dog of that name was " Bull Harbison."

pie 'longside o' what *I* am. Oh, *Lordy*, Lordy, Lordy, I wisht I only had half your chance."

Tom choked off and whispered :

" Look, Hucky, look ! He's got his *back* to us ! "

Hucky looked with joy in his heart.

" Well, he has, by jingoes ! Did he before ? "

" Yes, he did. But I, like a fool, never thought. Oh, this is bully, you know. *Now*, who can he mean ? "

The howling stopped. Tom pricked up his ears.

" *Sh !* What's that ? " he whispered.

" Sounds like—like hogs grunting. No—it's somebody snoring, Tom.

" That *is* it ? Where'bouts is it, Huck ?

" I b'leeve it's down at t'other end. Sounds so, anyway. Pap used to sleep there sometimes, 'long with the hogs, but laws bless you, he just lifts things when he snores. Besides, I reckon he ain't ever coming back to this town any more."

The spirit of adventure rose in the boys' souls once more.

" Hucky, do you das't to go if I lead ? "

" I don't like to, much, Tom. S'pose it's Injun Joe ! "

Tom quailed. But presently the temptation rose up strong again and the boys agreed to try, with the understanding that they would take to their heels if the snoring stopped. So they went tip-toeing stealthily down, the one behind the other. When they had got to within five steps of the snorer, Tom stepped on a stick, and it broke with a sharp snap. The man moaned, writhed a little, and his face came into the moonlight. It was Muff Potter. The boys' hearts had stood still, and their bodies too, when the man moved, but their fears passed away now. They tip-toed out, through the broken weather-boarding, and stopped at a little distance to exchange a parting word. That long, lugubrious howl rose on the night air again! They turned and saw the strange dog standing within a few feet of where Potter was lying, and facing Potter with his nose pointing heavenward.

" Oh, geeminy, it's *him !* " exclaimed both boys in a breath.

" Say, Tom, they say a stray dog come howling around Johnny Miller's house, 'bout midnight, as much as two weeks ago ; and a whippowill come in and lit on the banisters and sung, the very same evening ; and there ain't anybody dead there yet."

" Well, I know that. And suppose there ain't. Didn't Gracie Miller fall in the kitchen fire and burn herself terrible the very next Saturday ? "

" Yes, but she ain't *dead*. And what's more, she's getting better too."

" All right ; you wait and see. She's a goner, just as dead sure as Muff Potter's a goner. That's what the niggers say, and they know all about these kind of things, Huck."

Then they separated, cogitating.

When Tom crept in at his bedroom window, the night was almost spent. He undressed with excessive caution, and fell asleep congratulating himself that nobody knew of his escapade. He was not aware that the gentle snoring Sid was awake, and had been so for an hour.

When Tom awoke, Sid was dressed and gone. There was a late look in the light, a late atmosphere. He was startled. Why had he not been called—persecuted till he was up as usual ? The thought filled him with bodings. Within five minutes he was dressed and downstairs, feeling sore and drowsy. The family were still at table, but they had finished breakfast. There was no voice of rebuke; but there were averted eyes; there was a silence and an air of solemnity that struck a chill to the culprit's heart. He sat down and tried to seem gay, but it was uphill work; it roused no smile, no response, and he lapsed into silence and let his heart sink down to the depths.

After breakfast his aunt took him aside, and Tom almost brightened in the hope that he was going to be flogged; but it was not so. His aunt wept over him and asked him how he could go and break her old heart so; and finally told him to go on, and ruin himself and bring her grey hairs with sorrow to the grave, for it was no use for her to try any more. This was worse than a thousand whippings, and Tom's heart was sorer now than his body. He cried, he pleaded for forgiveness, promised reform over and over again, and then received his dismissal, feeling that he had won but an imperfect forgiveness and established but a feeble confidence.

He left the presence too miserable to even feel vengeful toward Sid; and so the latter's prompt retreat through the back gate was unnecessary. He moped to school gloomy and sad, and took his flogging along with Joe Harper for playing hookey the day before, with the air of one whose heart was busy with heavier woes and wholly dead to trifles. Then he betook himself to his seat, rested his elbows on his desk and his jaws in his hands, and stared at the wall with the stony stare of suffering that has reached the limit and can no further go. His elbow was pressing against some hard substance.

After a long time he slowly and sadly changed his position, and took up this object with a sigh. It was in a paper. He unrolled it. A long, lingering colossal sigh followed, and his heart broke. It was his brass andiron knob! This final feather broke the camel's back.

CHAPTER XI

CLOSE upon the hour of noon the whole village was suddenly electrified with the ghastly news. No need of the as yet undreamed of telegraph, the tale flew from man to man, from group to group, from house to house, with little less than telegraphic speed. Of course the schoolmaster gave holiday for that afternoon; the town would have thought strangely of him if he had not. A gory knife had been found close to the murdered man, and it had been recognised by somebody as belonging to Muff Potter— so the story ran. And it was said that a belated citizen had come upon Potter washing himself in the " branch " about one or two o'clock in the morning, and that Potter had at once sneaked off—suspicious circumstances, especially the washing, which was not a habit with Potter. It was also said that the town had been ransacked for this " murderer " (the public are not slow in the matter of sifting evidence and arriving at a verdict), but that he could not be found. Horsemen had departed down all the roads in every direction, and the Sheriff was confident that he would be captured before night.

All the town was drifting towards the graveyard. Tom's heartbreak vanished, and he joined the procession, not because he would not a thousand times rather go anywhere else, but because an awful, unaccountable fascination drew him on. Arrived at the dreadful place, he wormed his small body through the crowd and saw the dismal spectacle. It seemed to him an age since he was there before. Somebody pinched his arm. He turned, and his eyes met Huckleberry's. Then both looked elsewhere at once, and wondered if anybody had noticed anything in their mutual glance. But everybody was talking, and intent upon the grisly spectacle before them.

" Poor fellow ! " " Poor young fellow ! " " This ought to be a lesson to grave-robbers ! " " Muff Potter'll hang for this if they catch him ! " This was the drift of remark, and the minister said, " It was a judgment ; His hand is here."

Now Tom shivered from head to heel ; for his eye fell upon the stolid face of Injun Joe. At this moment the crowd began to sway and struggle, and voices shouted, " It's him ! it's him ! he's coming himself ! "

" Who ? who ? " from twenty voices.

" Muff Potter ! "

" Hallo, he's stopped ! Look out, he's turning ! Don't let him get away ! "

People in the branches of the trees over Tom's head said he wasn't trying to get away—he only looked doubtful and perplexed.

" Infernal impudence ! " said a bystander ; " wanted to come and take a quiet look at his work—didn't expect any company."

The crowd fell apart now, and the Sheriff came through ostentatiously, leading Potter by the arm. The poor fellow's face was haggard, and his eyes showed the fear that was upon him. When he stood before the murdered man, he shook as with a palsy, and he put his face in his hands and burst into tears.

" I didn't do it, friends," he sobbed ; " 'pon my word and honour I never done it."

" Who's accused you ? " shouted a voice.

This shot seemed to carry home. Potter lifted his face and looked around him with a pathetic hopelessness in his eyes. He saw Injun Joe, and exclaimed :

" Oh, Injun Joe, you promised me you'd never——"

" Is that your knife ? " and it was thrust before him by the Sheriff.

Potter would have fallen if they had not caught him and eased him to the ground. Then he said :

" Something told me 't if I didn't come back and get—" He shuddered ; then waved his nerveless hand with a vanquished gesture and said. " Tell 'em, Joe, tell 'em—it ain't no use any more."

Then Huckleberry and Tom stood dumb and staring, and heard the stony-hearted liar reel off his serene statement, they expecting every moment that the clear sky would deliver God's lightnings upon his head, and wondering to see how long the stroke was delayed. And when he had finished and still stood alive and whole, their wavering impulse to break their oath and save the poor betrayed prisoner's life, faded and vanished away, for plainly this miscreant had sold himself to Satan, and it would be fatal to meddle with the property of such a power as that.

" Why didn't you leave ? What did you want to come here for ? " somebody said.

" I couldn't help it—I couldn't help it," Potter moaned. " I wanted to run away, but I couldn't seem to come anywhere but here." And he fell to sobbing again.

Injun Joe repeated his statement, just as calmly, a few minutes afterwards on the inquest, under oath ; and the boys, seeing that the lightnings were still withheld, were confirmed in their belief that Joe had sold himself to the devil. He was now become, to them, the most balefully interesting object they had ever looked upon, and they could not take their fascinated eyes from his face. They inwardly resolved to watch him, nights, when opportunity should offer, in the hope of getting a glimpse of his dread master.

Injun Joe helped to raise the body of the murdered man, and put it in a waggon for removal ; and it was whispered through the shuddering crowd that the wound bled a little ! The boys thought that this happy circumstance would turn suspicion in the right direction ; but they were disappointed, for more than one villager remarked :

" It was within three feet of Muff Potter when it done it."

Tom's fearful secret and gnawing conscience disturbed his sleep for as much as a week after this ; and at breakfast one morning, Sid said :

" Tom, you pitch around and talk in your sleep so much that you keep me awake about half the time."

Tom blanched and dropped his eyes.

" It's a bad sign," said Aunt Polly gravely. " What you got on your mind, Tom ? "

" Nothing. Nothing 't I know of." But the boy's hand shook so that he spilled his coffee.

" And you do talk such stuff," Sid said. " Last night you said, ' It's blood, it's blood, that's what it is ! ' You said that over and over. And you

said, ' Don't torment me so—I'll tell.   Tell what ?
What is it you'll tell ? "

Everything was swimming before Tom.   There is
no telling what might have happened now, but
luckily the concern passed out of Aunt Polly's face,
and she came to Tom's relief without knowing it.
She said :

" Sho ! It's that dreadful murder.   I dream
about it most every night myself.   Sometimes I
dream it's me that done it."

Mary said she had been affected much the same
way.   Sid seemed satisfied.   Tom got out of the
presence as quickly as he plausibly could, and after
that he complained of toothache for a week, and
tied up his jaws every night.   He never knew that
Sid lay nightly watching, and frequently slipped the
bandage free, and then leaned on his elbow listening
a good while at a time, and afterwards slipped the
bandage back to its place again.   Tom's distress of
mind wore off gradually, and the toothache grew irk-
some and was discarded.   If Sid really managed to
make anything out of Tom's disjointed mutterings
he kept it to himself.   It seemed to Tom that his
schoolmates never would get done holding inquests
on dead cats, and thus keeping his trouble present
to his mind.   Sid noticed that Tom never was
coroner at one of these inquiries, though it had been
his habit to take the lead in all new enterprises ; he
noticed, too, that Tom never acted as a witness—
and that was strange ; and Sid did not overlook the
fact that Tom even showed a marked aversion to
these inquests, and always avoided them when he
could.   Sid marvelled, but said nothing.   However,
even inquests went out of vogue at last, and ceased
to torture Tom's conscience.

Every day or two during this time of sorrow, Tom watched his opportunity and went to the little grated jail window and smuggled such small comforts through to the " murderer " as he could get hold of. The jail was a trifling little brick den that stood in a marsh at the edge of the village, and no guards were afforded for it ; indeed, it was seldom occupied. These offerings greatly helped to ease Tom's conscience. The villagers had a strong desire to tar-and-feather Injun Joe and ride him on a rail for body-snatching, but so formidable was his character that nobody could be found who was willing to take the lead in the matter, so it was dropped. He had been careful to begin both of his inquest-statements with the fight, without confessing the grave-robbery that preceded it ; therefore it was deemed wisest not to try the case in the courts at present.

CHAPTER XII

ONE of the reasons why Tom's mind had drifted away from its secret troubles was that it had found a new and weighty matter to interest itself about. Becky Thatcher had stopped coming to school. Tom had struggled with his pride a few days, and tried to "whistle her down the wind," but failed. He began to find himself hanging around her father's house, nights, and feeling very miserable. She was sick. What if she should die! There was distraction in the thought. He no longer took an interest in war, or even in piracy. The charm of life was gone, there was nothing but dreariness left. He put his hoop away, and his bat; there was no joy in them any more. His aunt was concerned; she began to try all manner of medicines on him. She was one of those people who are infatuated with patent medicines and all new-fangled methods of producing health or mending it. She was an inveterate experimenter in these things. When something fresh in this line came out she was in a fever right away to try it; not on herself, for she was never ailing; but on anybody else that came handy. She was a subscriber for all the "Health" periodicals and phrenological frauds; and the solemn ignorance they were inflated with was breath to her nostrils. All the rot they contained about ventilation, and how to go to bed, and how to get up, and what to eat, and what to drink, and how much exercise to take, and what frame of mind to keep oneself in, and what sort of clothing to wear, was all gospel to her, and she never observed that her health journals of the current month customarily upset everything they had recommended the month before. She was as simple-hearted and honest as the day was long, and so she was an easy victim. She gathered together her quack periodicals and her quack medicines, and thus armed with death, went about on her pale horse, metaphorically speaking, with " hell following after." But she never suspected that she was not an angel of healing and the balm of Gilead in disguise to the suffering neighbours.

The water treatment was new, now, and Tom's low condition was a windfall to her. She had him out at daylight every morning, stood him up in the wood-shed and drowned him with a deluge of cold water ; then she scrubbed him down with a towel like a file, and so brought him to ; then she rolled him up in a wet sheet and put him away under blankets till she sweated his soul clean and " the yellow stains of it came through his pores," as Tom said.

Yet notwithstanding all this the boy grew more and more melancholy and pale and dejected. She added hot baths, sitz baths, shower baths, and plunges. The boy remained as dismal as a hearse. She began to assist the water with a slim oatmeal diet and blister plasters. She calculated his capacity as she would a jug's, and filled him up every day with quack cure-alls.

Tom had become indifferent to persecution by this time. This phase filled the old lady's heart with consternation. This indifference must be broken up at any cost. Now she heard of Pain-killer for the first time. She ordered a lot at once. She tasted it and was filled with gratitude. It was simply fire in a liquid form. She dropped the water treatment and everything else, and pinned her faith to Pain-killer. She gave Tom a teaspoonful and watched with the deepest anxiety for the result. Her troubles were instantly at rest, her soul at peace again ; for the " indifference " was broken up. The boy could not have shown a wilder, heartier interest if she had built a fire under him.

Tom felt that it was time to wake up ; this sort of life might be romantic enough in his blighted condition, but it was getting to have too little senti-ment and too much distracting variety about it. So he thought over various plans for relief, and finally hit upon that of professing to be fond of Pain-killer. He asked for it so often that he became a nuisance, and his aunt ended by telling him to help himself and quit bothering her. If it had been Sid she would have had no misgivings to alloy her delight ; but since it was Tom she watched the bottle clandestinely. She found that the medicine did really diminish, but it did not occur to her that the boy was mending the health of a crack in the sitting-room floor with it.

One day Tom was in the act of dosing the crack when his aunt's yellow cat came along, purring, eyeing the tea-spoon avariciously, and begging for a taste. Tom said :

" Don't ask for it unless you want it, Peter."

But Peter signified that he did want it.

" You better make sure."

Peter was sure.

" Now you've asked for it, and I'll give it to you, because there ain't anything mean about *me ;* but if you find you don't like it you mustn't blame anybody but your own self."

Peter was agreeable, so Tom prised his mouth open and poured down the Pain-killer. Peter sprang a couple of yards into the air, and then delivered a war-whoop and set off round and round the room, banging against furniture, upsetting flower-pots, and making general havoc. Next he rose on his hind feet and pranced around, in a frenzy of enjoyment, with his head over his shoulder and his voice proclaiming his unappeasable happiness. Then he went tearing around the house again, spreading chaos and destruction in his path. Aunt Polly entered in time to see him throw a few double summersets, deliver a final mighty hurrah, and sail through the open window, carrying the rest of the flower-pots with him. The old lady stood petrified with astonishment, peering over her glasses ; Tom lay on the floor, expiring with laughter.

" Tom, what on earth ails that cat ? "

" *I* don't know, aunt," gasped the boy.

" Why I never see anything like it. What *did* make him act so ? "

" 'Deed I don't know, Aunt Polly ; cats always act so when they're having a good time."

" They do, do they ? " There was something in the tone that made Tom apprehensive.

" Yes'm. That is, I believe they do,"

" *You do ?* "

" Yes'm."

The old lady was bending down, Tom watching with interest emphasised by anxiety. Too late he divined her " drift." The handle of the tell-tale tea-spoon was visible under the bed-valance. Aunt Polly took it, held it up. Tom winced, and dropped

his eyes. Aunt Polly raised him by the usual handle
—his ear—and cracked his head soundly with her
thimble.

" Now, sir, what did you want to treat that poor
dumb beast so for ? "

" I done it out of pity for him—because he hadn't
any aunt."

" Hadn't any aunt !—you numbskull. What has
that got to do with it ? "

" Heaps. Because if he'd a had one she'd a
burnt him out herself ! She'd a roasted his bowels
out of him 'thout any more feeling than if he was
a human ! "

Aunt Polly felt a sudden pang of remorse. This
was putting the thing in a new light ; what was
cruelty to a cat *might* be cruelty to a boy too. She
began to soften : she felt sorry. Her eyes watered
a little, and she put her hand on Tom's head and
said gently :

" I was meaning for the best, Tom. And Tom,
it *did* do you good."

Tom looked up in her face with just a perceptible
twinkle peeping through his gravity :

" I know you was meaning for the best, aunty,
and so was I with Peter. It done *him* good, too. I
never see him get around so nice——"

" Oh, go 'long with you, Tom, before you aggra-
vate me again. And you try and see if you can't
be a good boy for once, and you needn't take any
more medicine."

Tom reached school ahead of time. It was noticed
that this strange thing had been occurring every
day latterly. And now, as usual of late, he hung
about the gate of the school-yard instead of playing
with his comrades. He was sick, he said ; and he

looked it. He tried to seem to be looking everywhere but whither he was really looking—down the road. Presently Jeff Thatcher hove in sight, and Tom's face lighted ; he gazed a moment, and then turned sorrowfully away. When Jeff Thatcher arrived, Tom accosted him, and "led up" warily to opportunities for remark about Becky, but the giddy lad never could see the bait. Tom watched and watched, hoping whenever a frisking frock came in sight, and hating the owner of it as soon as he saw she was not the right one. At last frocks ceased to appear, and he dropped hopelessly into the dumps ; he entered the empty school-house and sat down to suffer. Then one more frock passed in at the gate, and Tom's heart gave a great bound. The next instant he was out, and "going on" like an Indian ; yelling, laughing, chasing boys, jumping over the fence at risk of life and limb, throwing handsprings, standing on his head—doing all the heroic things he could conceive of, and keeping a furtive eye out, all the while, to see if Becky Thatcher was noticing. But she seemed to be unconscious of it all ; she never looked. Could it be possible that she was not aware that he was there ? He carried his exploits to her immediate vicinity ; came war-whooping around, snatched a boy's cap, hurled it to the roof of the school house, broke through a group of boys, tumbling them in every direction, and fell sprawling himself under Becky's nose, almost upsetting her—and she turned, with her nose in the air, and he heard her say, "Mf ! some people think they're mighty smart—always showing off ! "

Tom's cheeks burned. He gathered himself up and sneaked off, crushed and crestfallen.

CHAPTER XIII

Tom's mind was made up now. He was gloomy and
desperate. He was a forsaken, friendless boy, he
said; nobody loved him: when they found out
what they had driven him to, perhaps they would
be sorry; he had tried to do right and get along,
but they would not let him; since nothing would do
them but to be rid of him, let it be so; and let them
blame him for the consequences—why shouldn't
they? what right had the friendless to complain?
Yes, they had forced him to it at last; he would lead
a life of crime. There was no choice. By this time
he was far down Meadow Land, and the bell for
school to "take up" tinkled faintly upon his ear.
He sobbed, now, to think he should never, never
hear that old familiar sound any more—it was
very hard, but it was forced on him; since he was
driven out into the cold world, he must submit
—but he forgave them. Then the sobs came thick
and fast.

Just at this point he met his soul's sworn comrade, Joe Harper—hard-eyed, and with evidently a
great and dismal purpose in his heart. Plainly
here were "two souls with but a single thought."
Tom, wiping his eyes with his sleeve, began to
blubber out something about a resolution to escape
from hard usage and lack of sympathy at home
by roaming abroad into the great world, never to

return ; and ended by hoping that Joe would not forget him.

But it transpired that this was a request which Joe had just been going to make of Tom, and had come to hunt him up for that purpose. His mother had whipped him for drinking some cream which he had never tasted and knew nothing about ; it was plain that she was tired of him and wished him to go ; if she felt that way, there was nothing for him to do but to succumb : he hoped she would be happy, and never regret having driven her poor boy out into the unfeeling world to suffer and die.

As the two boys walked sorrowing along, they made a new compact to stand by each other and be brothers, and never separate till death relieved them of their troubles. Then they began to lay their plans. Joe was for being a hermit, and living on crusts in a remote cave, and dying, sometime, of cold, and want, and grief ; but after listening to Tom, he conceded that there were some conspicuous advantages about a life of crime, and so he consented to be a pirate.

Three miles below St. Petersburg, at a point where the Mississippi River was a trifle over a mile wide, there was a long, narrow, wooded island, with a shallow bar at the head of it, and this offered well as a rendezvous. It was not inhabited ; it lay far over towards the farther shore, abreast a dense and almost wholly unpeopled forest. So Jackson's Island was chosen. Who were to be the subjects of their piracies was a matter that did not occur to them. Then they hunted up Huckleberry Finn, and he joined them promptly, for all careers were one to him ; he was indifferent. They presently separated, to meet at a lonely spot on the river bank two miles above the village, at the favourite hour, which was midnight. There was a small log raft there which they meant to capture. Each would bring hooks and lines, and such provisions as he could steal in the most dark and mysterious way—as became outlaws; and before the afternoon was done, they had all managed to enjoy the sweet glory of spreading the fact that pretty soon the town would " hear something." All who got this vague hint were cautioned to " be mum and wait."

About midnight Tom arrived with a boiled ham and a few trifles, and stopped in a dense undergrowth on a small bluff overlooking the meetingplace. It was starlight, and very still. The mighty river lay like an ocean at rest. Tom listened a moment, but no sound disturbed the quiet. Then he gave a low, distinct whistle. It was answered from under the bluff. Tom whistled twice more; these signals were answered in the same way. Then a guarded voice said :

" Who goes there ? "

" Tom Sawyer, the Black Avenger of the Spanish Main. Name your names."

" Huck Finn the Red-handed, and Joe Harper the Terror of the Seas." Tom had furnished these titles from his favourite literature.

" 'Tis well. Give the countersign."

Two hoarse whispers delivered the same awful word simultaneously to the brooding night :—

" BLOOD ! "

Then Tom tumbled his ham over the bluff and let himself down after it, tearing both skin and clothes to some extent in the effort. There was an easy, comfortable path along the shore under the bluff, but it lacked the advantages of difficulty and danger so valued by a pirate.

The Terror of the Seas had brought a side of bacon, and had about worn himself out with getting it there. Finn the Red-handed had stolen a skillet, and a quantity of half-cured leaf tobacco, and had also brought a few corn-cobs to make pipes with. But none of the pirates smoked or " chewed " but himself. The Black Avenger of the Spanish Main said it would never do to start without some fire. That was a wise thought ; matches were hardly known there in that day. They saw a fire smouldering upon a great raft a hundred yards above, and they went stealthily thither and helped themselves to a chunk. They made an imposing adventure of it, saying " hist " every now and then and suddenly halting with finger on lip ; moving with hands on imaginary dagger-hilts ; and giving orders in dismal whispers that if " the foe " stirred to " let him have it to the hilt," because " dead men tell no tales." They knew well enough that the raftmen were all down at the village laying in stores or having a spree, but still that was no excuse for their conducting this thing in an unpiratical way.

They shoved off presently. Tom in command, Huck at the after oar and Joe at the forward. Tom stood amidships, gloomy browed and with folded arms, and gave his orders in a low, stern whisper.

" Luff, and bring her to the wind ! "

" Aye, aye, sir ! "

" Steady, stead-y-y-y ! "

" Steady it is, sir ! "

" Let her go off a point ! "

" Point it is, sir ! "

As the boys steadily and monotonously drove the

raft toward mid-stream, it was no doubt understood that these orders were given only for " style," and were not intended to mean anything in particular.

" What sail's she carrying ? "

" Courses, tops'ls, and flying-jib, sir ! "

" Send the r'yals up ! Lay out aloft there, half-a-dozen of ye, foretomast-stuns'l ! Lively, now ! "

" Aye, aye, sir ! "

" Shake out that mainto-galans'l ! Sheets and braces ! *Now*, my hearties ! "

" Aye, aye, sir ! "

" Hellum-a-lee—hard a-port ! Stand by to meet her when she comes ! Port, port ! *Now*, men ! With a will ! Stead-y-y ! "

" Steady it is, sir ! "

The raft drew beyond the middle of the river ; the boys pointed her head right and then lay on their oars.   The river was not high, so there was not more than a two or three mile current.   Hardly a word was said during the next three-quarters of an hour.   Now the raft was passing before the distant town.   Two or three glimmering lights showed where it lay, peacefully sleeping, beyond the vague vast sweep of star-gemmed water, unconscious of the tremendous event that was happening.   The Black Avenger stood still with folded arms, " looking his last " upon the scene of his former joys and his later sufferings, and wishing " she " could see him now, abroad on the wild sea, facing peril and death with dauntless heart, going to his doom with a grim smile on his lips.   It was but a small strain on his imagination to remove Jackson's Island beyond eye-shot of the village, and so he " looked his last " with a broken and satisfied heart.   The other pirates were looking their last, too ; and they all looked so long that they came near letting the current drift them out of the range of the island. But they discovered the danger in time, and made shift to avert it. About two o'clock in the morning the raft grounded on the bar two hundred yards above the head of the island, and they waded back and forth until they had landed their freight. Part of the little raft's belongings consisted of an old sail, and this they spread over a nook in the bushes for a tent to shelter their provisions; but they themselves would sleep in the open air in good weather, as became outlaws.

They built a fire against the side of a great log twenty or thirty steps within the sombre depths of the forest, and then cooked some bacon in the frying-pan for supper, and used up half of the corn "pone" stock they had brought. It seemed glorious sport to be feasting in that wild free way in the virgin forest of an unexplored and uninhabited island, far from the haunts of men, and they said they would never return to civilisation. The climbing fire lit up their faces and threw its ruddy glare upon the pillared tree-trunks of their forest temple, and upon the varnished foliage and festooning vines. When the last crisp slice of bacon was gone, and the last allowance of corn pone devoured, the boys stretched themselves out on the grass, filled with contentment. They could have found a cooler place, but they would not deny themselves such a romantic feature as the roasting camp-fire.

"*Ain't* it jolly?" said Joe.

"It's *nuts*," said Tom.

"What would the boys say if they could see us?"

"Say? Well, they'd just die to be here—hey, Hucky?"

"I reckon so," said Huckleberry; "anyways *I'm* suited. I don't want nothing better'n this. I don't ever get enough to eat gen'ally—and here they can't come and kick at a feller and bullyrag him so."

"It's just the life for me," said Tom. "You don't have to get up, mornings, and you don't have to go to school, and wash, and all that blame foolishness."

"You see a pirate don't have to do *anything*, Joe, when he's ashore, but a hermit *he* has to be praying considerable, and then he don't have any fun, any way, all by himself that way."

"Oh yes, that's so," said Joe, "but I hadn't thought much about it, you know. I'd a good deal ruther be a pirate now that I've tried it."

"You see," said Tom, "people don't go much on hermits, nowadays, like they used to in old times, but a pirate's always respected. And a hermit's got to sleep on the hardest place he can find, and put sackcloth and ashes on his head, and stand out in the rain, and——"

"What does he put sackcloth and ashes on his head for?" inquired Huck.

"*I* dunno. But they've *got* to do it. Hermits always do. You'd have to do that if you was a hermit."

"Dern'd if I would," said Huck.

"Well, what would you do?"

"I dunno. But I wouldn't do that."

"Why, Huck, you'd *have* to. How'd you get around it?"

"Why I just wouldn't stand it. I'd run away."

"Run away! Well, you *would* be a nice old slouch of a hermit. You'd be a disgrace."

The Red-handed made no response, being better

employed. He had finished gouging out a cob, and now he fitted a weed stem to it, loaded it with tobacco, and was pressing a coal to the charge and blowing a cloud of fragrant smoke; he was in the full bloom of luxurious contentment. The other pirates envied him this majestic vice, and secretly resolved to acquire it shortly. Presently Huck said:

" What does pirates have to do ? "

Tom said :

" Oh, they have just a bully time—take ships, and burn them, and get the money and bury it in awful places in their island where there's ghosts and things to watch it, and kill everybody in the ships —make 'em walk a plank."

" And they carry the women to the island," said Joe ; " they don't kill the women."

" No," assented Tom, " they don't kill the women —they're too noble. And the women's always beautiful, too."

" And don't they wear the bulliest clothes ! Oh no ! All gold and silver and di'monds," said Joe with enthusiasm.

" Who ? " said Huck.

" Why the pirates."

Huck scanned his own clothing forlornly.

" I reckon I ain't dressed fitten for a pirate," said he, with a regretful pathos in his voice ; " but I ain't got none but these."

But the other boys told him the fine clothes would come fast enough after they should have begun their adventures. They made him understand that his poor rags would do to begin with, though it was customary for wealthy pirates to start with a proper wardrobe.

Gradually their talk died out and drowsiness began

to steal upon the eyelids of the little waifs. The
pipe dropped from the fingers of the Red-handed,
and he slept the sleep of the conscience-free and the
weary. The Terror of the Seas and the Black
Avenger of the Spanish Main had more difficulty
in getting to sleep. They said their prayers inwardly, and lying down, since there was nobody
there with authority to make them kneel and recite
aloud ; in truth they had a mind not to say them
at all, but they were afraid to proceed to such
lengths as that, lest they might call down a sudden
and special thunderbolt from heaven. Then at once
they reached and hovered upon the imminent verge
of sleep—but an intruder came now that would not
" down." It was conscience. They began to feel
a vague fear that they had been doing wrong to
run away ; and next they thought of the stolen
meat, and then the real torture came. They tried
to argue it away by reminding conscience that they
had purloined sweetmeats and apples scores of times ;
but conscience was not to be appeased by such thin
plausibilities. It seemed to them, in the end, that
there was no getting around the stubborn fact that
taking sweetmeats was only " hooking," while taking
bacon and ham and such valuables was plain, simple
stealing—and there was a command against that in
the Bible. So they inwardly resolved that so long
as they remained in the business, their piracies should
not again be sullied with the crime of stealing.
Then conscience granted a truce, and these curiously
inconsistent pirates fell peacefully to sleep.

CHAPTER XIV

WHEN Tom awoke in the morning, he wondered where he was. He sat up and rubbed his eyes and looked around; then he comprehended. It was the cool grey dawn, and there was a delicious sense of repose and peace in the deep pervading calm and silence of the woods. Not a leaf stirred; not a sound obtruded upon great Nature's meditation. Beaded dew-drops stood upon the leaves and grasses. A white layer of ashes covered the fire, and a thin blue wreath of smoke rose straight into the air. Joe and Huck still slept. Now, far away in the woods, a bird called; another answered; presently the hammering of a woodpecker was heard. Gradually the cool dim grey of the morning whitened, and as gradually sounds multiplied and life manifested itself. The marvel of Nature shaking off sleep and going to work unfolded itself to the musing boy. A little green worm came crawling over a dewy leaf, lifting two-thirds of his body into the air from time to time, " sniffling around," then proceeding again, for he was measuring, Tom said; and when the worm approached him of its own accord, he sat as still as a stone, with his hopes rising and falling by turns as the creature still came towards him or seemed inclined to go elsewhere; and when at last it considered a painful moment with its curved body in the air and then came decisively down upon Tom's

leg and began a journey over him, his whole heart
was glad—for that meant that he was going to have
a new suit of clothes—without the shadow of a
doubt, a gaudy piratical uniform. Now a procession of ants appeared, from nowhere in particular,
and went about their labours; one struggled man-
fully by with a dead spider five times as big as itself
in its arms, and lugged it straight up a tree trunk.
A brown spotted lady-bug climbed the dizzy height
of a grass-blade, and Tom bent down close to it and
said ;—

> "Lady-bug, lady-bug, fly away home,
> Your house is on fire, your children's alone ; "

and she took wing and went off to see about it—
which did not surprise the boy, for he knew of old
that this insect was credulous about conflagrations,
and he had practised upon its simplicity more than
once. A tumble-bug came next, heaving sturdily
at its ball, and Tom touched the creature, to see
it shut its legs against its body and pretend to be
dead. The birds were fairly rioting by this time.
A cat-bird, the northern mocker, lit in a tree over
Tom's head, and trilled out her imitations of her
neighbours in a rapture of enjoyment ; then a shrill
jay swept down, a flash of blue flame, and stopped on
a twig almost within the boy's reach, cocked his head
to one side and eyed the strangers with a consuming
curiosity ; a grey squirrel and a big fellow of the
" fox " kind came skurrying along, sitting up at
intervals to inspect and chatter at the boys, for the
wild things had probably never seen a human being
before, and scarcely knew whether to be afraid or
not. All Nature was wide awake and stirring now,
long lances of sunlight pierced down through the

dense foliage far and near, and a few butterflies
came fluttering upon the scene.

Tom stirred up the other pirates and they all
clattered away with a shout, and in a minute or
two were stripped and chasing after and tumbling
over each other in the shallow limpid water of the
white sand-bar. They felt no longing for the little
village sleeping in the distance beyond the majestic
waste of water. A vagrant current or a slight rise
in the river had carried off their raft, but this only
gratified them, since its going was something like
burning the bridge between them and civilisation.

They came back to camp wonderfully refreshed,
glad-hearted, and ravenous; and they soon had the
camp-fire blazing up again. Huck found a spring
of clear cold water close by, and the boys made cups
of broad oak or hickory leaves, and felt that water,
sweetened with such a wild-wood charm as that,
would be a good enough substitute for coffee. While
Joe was slicing bacon for breakfast, Tom and Huck
asked him to hold on a minute; they stepped to a
promising nook in the river bank and threw in their
lines; almost immediately they had reward. Joe
had not had time to get impatient before they were
back again with some handsome bass, a couple of
sun perch, and a small cat-fish—provision enough
for quite a family. They fried the fish with the
bacon and were astonished; for no fish had ever
seemed so delicious before. They did not know that
the quicker a freshwater fish is on the fire after he is
caught the better he is; and they reflected little
upon what a sauce open-air sleeping, open-air exercise, bathing, and a large ingredient of hunger make
too.

They lay around in the shade after breakfast, while Huck had a smoke, and then went off through the woods on an exploring expedition. They tramped gaily along, over decaying logs, through tangled underbrush, among solemn monarchs of the forest, hung from their crowns to the ground with a drooping regalia of grape-vines. Now and then they came upon snug nooks carpeted with grass and jewelled with flowers.

They found plenty of things to be delighted with, but nothing to be astonished at. They discovered that the island was about three miles long and a quarter of a mile wide, and that the shore it lay closest to was only separated from it by a narrow channel hardly two hundred yards wide. They took a swim about every hour, so it was close upon the middle of the afternoon when they got back to camp. They were too hungry to stop to fish, but they fared sumptuously upon cold ham, and then threw themselves down in the shade to talk. But the talk soon began to drag, and then died. The stillness, the solemnity, that brooded in the woods, and the sense of loneliness, began to tell upon the spirits of the boys. They fell to thinking. A sort of undefined longing crept upon them. This took dim shape presently—it was budding home-sickness. Even Finn the Red-handed was dreaming of his doorsteps and empty hogsheads. But they were all ashamed of their weakness, and none was brave enough to speak his thought.

For some time, now, the boys had been dully conscious of a peculiar sound in the distance, just as one sometimes is of the ticking of a clock which he takes no distinct note of. But now this mysterious sound became more pronounced, and forced a recognition. The boys started, glanced at each other, and then each assumed a listening attitude. There was a long silence, profound and unbroken ; then a deep, sullen boom came floating down out of the distance.

" What is it ! " exclaimed Joe, under his breath.

" I wonder ? " said Tom in a whisper.

" 'Tain't thunder," said Huckleberry, in an awed tone, " becuz thunder——"

" Hark ! " said Tom : " listen—don't talk."

They waited a time that seemed an age, and then the same muffled boom troubled the solemn hush.

" Let's go and see."

They sprang to their feet and hurried to the shore towards the town. They parted the bushes on the bank and peered out over the water. The little steam ferry-boat was about a mile below the village, drifting with the current. Her broad deck seemed crowded with people. There were a great many skiffs rowing about or floating with the stream in the neighbourhood of the ferry-boat, but the boys could not determine what the men in them were doing. Presently a great jet of white smoke burst from the ferry-boat's side, and as it expanded and rose in a lazy cloud, that same dull throb of sound was borne to the listeners again.

" I know now ! " exclaimed Tom ; " somebody's drownded ! "

" That's it," said Huck ; " they done that last summer when Bill Turner got drownded ; they shoot a cannon over the water, and that makes him come up to the top. Yes, and they take loaves of bread and put quicksilver in 'em and set 'em afloat, and wherever there's anybody that's drownded, they'll float right there and stop."

"Yes, I've heard about that," said Joe. "I wonder what makes the bread do that."

"Oh, it ain't the bread so much," said Tom; "I reckon it's mostly what they *say* over it before they start it out."

"But they don't say anything over it," said Huck. "I've seen 'em, and they don't."

"Well, that's funny," said Tom. "But maybe they say it to themselves. Of *course* they do. Anybody might know that."

The other boys agreed that there was reason in what Tom said, because an ignorant lump of bread, uninstructed by an incantation, could not be expected to act very intelligently when sent upon an errand of such gravity.

"By jings I wish I was over there now," said Joe.

"I do too," said Huck. "I'd give heaps to know who it is."

The boys listened still and watched. Presently a revealing thought flashed through Tom's mind, and he exclaimed:

"Boys, I know who's drownded; it's us!"

They felt like heroes in an instant. Here was a gorgeous triumph; they were missed; they were mourned; hearts were breaking on their account; tears were being shed; accusing memories of unkindnesses to these poor lost lads were rising up, and unavailing regrets and remorse were being indulged; and best of all, the departed were the talk of the whole town, and the envy of all the boys, as far as this dazzling notoriety was concerned. This was fine. It was worth while to be a pirate, after all.

As twilight drew on, the ferry-boat went back to her accustomed business and the skiffs disappeared. The pirates returned to camp. They were jubilant with vanity over their new grandeur and the illustrious trouble they were making. They caught fish, cooked supper and ate it, and then fell to guessing at what the village was thinking and saying about them; and the pictures they drew of the public distress on their account were gratifying to look upon from their point of view. But when the shadows of night closed them in, they gradually ceased to talk, and sat gazing into the fire, with their minds evidently wandering elsewhere. The excitement was gone, now, and Tom and Joe could not keep back thoughts of certain persons at home who were not enjoying this fine frolic as much as they were. Misgivings came; they grew troubled and unhappy; a sigh or two escaped unawares. By-and-by Joe timidly ventured upon a roundabout "feeler" as to how the others might look upon a return to civilisation—not right now, but——

Tom withered him with derision! Huck, being uncommitted as yet, joined in with Tom, and the waverer quickly "explained," and was glad to get out of the scrape with as little taint of chicken-hearted home-sickness clinging to his garments as he could. Mutiny was effectually laid to rest for the moment.

As the night deepened, Huck began to nod, and presently to snore; Joe followed next. Tom lay upon his elbow motionless for some time, watching the two intently. At last he got up cautiously on his knees, and went searching among the grass and the flickering reflections flung by the camp-fire. He picked up and inspected several large semi-cylinders of the thin white bark of a sycamore, and finally chose two which seemed to suit him. Then he knelt by the fire and painfully wrote something upon each of these with his "red keel"; one he rolled up and put in his jacket-pocket, and the other he put in Joe's hat and removed it to a little distance from the owner. And he also put into the hat certain schoolboy treasures of almost inestimable value, among them a lump of chalk, an india-rubber ball, three fish-hooks, and one of that kind of marbles known as a "sure 'nough crystal." Then he tip-toed his way cautiously among the trees till he felt that he was out of hearing, and straightway broke into a keen run in the direction of the sand-bar.

CHAPTER XV

A FEW minutes later Tom was in the shoal water
of the bar, wading towards the Illinois shore.   Before
the depth reached his middle he was half-way over :
the current would permit no more wading now, so
he struck out confidently to swim the remaining
hundred yards.   He swam quartering up stream,
but still was swept downward rather faster than he
had expected.   However, he reached the shore
finally, and drifted along till he found a low place
and drew himself out.   He put his hand on his
jacket pocket, found his piece of bark safe, and
then struck through the woods, following the shore
with streaming garments.   Shortly before ten o'clock
he came out into an open place opposite the village,
and saw the ferry-boat lying in the shadow of the
trees and the high bank.   Everything was quiet under
the blinking stars.   He crept down the bank, watching with all his eyes, slipped into the water, swam
three or four strokes and climbed into the skiff that
did " yawl " duty at the boat's stern.   He laid himself down under the thwarts and waited, panting.
Presently the cracked bell tapped, and a voice gave
the order to " cast off."   A minute or two later
the skiff's head was standing high up against the
boat's swell, and the voyage was begun.   Tom felt
happy in his success, for he knew it was the boat's
last trip for the night.   At the end of a long twelve

or fifteen minutes the wheels stopped, and Tom
slipped overboard and swam ashore in the dusk,
landing fifty yards down stream, out of danger of
possible stragglers. He flew along unfrequented
alleys, and shortly found himself at his aunt's back
fence. He climbed over, approached the " ell " and
looked in at the sitting-room window, for a light
was burning there. There sat Aunt Polly, Sid,
Mary, and Joe Harper's mother, grouped together,
talking. They were by the bed, and the bed was
between them and the door. Tom went to the door
and began to softly lift the latch ; then he pressed
gently and the door yielded a crack ; he continued
pushing cautiously, and quaking every time it
creaked, till he judged he might squeeze through
on his knees ; and so he put his head through and
began warily.

" What makes the candle blow so ? " said Aunt
Polly. Tom hurried up. " Why, that door's open,
I believe. Why, of course it is. No end of strange
things now. Go along and shut it, Sid."

Tom disappeared under the bed just in time.
He lay and " breathed " himself for a time, and then
crept to where he could almost touch his aunt's foot.

" But as I was saying," said Aunt Polly, " he
warn't *bad*, so to say—only mischeevous. Only just
giddy, and harum-scarum, you know. He warn't
any more responsible than a colt. *He* never meant
any harm, and he was the best-hearted boy that
ever was "—and she began to cry.

" It was just so with my Joe—always full of his
devilment, and up to every kind of mischief, but he
was just as unselfish and kind as he could be—and
laws bless me, to think I went and whipped him for
taking that cream, never once recollecting that I

throwed it out myself because it was sour, and I never to see him again in this world, never, never, never, poor abused boy!" And Mrs. Harper sobbed as if her heart would break.

"I hope Tom's better off where he is," said Sid; "but if he'd been better in some ways——"

"*Sid!*" Tom felt the glare of the old lady's eye, though he could not see it. "Not a word against my Tom, now that he's gone! God'll take care of *him*—never you trouble *your*self, sir. Oh, Mrs. Harper, I don't know how to give him up, I don't know how to give him up! He was such a comfort to me, although he tormented my old heart out of me, 'most."

"The Lord giveth, and the Lord taketh away. Blessed be the name of the Lord! But it's *so* hard —oh, it's so hard! Only last Saturday my Joe bursted a shooting-cracker right under my nose, and I knocked him sprawling. Little did I know then, how soon—oh, if it was to do over again I'd hug him and bless him for it."

"Yes, yes, yes, I know just how you feel, Mrs. Harper, I know just exactly how you feel. No longer ago than yesterday noon, my Tom took and filled the cat full of Pain-killer, and I did think the cretur would tear the house down. And God forgive me, I cracked Tom's head with my thimble, poor boy, poor dead boy. But he's out of all his troubles now. And the last words I ever heard him say was to reproach——"

But this memory was too much for the old lady, and she broke entirely down. Tom was snuffling now himself—and more in pity of himself than anybody else. He could hear Mary crying, and putting in a kindly word for him from time to time. He began to have a nobler opinion of himself than ever before. Still he was sufficiently touched by his aunt's grief to long to rush out from under the bed and overwhelm her with joy—and the theatrical gorgeousness of the thing appealed strongly to his nature, too, but he resisted and lay still. He went on listening, and gathered by odds and ends that it was conjectured at first that the boys had got drowned while taking a swim ; then the small raft had been missed ; next, certain boys said the missing lads had promised that the village should " hear something " soon ; the wise heads had " put this and that together," and decided that the lads had gone off on that raft, and would turn up at the next town below presently ; but towards noon the raft had been found, lodged against the Missouri shore some five or six miles below the village, and then hope perished ; they must be drowned, else hunger would have driven them home by nightfall if not sooner. It was believed that the search for the bodies had been a fruitless effort merely because the drowning must have occurred in mid-channel, since the boys, being good swimmers, would otherwise have escaped to shore. This was Wednesday night. If the bodies continued missing until Sunday, all hope would be given over, and the funerals would be preached on that morning. Tom shuddered.

Mrs. Harper gave a sobbing good-night and turned to go. Then with a mutual impulse the two bereaved women flung themselves into each other's arms and had a good consoling cry, and then parted. Aunt Polly was tender far beyond her wont in her good-night to Sid and Mary. Sid snuffled a bit, and Mary went off crying with all her heart.

Aunt Polly knelt down and prayed for Tom so

touchingly, so appealingly, and with such measureless love in her words and her old, trembling voice, that he was weltering in tears again long before she was through.

He had to keep still long after she went to bed, for she kept making broken-hearted ejaculations from time to time, tossing unrestfully, and turning over. But at last she was still, only moaning a little in her sleep. Now the boy stole out, rose gradually by the bedside, shaded the candle-light with his hand, and stood regarding her. His heart was full of pity for her. He took out his sycamore scroll and placed it by the candle. But something occurred to him, and he lingered considering. His face lighted with a happy solution of his thought; he put the bark hastily in his pocket, then he bent over and kissed the faded lips, and straightway made his stealthy exit, latching the door behind him.

He threaded his way back to the ferry landing, found nobody at large there, and walked boldly on board the boat, for he knew she was tenantless except that there was a watchman, who always turned in and slept like a graven image. He untied the skiff at the stern, slipped into it, and was soon rowing cautiously up stream. When he had pulled a mile above the village, he started quartering across, and bent himself stoutly to his work. He hit the landing on the other side neatly, for this was a familiar bit of work to him. He was moved to capture the skiff, arguing that it might be considered a ship and therefore legitimate prey for a pirate · but he knew a thorough search would be made for it, and that might end in revelations. So he stepped ashore and entered the wood. He sat down and took a long rest, torturing himself mean-

time to keep awake, and then started wearily
down the home stretch. The night was far spent.
It was broad daylight before he found himself
fairly abreast the island bar. He rested again until
the sun was well up and gilding the great river with
its splendour, and then he plunged into the stream.
A little later he paused, dripping, upon the threshold of the camp, and heard Joe say :

"No, Tom's true-blue, Huck, and he'll come back.
He won't desert. He knows that would be a disgrace to a pirate, and Tom's too proud for that sort
of thing. He's up to something or other. Now I
wonder what ? "

"Well, the things is ours anyway, ain't they ? "

"Pretty near, but not yet, Huck. The writing
says they are if he ain't back to breakfast."

"Which he is ! " exclaimed Tom, with fine dramatic effect, stepping grandly into camp.

A sumptuous breakfast of bacon and fish was
shortly provided, and as the boys set to work upon
it, Tom recounted (and adorned) his adventures.
They were a vain and boastful company of heroes
when the tale was done. Then Tom hid himself
away in a shady nook to sleep till noon, and the
other pirates got ready to fish and explore

CHAPTER XVI

AFTER dinner, all the gang turned out to hunt for turtle eggs on the bar. They went about poking sticks into the sand, and when they found a soft place they went down on their knees and dug with their hands. Sometimes they would take fifty or sixty eggs out of one hole. They were perfectly round, white things, a trifle smaller than an English walnut. They had a famous fried-egg feast that night, and another on Friday morning. After breakfast they went whooping and prancing out on the bar, and chased each other round and round, shedding clothes as they went, until they were naked, and then continued the frolic far away up the shoal water of the bar, against the stiff current, which latter tripped their legs from under them from time to time, and greatly increased the fun. And now and then they stood in a group and splashed water in each other's faces with their palms, gradually approaching each other with averted faces, to avoid the straggling sprays, and finally gripping and struggling till the best man ducked his neighbour, and then they all went under in a tangle of white legs and arms, and came up blowing, sputtering, laughing, and gasping for breath at one and the same time.

When they were well exhausted, they would run

out and sprawl on the dry, hot sand, and lie there and cover themselves up with it, and by-and-by break for the water again and go through the original performance once more. Finally it occurred to them that their naked skin represented flesh-coloured " tights " very fairly ; so they drew a ring in the sand and had a circus—with three clowns in it, for none would yield this proudest post to his neighbour.

Next they got their marbles. and played " knucks " and " ring-taw " and " keeps," till that amusement grew stale. Then Joe and Huck had another swim, but Tom would not venture, because he found that in kicking off his trousers he had kicked his string of rattlesnake rattles off his ankle, and he wondered how he had escaped cramp so long without the protection of this mysterious charm. He did not venture again until he had found it, and by that time the other boys were tired and ready to rest. They gradually wandered apart, dropped into the " dumps," and fell to gazing longingly across the wide river to where the village lay drowsing in the sun. Tom found himself writing *Becky* in the sand with his big toe ; he scratched it out and was angry with himself for his weakness. But he wrote it again, nevertheless ; he could not help it. He erased it once more, and then took himself out of temptation by driving the other boys together, and then joining them.

But Joe's spirits had gone down almost beyond resurrection. He was so home-sick that he could hardly endure the misery of it. The tears lay very near the surface. Huck was melancholy too. Tom was down-hearted, but tried hard not to show it. He had a secret which he was not ready to tell yet, but if this mutinous depression was not broken up soon, he would have to bring it out. He said with a great show of cheerfulness :

" I bet there's been pirates on this island before, boys. We'll explore it again. They've hid treasures here somewhere. How'd you feel to light on a rotten chest full of gold and silver—hey ? "

But it roused only a faint enthusiasm, which faded out with no reply. Tom tried one or two other seductions ; but they failed too. It was discouraging work. Joe sat poking up the sand with a stick, and looking very gloomy. Finally he said :

" Oh, boys, let's give it up. I want to go home. It's so lonesome."

" Oh no, Joe, you'll feel better by-and-by," said Tom. " Just think of the fishing that's here."

" I don't care for the fishing. I want to go home."

" But, Joe, there ain't such another swimming-place anywhere."

" Swimming's no good ; I don't seem to care for it, somehow, when there ain't anybody to say I shan't go in. I mean to go home."

" Oh, shucks ! baby ! You want to see your mother, I reckon."

" Yes, I *do* want to see my mother, and you would too, if you had one. I ain't any more baby than you are." And Joe snuffled a little.

" Well, we'll let the cry-baby go home to his mother, won't we, Huck ? Poor thing—does it want to see its mother ? And so it shall. *You* like it here, don't you, Huck ? We'll stay, won't we ? "

Huck said " Y-e-s—" without any heart in it.

" I'll never speak to you again as long as I live," said Joe, rising. " There now ! " And he moved moodily away and began to dress himself.

" Who cares ? " said Tom. " Nobody wants you

to. Go 'long home and get laughed at. Oh, you're a nice pirate. Huck and me ain't cry-babies. We'll stay, won't we, Huck? Let him go if he wants to. I reckon we can get along without him, per'aps."

But Tom was uneasy nevertheless, and was alarmed to see Joe go sullenly on with his dressing. And then it was discomforting to see Huck eyeing Joe's preparations so wistfully and keeping up such an ominous silence. Presently, without a parting word, Joe began to wade off towards the Illinois shore. Tom's heart began to sink He glanced at Huck. Huck could not bear the look, and dropped his eyes. Then he said:

" I want to go, too, Tom ; it was getting so lonesome anyway, and now it'll be worse. Let's us go too, Tom."

" I won't ; you can all go if you want to. I mean to stay."

" Tom, I better go."

" Well, go 'long—who's hindering you ? "

Huck began to pick up his scattered clothes. He said :

" Tom, I wisht you'd come too. Now you think it over. We'll wait for you when we get to shore."

" Well, you'll wait a blame long time, that's all."

Huck started sorrowfully away, and Tom stood looking after him, with a strong desire tugging at his heart to yield his pride and go along too. He hoped the boys would stop, but they still waded slowly on. It suddenly dawned on Tom that it was become very lonely and still. He made one final struggle with his pride, and then he darted after his comrades, yelling :

" Wait ! wait ! I want to tell you something ! "

They presently stopped and turned round. When

he got to where they were, he began unfolding his
secret, and they listened moodily till at last they
saw the " point " he was driving at, and then they
set up a war-whoop of applause and said it was "splendid ! " and said if he had told them that at first, they
wouldn't have started away.   He made a plausible
excuse ; but his real reason had been the fear that
not even the secret would keep them with him any
very great length of time, and so he had meant to
hold it in reserve as a last seduction.

The lads came gaily back and went at their sports
again with a will, chatting all the time about Tom's
stupendous plan and admiring the genius of it.
After a dainty egg-and fish dinner, Tom said he
wanted to learn to smoke now.   Joe caught at the
idea, and said he would like to try too.   So Huck
made pipes and filled them.   These novices had
never smoked anything before but cigars made of
grape-vine, and they " bit " the tongue, and were
not considered manly, anyway.

Now they stretched themselves out on their elbows
and began to puff charily, and with slender confidence.   The smoke had an unpleasant taste, and
they gagged a little, but Tom said :

" Why, it's just as easy !   If I'd a knowed *this*
was all, I'd a learnt long ago."

" So would I," said Joe.   " It's just nothing."

" Why, many a time I've looked at people smoking and thought, Well, I wish I could do that ; but
I never thought I could," said Tom.   " That's just
the way with me, ain't it, Huck ?   You've heard
me talk just that way, haven't you, Huck ?   I'll
leave it to Huck if I haven't."

" Yes, heaps of times," said Huck.

" Well, I have too," said Tom ; " oh, hundreds of

times. Once down there by the slaughter-house
Don't you remember, Huck? Bob Tanner was
there, and Johnny Miller, and Jeff Thatcher, when
I said it. Don't you remember, Huck, 'bout me
saying that?"

"Yes, that's so," said Huck. "That was the day
after I lost a white alley—no, 'twas the day before!"

"There, I told you so," said Tom. "Huck recol-
lects it."

"I believe I could smoke this pipe all day," said
Joe. "*I* don't feel sick."

"Neither do I," said Tom. "*I* could smoke it all
day, but I bet you Jeff Thatcher couldn't."

"Jeff Thatcher! Why, he'd keel over just with
two draws. Just let him try it once; *he'd* see!"

"I bet he would, and Johnny Miller—I wish I
could see Johnny Miller tackle it once."

"Oh, don't *I?*" said Joe. "Why, I bet you
Johnny Miller couldn't any more do this than nothing. Just one little snifter would fetch *him.*"

"'Deed it would, Joe. Say—I wish the boys could
see us now."

"So do I!"

"Say, boys, don't say anything about it, and
some time when they're around I'll come up to you
and say, 'Joe, got a pipe? I want a smoke!' And
you'll say, kind of careless like, as if it warn't anything, you'll say, 'Yes. I got my *old* pipe, and another one, but my tobacker ain't very good.' And
I'll say, 'Oh, that's all right, if it's *strong* enough.'
And then you'll out with the pipes, and we'll light up
just as ca'm, and then just see 'em look!"

"By jings that'll be gay, Tom; I wish it was
now!"

"So do I! And when we tell 'em we learned

when we was off pirating, won't they wish they'd been along!"

"Oh, I reckon not! I'll just *bet* they will!"

So the talk ran on; but presently it began to flag a trifle, and grow disjointed. The silences widened; the expectoration marvellously increased. Every pore inside the boys' cheeks became a spouting fountain; they could scarcely bale out the cellars under their tongues fast enough to prevent an inundation; little overflowings down their throats occurred in spite of all they could do, and sudden retchings followed every time. Both boys were looking very pale and miserable now. Joe's pipe dropped from his nerveless fingers. Tom's followed. Both fountains were going furiously, and both pumps baling with might and main. Joe said feebly:

"I've lost my knife. I reckon I better go and find it."

Tom said, with quivering lips and halting utterance:

"I'll help you. You go over that way, and I'll hunt around by the spring. No, you needn't come, Huck—we can find it."

So Huck sat down again, and waited an hour. Then he found it lonesome, and went to find his comrades. They were wide apart in the woods, both very pale, both fast asleep. But something informed him that if they had had any trouble they had got rid of it.

They were not talkative at supper that night; they had a humble look; and when Huck prepared his pipe after the meal, and was going to prepare theirs, they said no, they were not feeling very well —something they ate at dinner had disagreed with them.

CHAPTER XVII

ABOUT midnight Joe awoke, and called the boys.
There was a brooding oppressiveness in the air that
seemed to bode something. The boys huddled
themselves 'together, and sought the friendly com-
panionship of the fire, though the dull dead heat of
the breathless atmosphere was stifling. They sat still,
intent and waiting. Beyond the light of the fire,
everything was swallowed up in the blackness of
darkness. Presently there came a quivering glow
that vaguely revealed the foliage for a moment and
then vanished. By-and-by another came, a little
stronger. Then another. Then a faint moan came
sighing through the branches of the forest, and the
boys felt a fleeting breath upon their cheeks, and
shuddered with the fancy that the Spirit of the Night
had gone by. There was a pause. Now a weird flash
turned night into day, and showed every little grass-
blade separate and distinct, that grew about their
feet. And it showed three white, startled faces too.
A deep peal of thunder went rolling and tumbling
down the heavens, and lost itself in sullen rumblings
in the distance. A sweep of chilly air passed by,
rustling all the leaves and snowing the flaky ashes
broadcast about the fire. Another fierce glare lit
up the forest, and an instant crash followed that
seemed to rend the tree-tops right over the boys'
heads. They clung together in terror in the thick

gloom that followed. A few big rain-drops fell pat-
tering upon the leaves.

" Quick, boys, go for the tent ! " exclaimed Tom.

They sprang away, stumbling over roots and among
vines in the dark, no two plunging in the same direction. A furious blast roared through the trees,
making everything sing as it went. One blinding
flash after another came, and peal on peal of deafen-
ing thunder. And now a drenching rain poured down,
and the rising hurricane drove it in sheets along the
ground. The boys cried out to each other, but the
roaring wind and the booming thunder-blasts
drowned their voices utterly. However, one by one
they straggled in at last, and took shelter under the
tent, cold, scared, and streaming with water ; but
to have company in misery seemed something to be
grateful for. They could not talk, the old sail flapped
so furiously, even if the other noises would have
allowed them. The tempest rose higher and higher,
and presently the sail tore loose from its fastenings,
and went winging away on the blast. The boys
seized each other's hands, and fled, with many tum-
blings and bruises, to the shelter of a great oak that
stood upon the river bank. Now the battle was at
its highest. Under the ceaseless conflagration of
lightnings that flamed in the skies, everything below
stood out in clean-cut and shadowless distinctness ;
the bending trees, the billowy river white with foam,
the driving spray of spume-flakes, the dim outlines of
the high bluffs on the other side, glimpsed through
the drifting cloud-rack and the slanting veil of rain.
Every little while some giant tree yielded the fight
and fell crashing through the younger growth ; and
the unflagging thunder-peals came now in ear-
splitting explosive bursts, keen and sharp, and un-

speakably appalling. The storm culminated in one matchless effort that seemed likely to tear the island to pieces, burn it up, drown it to the tree-tops, blow it away and deafen every creature in it, all at one and the same moment. It was a wild night for homeless young heads to be out in.

But at last the battle was done, and the forces retired, with weaker and weaker threatenings and grumblings, and peace resumed her sway. The boys went back to camp a good deal awed; but they found there was still something to be thankful for, because the great sycamore, the shelter of their beds, was a ruin now, blasted by the lightnings, and they were not under it when the catastrophe happened.

Everything in camp was drenched, the camp fire as well; for they were but heedless lads, like their generation, and had made no provision against rain. Here was matter for dismay, for they were soaked through and chilled. They were eloquent in their distress: but they presently discovered that the fire had eaten so far up under the great log it had been built against (where it curved upward and separated itself from the ground), that a hand-breadth or so of it had escaped wetting; so they patiently wrought until, with shreds and bark gathered from the under sides of sheltered logs, they coaxed the fire to burn again. Then they piled on great dead boughs till they had a roaring furnace and were glad-hearted once more. They dried their boiled ham and had a feast, and after that they sat by the fire and expanded and glorified their midnight adventure until morning, for there was not a dry spot to sleep on anywhere around.

As the sun began to steal in upon the boys, drowsiness came over them and they went out on the sand-bar and lay down to sleep. They got scorched out by-and-by, and drearily set about getting breakfast. After the meal they felt rusty, and stiff-jointed, and a little homesick once more. Tom saw the signs, and fell to cheering up the pirates as well as he could. But they cared nothing for marbles, or circus, or swimming, or anything. He reminded them of the imposing secret, and raised a ray of cheer. While it lasted he got them interested in a new device. This was to knock off being pirates for a while, and be Indians for a change. They were attracted by this idea ; so it was not long before they were stripped, and striped from head to heel with black mud, like so many zebras, all of them chiefs, of course, and then they went tearing through the woods to attack an English settlement.

By-and-by they separated into three hostile tribes, and darted upon each other from ambush with dreadful war-whoops, and killed and scalped each other by thousands. It was a gory day. Consequently it was a satisfactory one.

They assembled in camp towards supper-time, hungry and happy. But now a difficulty arose— hostile Indians could not break the bread of hospitality together without first making peace, and this was a simple impossibility without smoking a pipe of peace. There was no other process that ever they had heard of. Two of the savages almost wished they had remained pirates. However, there was no other way, so with such show of cheerfulness as they could muster they called for the pipe and took their whiff, as it passed, in due form.

And behold they were glad they had gone into savagery, for they had gained something ; they found that they could now smoke a little without

having to go and hunt for a lost knife ; they did not
get sick enough to be seriously uncomfortable. They
were not likely to fool away this high promise for
lack of effort. No, they practised cautiously after
supper with right fair success, and so they spent a
jubilant evening. They were prouder and happier
in their new acquirement than they would have been
in the scalping and skinning of the Six Nations. We
will leave them to smoke and chatter and brag, since
we have no further use for them at present.

CHAPTER XVIII

BUT there was no hilarity in the little town that tranquil Saturday afternoon. The Harpers and Aunt Polly's family were being put into mourning with great grief and many tears. An unusual quiet possessed the village, although it was ordinarily quiet enough in all conscience. The villagers conducted their concerns with an abstracted air, and talked little ; but they sighed often. The Saturday holiday seemed a burden to the children. They had no heart in their sports, and gradually gave them up.

In the afternoon Becky Thatcher found herself moping about the deserted school-house yard, and feeling very melancholy. But she found nothing there to comfort her. She soliloquised :

" Oh, if I only had his brass andiron-knob again ! But I haven't got anything now to remember him by," and she choked back a little sob.

Presently she stopped, and said to herself :

" It was right here. Oh, if it was to do over again, I wouldn't say that—I wouldn't say it for the whole world. But he's gone now ; I'll never, never, never see him any more."

This thought broke her down, and she wandered away with the tears rolling down her cheeks. Then quite a group of boys and girls—playmates of Tom's and Joe's—came by, and stood looking over the paling fence and talking in reverent tones of how Tom did

so-and-so the last time they saw him, and how Joe
said this and that small trifle (pregnant with awful
prophecy, as they could easily see now !)—and each
speaker pointed out the exact spot where the lost
lads stood at the time, and then added something
like, " And I was a-standing just so—just as I am
now, and as if you was him—I was as close as that—
and he smiled, just this way—and then something
seemed to go all over me, like—awful, you know—
and I never thought what it meant, of course, but I
can see now ! "

Then there was a dispute about who saw the dead
boys last in life, and many claimed that dismal distinction, and offered evidences more or less tampered
with by the witness ; and when it was ultimately
decided who did see the departed last, and exchanged
the last words with them, the lucky parties took
upon themselves a sort of sacred importance, and
were gaped at and envied by all the rest. One poor
chap who had no other grandeur to offer, said, with
tolerably manifest pride in the remembrance :

" Well, Tom Sawyer he licked me once."

But that bid for glory was a failure. Most of the
boys could say that, and so that cheapened the distinction too much. The group loitered away, still
recalling memories of the lost heroes in awed voices.

When the Sunday-school hour was finished the
next morning, the bell began to toll, instead of ring-
ing in the usual way. It was a very still Sabbath,
and the mournful sound seemed in keeping with the
musing hush that lay upon nature. The villagers
began to gather, loitering a moment in the vestibule
to converse in whispers about the sad event. But
there was no whispering in the house ; only the
funereal rustling of dresses, as the women gathered to

their seats, disturbed the silence there. None could remember when the little church had been so full before. There was finally a waiting pause, an expectant dumbness, and then Aunt Polly entered, followed by Sid and Mary, and then by the Harper family, all in deep black, and the whole congregation, the old minister as well, rose reverently and stood, until the mourners were seated in the front pew. There was another communing silence, broken at intervals by muffled sobs, and then the minister spread his hands abroad and prayed. A moving hymn was sung, and the text followed : " I am the resurrection and the life."

As the service proceeded, the clergyman drew such pictures of the graces, the winning ways, and the rare promise of the lost lads, that every soul there, thinking he recognised these pictures, felt a pang in remembering that he had persistently blinded himself to them always before, and had as persistently seen only faults and flaws in the poor boys. The minister related many a touching incident in the lives of the departed, too, which illustrated their sweet, generous natures, and the people could easily see, now, how noble and beautiful those episodes were, and remembered with grief that at the time they occurred they had seemed rank rascalities, well deserving of the cowhide. The congregation became more and more moved as the pathetic tale went on, till at last the whole company broke down and joined the weeping mourners in a chorus of anguished sobs, the preacher himself giving way to his feelings, and crying in the pulpit.

There was a rustle in the gallery which nobody noticed ; a moment later the church door creaked ; the minister raised his streaming eyes above his handkerchief, and stood transfixed ! First one and then another pair of eyes followed the minister's, and then, almost with one impulse, the congregation rose and stared while the three dead boys came marching up the aisle, Tom in the lead, Joe next, and Huck, a ruin of drooping rags, sneaking sheepishly in the rear. They had been hid in the unused gallery, listening to their own funeral sermon !

Aunt Polly, Mary, and the Harpers threw themselves upon their restored ones, smothered them with kisses and poured out thanksgivings, while poor Huck stood abashed and uncomfortable, not knowing exactly what to do or where to hide from so many unwelcoming eyes. He wavered, and started to slink away, but Tom seized him and said :

" Aunt Polly, it ain't fair. Somebody's got to be glad to see Huck."

" And so they shall ! I'm glad to see him, poor motherless thing ! " And the loving attentions Aunt Polly lavished upon him were the one thing capable of making him more uncomfortable than he was before.

Suddenly the minister shouted at the top of his voice :

" ' Praise God, from whom all blessings flow '—SING !—and put your hearts in it ! "

And they did. Old Hundred swelled up with a triumphant burst, and while it shook the rafters Tom Sawyer the Pirate looked around upon the envying juveniles about him, and confessed in his heart that this was the proudest moment of his life.

As the " sold " congregation trooped out, they said they would almost be willing to be made ridiculous again to hear Old Hundred sung like that once more.

Tom got more cuffs and kisses that day—according to Aunt Polly's varying moods—than he had earned before in a year; and he hardly knew which expressed the most gratefulness to God and affection for himself.

CHAPTER XIX

THAT was Tom's great secret—the scheme to return home with his brother pirates and attend their own funerals. They had paddled over to the Missouri shore on a log, at dusk on Saturday, landing five or six miles below the village; they had slept in the woods at the edge of the town till nearly daylight, and had then crept through back lanes and alleys and finished their sleep in the gallery of the church among a chaos of invalid benches.

At breakfast, Monday morning, Aunt Polly and Mary were very loving to Tom, and very attentive to his wants. There was an unusual amount of talk. In the course of it Aunt Polly said:

"Well, I don't say it wasn't a fine joke, Tom, to keep everybody suffering 'most a week so you boys had a good time, but it is a pity you could be so hard-hearted as to let me suffer so. If you could come over on a log to go to your funeral, you could have come over and give me a hint some way that you warn't dead, but only run off."

"Yes, you could have done that, Tom," said Mary; "and I believe you would if you had thought of it."

"Would you, Tom?" said Aunt Polly, her face lighting wistfully. "Say, now, would you, if you'd thought of it?"

" I—well, I don't know. 'Twould a spoiled every-thing."

"Tom, I hoped you loved me that much," said Aunt Polly, with a grieved tone that discomforted the boy. "It would been something if you'd cared enough to think of it, even if you didn't do it."

"Now, auntie, that ain't any harm," pleaded Mary; "it's only Tom's giddy way—he is always in such a rush that he never thinks of anything."

"More's the pity. Sid would have thought. And Sid would have come and done it, too. Tom, you'll look back some day, when it's too late, and wish you'd cared a little more for me when it would have cost you so little."

"Now, auntie, you know I do care for you," said Tom.

"I'd know it better if you acted more like it."

"I wish now I'd thought," said Tom, with a repentant tone; "but I dreamed about you, any-way. That's something, ain't it?"

"It ain't much—a cat does that much—but it's better than nothing. What did you dream?"

"Why, Wednesday night I dreamt that you was sitting over there by the bed, and Sid was sitting by the wood-box, and Mary next to him."

"Well, so we did. So we always do. I'm glad your dreams could take even that much trouble about us."

"And I dreamt that Joe Harper's mother was here."

"Why, she was here! Did you dream any more?"

"Oh, lots. But it's so dim now."

"Well, try to recollect—can't you?"

"Somehow it seems to me that the wind—the wind blowed the—the——"

"Try harder, Tom! The wind did blow something, come!"

Tom pressed his fingers on his forehead an anxious minute, and then said:

"I've got it now! I've got it now! It blowed the candle!"

"Mercy on us! Go on, Tom, go on!"

"And it seems to me that you said, 'Why, I believe that that door——'"

"Go on, Tom!"

"Just let me study a moment—just a moment. Oh yes—you said you believed the door was open."

"As I'm a sitting here, I did! Didn't I, Mary? Go on!"

"And then—and then—well, I won't be certain, but it seems like as if you made Sid go and—and——"

"Well? Well? What did I make him do, Tom? What did I make him do?"

"You made him—you——Oh, you made him shut it!"

"Well, for the laud's sake! I never heard the beat of that in all my days! Don't tell me there ain't anything in dreams any more. Sereny Harper shall know of this before I'm an hour older. I'd like to see her get around this with her rubbage about superstition. Go on, Tom!"

"Oh, it's all getting just as bright as day now. Next you said I warn't bad, only mischeevous and harum-scarum, and not any more responsible than—than—I think it was a colt, or something."

"And so it was! Well, Goodness gracious! Go on, Tom!"

"And then you began to cry."

"So I did. So I did. Not the first time, neither. And then——"

" Then Mrs. Harper she began to cry, and said Joe was just the same, and she wished she hadn't whipped him for taking cream when she'd throwed it out her ownself——"

"Tom! The sperrit was upon you! You was a prophesying—that's what you was doing! Laud alive!—go on, Tom!"

" Then Sid he said—he said——"

" I don't think I said anything," said Sid.

" Yes, you did, Sid," said Mary.

" Shut your heads and let Tom go on! What did he say, Tom?"

" He said—I think he said he hoped I was better off where I was gone to, but if I'd been better sometimes——"

"There, d'you hear that? It was his very words!"

" And you shut him up sharp."

" I lay I did! There must a been an angel there. There was an angel there, somewheres!"

" And Mrs. Harper told about Joe scaring her with a fire-cracker, and you told about Peter and the " Pain-killer——"

" Just as true as I live!"

"And then there was a whole lot of talk 'bout dragging the river for us, and 'bout having the funeral Sunday, and then you and old Mrs. Harper hugged and cried, and she went."

" It happened just so! It happened just so, as sure as I'm a sitting in these very tracks. Tom, you couldn't told it more like if you'd a seen it! And then what? Go on, Tom."

" Then I thought you prayed for me—and I could see you and hear every word you said. And you went to bed, and I was so sorry that I took and wrote on a piece of sycamore bark, ' We ain't dead—we are only off being pirates," and put it on the table by the candle ; and then you looked so good, laying there asleep, that I thought I went and leaned over and kissed you on the lips."

" Did you, Tom, did you ? I just forgive you everything for that ! " And she seized the boy in a crushing embrace that made him feel like the guiltiest of villains.

" It was very kind, even though it was only a dream," Sid soliloquised just audibly.

" Shut up, Sid ! A body does just the same in a dream as he'd do if he was awake. Here's a big Milum apple I've been saving for you, Tom, if you was ever found again—now go 'long to school. I'm thankful to the good God and Father of us all I've got you back, that's long-suffering and merciful to them that believe on Him and keep His word, though goodness knows I'm unworthy of it ; but if only the worthy ones got His blessings and had His hand to help them over the rough places, there's few enough would smile here or ever enter into His rest when the long night comes. Go 'long, Sid, Mary, Tom— take yourselves off—you've hendered me long enough."

The children left for school, and the old lady to call on Mrs. Harper, and vanquish her realism with Tom's marvellous dream. Sid had better judgment than to utter the thought that was in his mind as he left the house. It was this :

" Pretty thin—so long a dream as that, without any mistakes in it ! "

What a hero Tom was become now ! He did not go skipping and prancing, but moved with a dignified swagger, as became a pirate who felt that the public eye was on him. And indeed it was ; he tried not to seem to see the looks or hear the remarks as he passed along, but they were food and drink to him. Smaller boys than himself flocked at his heels, as proud to be seen with him and tolerated by him as if he had been the drummer at the head of a procession, or the elephant leading a menagerie into town. Boys of his own size pretended not to know he had been away at all, but they were consuming with envy, nevertheless. They would have given anything to have that swarthy, sun-tanned skin of his, and his glittering notoriety; and Tom would not have parted with either for a circus.

At school the children made so much of him and Joe, and delivered such eloquent admiration from their eyes, that the two heroes were not long in becoming insufferably "stuck-up." They began to tell their adventures to hungry listeners—but they only began; it was not a thing likely to have an end, with imaginations like theirs to furnish material. And finally, when they got out their pipes and went serenely puffing around, the very summit of glory was reached.

Tom decided that he could be independent of Becky Thatcher now. Glory was sufficient. He would live for glory. Now that he was distinguished, maybe she would be wanting to "make up." Well, let her—she should see that he could be as indifferent as some other people. Presently she arrived. Tom pretended not to see her. He moved away and joined a group of boys and girls, and began to talk. Soon he observed that she was tripping gaily back and forth with flushed face and dancing eyes, pretending to be busy chasing schoolmates, and screaming with laughter when she made a capture, but he noticed that she always made her captures in his vicinity, and that she seemed to cast a conscious eye in his direction at such times, too. It gratified all the vicious vanity that was in him; and so, instead of winning him, it only "set him up" the more and made him the more diligent to avoid betraying that he knew she was about. Presently she gave over skylarking, and moved irresolutely about, sighing once or twice and glancing furtively and wistfully towards Tom. Then she observed that now Tom was talking more particularly to Amy Lawrence than to any one else. She felt a sharp pang and grew disturbed and uneasy at once. She tried to go away, but her feet were treacherous, and carried her to the group instead. She said to a girl almost at Tom's elbow—with sham vivacity:

"Why, Mary Austin! you bad girl, why didn't you come to Sunday-school?"

"I did come—didn't you see me?"

"Why, no! Did you? Where did you sit?"

"I was in Miss Peters's class, where I always go. I saw you."

"Did you? Why, it's funny I didn't see you. I wanted to tell you about the picnic."

"Oh, that's jolly. Who's going to give it?"

"My ma's going to let me have one."

"Oh, goody; I hope she'll let me come."

"Well, she will. The picnic's for me. She'll let anybody come that I want, and I want you."

"That's ever so nice. When is it going to be?"

"By-and-by. Maybe about vacation."

"Oh, won't it be fun! You going to have all the girls and boys?"

"Yes, every one that's friends to me—or wants to be," and she glanced ever so furtively at Tom, but he talked right along to Amy Lawrence about the terrible storm on the island, and how the lightning tore the great sycamore tree " all to flinders " while he was "standing within three feet of it."

" Oh, may I come ? " said Gracie Miller.

" Yes."

" And me ? " said Sally Rogers.

" Yes."

" And me too ? " said Susy Harper. " And Joe ? "

" Yes."

And so on, with clapping of joyful hands, till all the group had begged for invitations but Tom and Amy. Then Tom turned coolly away, still talking, and took Amy with him. Becky's lips trembled and the tears came to her eyes ; she hid these signs with a forced gaiety and went on chattering, but the life had gone out of the picnic, now, and out of everything else ; she got away as soon as she could and hid herself, and had what her sex call " a good cry." Then she sat moody, with wounded pride, till the bell rang. She roused up, now, with a vindictive cast in her eye, and gave her plaited tails a shake, and said she knew what she'd do.

At recess Tom continued his flirtation with Amy with jubilant self-satisfaction. And he kept drifting about to find Becky and lacerate her with the performance. At last he spied her, but there was a sudden falling of his mercury. She was sitting cosily on a little bench behind the school-house, looking at a picture-book with Alfred Temple ; and so absorbed were they, and their heads so close together over the book, that they did not seem to be conscious of anything in the world beside. Jealousy ran red-hot through Tom's veins. He began to hate himself for throwing away the chance

Becky had offered for a reconciliation. He called himself a fool, and all the hard names he could think of. He wanted to cry with vexation. Amy chatted happily along, as they walked, for her heart was singing, but Tom's tongue had lost its function. He did not hear what Amy was saying, and whenever she paused expectantly, he could only stammer an awkward assent, which was as often misplaced as otherwise. He kept drifting to the rear of the school-house again and again, to sear his eyeballs with the hateful spectacle there. He could not help it. And it maddened him to see, as he thought he saw, that Becky Thatcher never once suspected that he was even in the land of the living. But she did see, nevertheless ; and she knew she was winning her fight, too, and was glad to see him suffer as she had suffered. Amy's happy prattle became intolerable. Tom hinted at things he had to attend to ; things that must be done ; and time was fleeting. But in vain—the girl chirped on. Tom thought, " Oh, hang her, ain't I ever going to get rid of her ? " At last he must be attending to those things ; she said artlessly that she would be " around " when school let out. And he hastened away, hating her for it.

" Any other boy ! " Tom thought, grating his teeth. " Any boy in the whole town but that Saint Louis smarty, that thinks he dresses so fine and is aristocracy ! Oh, all right. I licked you the first day you ever saw this town, mister, and I'll lick you again ! You just wait till I catch you out ! I'll just take and——"

And he went through the motions of thrashing an imaginary boy—pummelling the air, and kicking and gouging.

" Oh, you do, do you ? you holler 'nough, do you Now then, let that learn you ! "

And so the imaginary flogging was finished to his satisfaction.

Tom fled home at noon. His conscience could not endure any more of Amy's grateful happiness, and his jealousy could bear no more of the other distress. Becky resumed her picture-inspections with Alfred, but as the minutes dragged along and no Tom came to suffer, her triumph began to cloud and she lost interest ; gravity and absent-mindedness followed, and then melancholy ; two or three times she pricked up her ear at a footstep, but it was a false hope ; no Tom came. At last she grew entirely miserable, and wished she hadn't carried it so far. When poor Alfred, seeing that he was losing her he did not know how, and kept exclaiming : " Oh, here's a jolly one ! look at this ! " she lost patience at last and said, " Oh, don't bother me ! I don't care for them ! " and burst into tears, and got up and walked away.

Alfred dropped alongside and was going to try and comfort her, but she said :

" Go away and leave me alone, can't you ? I hate you ! "

So the boy halted, wondering what he could have done—for she had said she would look at pictures all through the nooning—and she walked on, crying. Then Alfred went musing into the deserted schoolhouse. He was humiliated and angry. He easily guessed his way to the truth—the girl had simply made a convenience of him to vent her spite upon Tom Sawyer. He was far from hating Tom the less when this thought occurred to him. He wished there was some way to get that boy into trouble without much risk to himself. Tom's spelling-book fell under his eye. Here was his opportunity. He gratefully opened to the lesson for the afternoon, and poured ink upon the page. Becky, glancing in at a window behind him at the moment, saw the act and moved on without discovering herself. She started homeward, now, intending to find Tom and tell him : Tom would be thankful, and their troubles would be healed. Before she was half-way home, however, she had changed her mind. The thought of Tom's treatment of her when she was talking about her picnic came scorching back, and filled her with shame. She resolved to let him get whipped on the damaged spelling-book's account, and to hate him for ever into the bargain.

CHAPTER XX

Tom arrived at home in a dreary mood, and the first thing his aunt said to him showed him that he had brought his sorrows to an unpromising market :

" Tom, I've a notion to skin you alive."

" Auntie, what have I done ? "

" Well, you've done enough. Here I go over to Sereny Harper like an old softy, expecting I'm going to make her believe all that rubbage about that dream, when, lo and behold you, she'd found out from Joe that you was over here and heard all the talk we had that night. Tom, I don't know what is to become of a boy that will act like that. It makes me feel so bad to think you could let me go to Sereny Harper, and make such a fool of myself, and never say a word."

This was a new aspect of the thing. His smartness of the morning had seemed to Tom a good joke before, and very ingenious. It merely looked mean and shabby now. He hung his head and could not think of anything to say for a moment ; then he said :

" Auntie, I wish I hadn't done it—but I didn't think."

" Oh, child, you never think. You never think of anything but your own selfishness. You could think to come all the way over here from Jackson's Island in the night to laugh at our troubles, and you could think to fool me with a lie about a dream :

but you couldn't ever think to pity us and save us from sorrow."

"Auntie, I know now it was mean, but I didn't mean to be mean; I didn't, honest. And besides, I didn't come over here to laugh at you that night."

"What did you come for, then?"

"It was to tell you not to be uneasy about us, because we hadn't got drownded."

"Tom, Tom, I would be the thankfullest soul in this world if I could believe you ever had as good a thought as that, but you know you never did—and *I* know it, Tom."

"Indeed and 'deed I did, auntie—I wish I may never stir if I didn't."

"Oh, Tom, don't lie—don't do it. It only makes things a hundred times worse."

"It ain't a lie, auntie; it's the truth. I wanted to keep you from grieving—that was all that made me come."

"I'd give the whole world to believe that—it would cover up a power of sins, Tom. I'd 'most be glad you'd run off and acted so bad. But it ain't reasonable; because why didn't you tell me, child?"

"Why, you see, auntie, when you got to talking about the funeral, I just got all full of the idea of our coming and hiding in the church, and I couldn't, somehow, bear to spoil it. So I just put the bark back in my pocket and kept mum."

"What bark?"

"The bark I had wrote on to tell you we'd gone pirating. "I wish, now, you'd waked up when I kissed you—I do, honest."

The hard lines in his aunt's face relaxed, and sudden tenderness dawned in her eyes.

" *Did* you kiss me, Tom ? "

" Why yes, I did."

" Are you sure you did, Tom ? "

" Why yes, I did, auntie—certain sure."

" What did you kiss me for, Tom ? "

" Because I loved you so, and you laid there moaning, and I was so sorry."

The words sounded like truth. The old lady could not hide a tremor in her voice when she said :

" Kiss me again, Tom !—and be off with you to school, now, and don't bother me any more."

The moment he was gone, she ran to a closet and got out the ruin of a jacket which Tom had gone pirating in. Then she stopped with it in her hand, and said to herself :

" No, I don't dare. Poor boy, I reckon he's lied about it—but it's a blessed, blessed lie, there's such comfort in it. I hope the Lord—I *know* the Lord will forgive him, because it was such good-heartedness in him to tell it. But I don't want to find out it's a lie. I won't look."

She put the jacket away, and stood by musing a minute. Twice she put out her hand to take the garment again, and twice she refrained. Once more she ventured, and this time she fortified herself with the thought : " It's a good lie—it's a good lie—I won't let it grieve me." So she sought the jacket pocket. A moment later she was reading Tom's piece of bark through flowing tears, and saying :

" I could forgive the boy, now, if he'd committed a million sins ! "

CHAPTER XXI

THERE was something about Aunt Polly's manner,
when she kissed Tom, that swept away his low spirits
and made him light-hearted and happy again. He
started to school, and had the luck of coming upon
Becky Thatcher at the head of Meadow Lane. His
mood always determined his manner. Without a
moment's hesitation he ran to her and said :

"I acted mighty mean to-day, Becky, and I'm so
sorry. I won't ever, ever do that way again as long
as ever I live—please make up, won't you ? "

The girl stopped and looked him scornfully in the
face :

"I'll thank you to keep yourself *to* yourself, Mr.
Thomas Sawyer. I'll never speak to you again."

She tossed her head and passed on. Tom was so
stunned that he had not even presence of mind
enough to say "Who cares, Miss Smarty ? " until
the right time to say it had gone by So he said
nothing. But he was in a fine rage, nevertheless.
He moped into the school-yard wishing she were a
boy, and imagining how he would trounce her if she
were. He presently encountered her and delivered
a stinging remark as he passed. She hurled one in
return, and the angry breach was complete. It
seemed to Becky, in her hot resentment, that she
could hardly wait for school to "take in," she was

so impatient to see Tom flogged for the injured spelling-book. If she had had any lingering notion of exposing Alfred Temple, Tom's offensive fling had driven it entirely away.

Poor girl, she did not know how fast she was nearing trouble herself. The master, Mr. Dobbins, had reached middle age with an unsatisfied ambition. The darling of his desires was to be a doctor, but poverty had decreed that he should be nothing higher than a village schoolmaster. Every day he took a mysterious book out of his desk, and absorbed himself in it at times when no classes were reciting. He kept that book under lock and key. There was not an urchin in school but was perishing to have a glimpse of it, but the chance never came. Every boy and girl had a theory about the nature of that book ; but no two theories were alike, and there was no way of getting at the facts in the case. Now as Becky was passing by the desk, which stood near the door, she noticed that the key was in the lock ! It was a precious moment. She glanced around ; found herself alone, and the next instant she had the book in her hands. The title-page—Professor somebody's "Anatomy"—carried no information to her mind ; so she began to turn the leaves. She came at once upon a handsomely engraved and coloured frontispiece—a human figure. At that moment a shadow fell on the page, and Tom Sawyer stepped in at the door and caught a glimpse of the picture. Becky snatched at the book to close it, and had the hard luck to tear the pictured page half down the middle. She thrust the volume into the desk, turned the key, and burst out crying with shame and vexation :

"Tom Sawyer, you are just as mean as you can be,

to sneak up on a person and look at what they're looking at."

"How could *I* know you was looking at anything?"

"You ought to be ashamed of yourself, Tom Sawyer; you know you're going to tell on me; and, oh, what shall I do, what shall I do! I'll be whipped, and I never was whipped in school."

Then she stamped her little foot and said:

"*Be* so mean if you want to! *I* know something that's going to happen. You just wait, and you'll see! Hateful, hateful, hateful!"—and she flung out of the house with a new explosion of crying.

Tom stood still, rather flustered by this onslaught. Presently he said to himself:

"What a curious kind of a fool a girl is. Never been licked in school! Shucks, what's a licking! That's just like a girl—they're so thin-skinned and chicken-hearted. Well, of course *I* ain't going to tell old Dobbins on this little fool, because there's other ways of getting even on her that ain't so mean; but what of it? Old Dobbins will ask who it was tore his book. Nobody'll answer. Then he'll do just the way he always does—ask first one and then t'other, and when he comes to the right girl he'll know it, without any telling. Girls' faces always tell on them. They ain't got any backbone. She'll get licked. Well, it's a kind of a tight place for Becky Thatcher, because there ain't any way out of it." Tom conned the thing a moment longer, and then added; "All right, though; she'd like to see me in just such a fix—let her sweat it out!"

Tom joined the mob of skylarking fellows outside. In a few moments the master arrived and school "took in." Tom did not feel a strong interest in his studies. Every time he stole a glance at the girls' side of the room, Becky's face troubled him. Considering all things, he did not want to pity her, and yet it was all he could do to help it. He could get up no exultation that was really worth the name. Presently the spelling-book discovery was made, and Tom's mind was entirely full of his own matters for a while after that. Becky roused up from her lethargy of distress, and showed good interest in the proceedings. She did not expect that Tom could get out of his trouble by denying that he spilt the ink on the book himself ; and she was right. The denial only seemed to make the thing worse for Tom. Becky supposed she would be glad of that, and she tried to believe she was glad of it, but she found she was not certain. When the worst came to the worst, she had an impulse to get up and tell on Alfred Temple, but she made an effort and forced herself to keep still, because, said she to herself, " he'll tell about me tearing the picture, sure. I wouldn't say a word, not to save his life ! "

Tom took his whipping and went back to his seat not at all broken-hearted, for he thought it was possible that he had unknowingly upset the ink on the spelling-book himself, in some skylarking bout— he had denied it for form's sake and because it was custom, and had stuck to the denial from principle.

A whole hour drifted by ; the master sat nodding in his throne, the air was drowsy with the hum of study. By-and-by Mr. Dobbins straightened himself up, yawned, then unlocked his desk, and reached for his book, but seemed undecided whether to take it out or leave it. Most of the pupils glanced up languidly, but there were two among them that watched his movements with intent eyes. Mr. Dobbins fingered his book absently for a while.

then took it out, and settled himself in his chair
to read.

Tom shot a glance at Becky. He had seen a
hunted and helpless rabbit look as she did, with a
gun levelled at its head. Instantly he forgot his
quarrel with her. Quick, something must be done !
done in a flash, too ! But the very imminence of
the emergency paralysed his invention. Good ! he
had an inspiration ! He would run and snatch the
book, spring through the door and fly ! but his resolution shook for one little instant, and the chance was
lost—the master opened the volume. If Tom only
had the wasted opportunity back again ! Too late ;
there was no help for Becky now, he said. The next
moment the master faced the school. Every eye
sank under his gaze ; there was that in it which
smote even the innocent with fear. There was
silence while one might count ten ; the master was
gathering his wrath. Then he spoke :

" Who tore this book ? "

There was not a sound. One could have heard a
pin drop. The stillness continued ; the master
searched face after face for signs of guilt.

" Benjamin Rogers, did you tear this book ? "

A denial. Another pause.

" Joseph Harper, did you ? "

Another denial. Tom's uneasiness grew more and
more intense under the slow torture of these proceedings. The master scanned the ranks of boys,
considered a while, then turned to the girls :

" Amy Lawrence ? "

A shake of the head.

" Gracie Miller ? "

The same sign.

" Susan Harper, did you do this ? "

Another negative. The next girl was Becky Thatcher. Tom was trembling from head to foot with excitement, and a sense of the hopelessness of the situation.

" Rebecca Thatcher "—(Tom glanced at her face ; it was white with terror)—" did you tear—no, look me in the face "—(her hands rose in appeal)—" did you tear this book ? "

A thought shot like lightning through Tom's brain. He sprang to his feet and shouted—

" *I* done it ! "

The school stared in perplexity at this incredible folly. Tom stood a moment to gather his dismembered faculties ; and when he stepped forward to go to his punishment, the surprise, the gratitude, the adoration that shone upon him out of poor Becky's eyes seemed pay enough for a hundred floggings. Inspired by the splendour of his own act, he took without an outcry the most merciless flogging that even Mr Dobbins had ever administered ; and also received with indifference the added cruelty of a command to remain two hours after school should be dismissed—for he knew who would wait for him outside till his captivity was done, and not count the tedious time as loss either.

Tom went to bed that night planning vengeance against Alfred Temple ; for with shame and repentance Becky had told him all, not forgetting her own treachery ; but even the longing for vengeance had to give way soon to pleasanter musings, and he fell asleep at last with Becky's latest words lingering dreamily in his ear :

" Tom, how *could* you be so noble !

CHAPTER XXII

VACATION was approaching. The schoolmaster, always severe, grew severer and more exacting than ever, for he wanted the school to make a good showing on " Examination " day. His rod and his ferule were seldom idle now—at least among the smaller pupils. Only the biggest boys, and young ladies of eighteen and twenty, escaped lashing. Mr. Dobbins's lashings were very vigorous ones too ; for although he carried, under his wig, a perfectly bald and shiny head, he had only reached middle age and there was no sign of feebleness in his muscle. As the great day approached, all the tryanny that was in him came to the surface ; he seemed to take a vindictive pleasure in punishing the least short-comings. The consequence was, that the smallest boys spent their days in terror and suffering and their nights in plotting revenge. They threw away no opportunity to do the master a mischief. But he kept ahead all the time. The retribution that fol-lowed every vengeful success was so sweeping and majestic that the boys always retired from the field badly worsted. At last they conspired together and hit upon a plan that promised a dazzling victory. They swore in the sign-painter's boy, told him the scheme, and asked his help. He had his own reasons for being delighted, for the master boarded in his father's family and had given the boy ample cause to hate him. The master's wife would go on a visit to the country in a few days, and there would be nothing to interfere with the plan; the master always prepared himself for great occasions by getting pretty well fuddled, and the sign-painter's boy said that when the dominie had reached the proper condition on Examination evening he would "manage the thing" while he napped in his chair; then he would have him awakened at the right time and hurried away to school.

In the fulness of time the interesting occasion arrived. At eight in the evening the school-house was brilliantly lighted and adorned with wreaths and festoons of foliage and flowers. The master sat throned in his great chair upon a raised platform, with his blackboard behind him. He was looking tolerably mellow. Three rows of benches on each side and six rows in front of him were occupied by the dignitaries of the town and by the parents of the pupils. To his left, back of the rows of citizens, was a spacious temporary platform upon which were seated the scholars who were to take part in the exercises of the evening; rows of small boys, washed and dressed to an intolerable state of discomfort; rows of gawky big boys; snow-banks of girls and young ladies clad in lawn and muslin, and conspicuously conscious of their bare arms, their grandmothers' ancient trinkets, their bits of pink and blue ribbon, and the flowers in their hair. All the rest of the house was filled with non-participating scholars.

The exercises began. A very little boy stood up and sheepishly recited " You'd scarce expect one of my age, to speak in public on the stage," &c., accompanying himself with the painfully exact and spasmodic gestures which a machine might have

used—supposing the machine to be a trifle out of
order.   But he got through safely, though cruelly
scared, and got a fine round of applause, when he
made his manufactured bow and retired.

A little shamefaced girl lisped " Mary had a little
lamb," &c., performed a compassion - inspiring
curtsey, got her meed of applause, and sat down
flushed and happy.

Tom Sawyer stepped forward with conceited confidence, and soared into the unquenchable and
indestructible " Give me liberty or give me death "
speech, with fine fury and frantic gesticulation, and
broke down in the middle of it.   A ghastly stage-
fright seized him, his legs quaked under him and he
was like to choke.   True, he had the manifest
sympathy of the house—but he had the house's
silence too, which was even worse than its sympathy.
The master frowned, and this completed the disaster.
Tom struggled a while and then retired, utterly
defeated.   There was a weak attempt at applause,
but it died early.

" The Boy stood on the Burning Deck " followed ;
also " The Assyrian Came Down," and other de-
clamatory gems.   Then there were reading exercises, and a spelling fight.   The meagre Latin class
recited with honour.   The prime feature of the
evening was in order, now—original " compositions "
by the young ladies.   Each in her turn stepped
forward to the edge of the platform, cleared her
throat, held up her manuscript (tied with dainty
ribbon) and proceeded to read, with laboured
attention to " expression " and punctuation.   The
themes were the same that had been illuminated
upon similar occasions by their mothers before them,
their grandmothers, and doubtless all their ancestors

in the female line clear back to the Crusades. "Friendship" was one; "Memories of other Days;" "Religion in History;" "Dream Land;" "The Advantages of Culture;" "Forms of Political Government Compared and Contrasted;" "Melancholy;" "Filial Love;" "Heart Longings," &c, &c.

A prevalent feature in these compositions was a nursed and petted melancholy; another was a wasteful and opulent gush of "fine language;" another was a tendency to lug in by the ears particularly prized words and phrases until they were worn entirely out; and a peculiarity that conspicuously marked and marred them was the inveterate and intolerable sermon that wagged its crippled tail at the end of each and every one of them. No matter what the subject might be, a brain-racking effort was made to squirm it into some aspect or other that the moral and religious mind could contemplate with edification. The glaring insincerity of these sermons was not sufficient to compass banishment of the fashion from the schools, and it is not sufficient to-day; it never will be sufficient while the world stands, perhaps. There is no school in all our land where the young ladies do not feel obliged to close their compositions with a sermon; and you will find that the sermon of the most frivolous and least religious girl in the school is always the longest and the most relentlessly pious. But enough of this. Homely truth is unpalatable. Let us return to the "Examination." The first composition that was read was one entitled, "Is this, then, Life?" Perhaps the reader can endure an extract from it.

"In the common walks of life, with what delightful emotions does the youthful mind look forward to

some anticipated scene of festivity! Imagination
is busy sketching rose-tinted pictures of joy. In
fancy, the voluptuous votary of fashion sees herself
amid the festive throng, ' the observed of all ob-
servers.' Her graceful form, arrayed in snowy
robes, is whirling through the mazes of the joyous
dance ; her eye is brightest, her step is lightest in
the gay assembly. In such delicious fancies time
quickly glides by, and the welcome hour arrives for
her entrance into the Elysian world, of which she
has had such bright dreams. How fairy-like does
everything appear to her enchanted vision! Each
new scene is more charming than the last. But
after a while she finds that beneath this goodly
exterior, all is vanity ; the flattery which once
charmed her soul, now grates harshly upon her ear ;
the ballroom has lost its charms ; and with wasted
health and embittered heart, she turns away with
the conviction that earthly pleasures cannot satisfy
the longings of the soul! "

And so forth and so on. There was a buzz of
gratification from time to time during the reading,
accompanied by whispered ejaculations of " How
sweet ! " " How eloquent ! " " So true ! " &c., and
after the thing had closed with a peculiarly afflicting
sermon, the applause was enthusiastic.

Then arose a slim, melancholy girl, whose face
had the " interesting " paleness that comes of pills
and indigestion, and read a " poem." Two stanzas of
it will do.

A MISSOURI MAIDEN'S FAREWELL
TO ALABAMA

" Alabama, good-bye ! I love thee well !
    But yet for a while do I leave thee now !
Sad, yes, sad thoughts of thee my heart doth swell,
    And burning recollections throng my brow !

> For I have wandered through thy flowery woods;
> Have roamed and read near Tallapoosa's stream;
> Have listened to Talassee's warring floods,
> And wooed on Coosa's side Aurora's beam.
>
> Yet shame I not to bear an o'er-full heart,
> Nor blush to turn behind my tearful eyes;
> 'Tis from no stranger land I now must part,
> 'Tis to no strangers left I yield these sighs.
> Welcome and home were mine within this State,
> Whose vales I leave, whose spires fade fast from me;
> And cold must be mine eyes, and heart, and tête,
> When, dear Alabama! they turn cold on thee!"

There were very few there who knew what *tête* meant, but the poem was very satisfactory nevertheless.

Next appeared a dark-complexioned, black-eyed, black-haired young lady, who paused an impressive moment, assumed a tragic expression, and began to read in a measured tone:

'A VISION

"Dark and tempestuous was the night. Around the throne on high not a single star quivered; but the deep intonations of the heavy thunder constantly vibrated upon the ear; whilst the terrific lightning revelled in angry mood through the cloudy chambers of heaven, seeming to scorn the power exerted over its terrors by the illustrious Franklin! Even the boisterous winds unanimously came forth from their mystic homes, and blustered about as if to enhance by their aid the wildness of the scene. At such a time, so dark, so dreary, for human sympathy my very spirit sighed; but instead thereof,

> "My dearest friend, my counsellor, my comforter and guide,
> My joy in grief, my second bliss in joy, came to my side.

"She moved like one of those bright beings pictured in the sunny walks of fancy's Eden by the romantic and young, a queen of beauty unadorned save by her own transcendent loveliness. So soft was her step, it failed to make even a sound, and but for the magical thrill imparted by her genial touch, as other unobtrusive beauties she would have glided away unperceived—unsought. A strange sadness rested upon her features, like icy tears upon the robe of December, as she pointed to the contending elements without, and bade me contemplate the two beings presented."

This nightmare occupied some ten pages of manuscript, and wound up with a sermon so destructive of all hope to non-Presbyterians, that it took the first prize. This composition was considered to be the very finest effort of the evening. The mayor of the village, in delivering the prize to the author of it, made a warm speech, in which he said that it was by far the most " eloquent thing he had ever listened to, and that Daniel Webster himself might well be proud of it."

It may be remarked in passing, that the number of compositions in which the word "beauteous" was over-fondled, and human experience referred to as " life's page," was up to the usual average.

Now the master, mellow almost to the verge of geniality, put his chair aside, turned his back to the audience, and began to draw a map of America on the blackboard, to exercise the geography class upon. But he made a sad business of it with his unsteady hand, and a smothered titter rippled over the house. He knew what the matter was, and set himself to right it. He sponged out lines and remade them ; but he only distorted them more than ever and the tittering was more pronounced. He threw his entire attention upon his work, now, as if determined not to be put down by the mirth. He felt that all eyes were fastened upon him; he imagined he was succeeding, and yet the tittering continued; it even manifestly increased. And well it might. There was a garret above, pierced with a scuttle over his head; down through this scuttle came a cat suspended around the haunches by a string; she had a rag tied about her head and jaws to keep her from mewing; as she slowly descended she curved upward and clawed at the string, she swung downward and clawed at the intangible air. The tittering rose higher and higher, the cat was within six inches of the absorbed teacher's head; down, down, a little lower, and she grabbed his wig with her desperate claws, clung to it, and was snatched up into the garret in an instant with her trophy still in her possession! And how the light did blaze abroad from the master's bald pate, for the sign-painter's boy had *gilded* it!

That broke up the meeting. The boys were avenged. Vacation was come.

NOTE.—The pretended "compositions" quoted above are taken without alteration from a volume entitled "Prose and Poetry, by a Western Lady," but they are exactly and precisely after the school-girl pattern, and hence are much happier than any mere imitations could be.

CHAPTER XXIII

TOM joined the new order of Cadets of Temperance, being attracted by the showy character of their "regalia." He promised to abstain from smoking, chewing, and profanity as long as he remained a member. Now he found out a new thing—namely, that to promise not to do a thing is the surest way in the world to make a body want to go and do that very thing. Tom soon found himself tormented with a desire to drink, and swear; the desire grew to be so intense that nothing but the hope of a chance to display himself in his red sash kept him from withdrawing from the order. Fourth of July was coming: but he soon gave that up—gave it up before he had worn his shackles over forty-eight hours, and fixed his hopes upon old Judge Frazer, justice of the peace, who was apparently on his death-bed, and would have a big public funeral, since he was so high an official. During three days Tom was deeply concerned about the Judge's condition, and hungry for news of it. Sometimes his hopes ran high, so high that he would venture to get out his regalia and practise before the looking-glass. But the Judge had a most discouraging way of fluctuating. At last he was pronounced upon the mend, and then convalescent. Tom was disgusted; and felt a sense of injury, too. He handed in his resignation at once, and that night the Judge suffered a relapse and died. Tom resolved that he would never trust a man like that again. The funeral was a fine thing. The Cadets paraded in a style calculated to kill the late member with envy.

Tom was a free boy again, however; there was something in that. He could drink and swear now, but found to his surprise that he did not want to. The simple fact that he could, took the desire away, and the charm of it.

Tom presently wondered to find that his coveted vacation was beginning to hang a little heavily on his hands.

He attempted a diary, but nothing happened during three days, and so he abandoned it.

The first of all the negro minstrel shows came to town, and made a sensation. Tom and Joe Harper got up a band of performers, and were happy for two days.

Even the Glorious Fourth was in some sense a failure, for it rained hard; there was no procession in consequence, and the greatest man in the world (as Tom supposed) Mr. Benton, an actual United States Senator, proved an overwhelming disappointment, for he was not twenty-five feet high, nor even anywhere in the neighbourhood of it.

A circus came. The boys played circus for three days afterwards in tents made of rag carpeting—admission, three pins for boys, two for girls—and then circusing was abandoned.

A phrenologist and a mesmeriser came—and went again and left the village duller and drearier than ever.

There were some boys' and girls' parties, but they were so few and so delightful that they only made the aching voids between ache the harder.

Becky Thatcher was gone to her Constantinople home to stay with her parents during vacation—so there was no bright side to life anywhere.

The dreadful secret of the murder was a chronic misery. It was a very cancer for permanency and pain.

Then came the measles.

During two long weeks Tom lay a prisoner, dead to the world and its happenings. He was very ill, he was interested in nothing. When he got upon his feet at last and moved feebly down town, a melancholy change had come over everything and every creature. There had been a " revival," and everybody had " got religion "; not only the adults, but even the boys and girls. Tom went about, hoping against hope for the sight of one blessed sinful face, but disappointment crossed him everywhere. He found Joe Harper studying a Testament, and turned sadly away from the depressing spectacle. He sought Ben Rogers, and found him visiting the poor with a basket of tracts. He hunted up Jim Hollis, who called his attention to the precious blessing of his late measles as a warning. Every boy he encountered added another ton to his depression; and when, in desperation, he flew for refuge at last to the bosom of Huckleberry Finn and was received with a scriptural quotation, his heart broke, and he crept home and to bed, realising that he alone of all the town was lost, for ever and for ever.

And that night there came on a terrific storm, with driving rain, awful claps of thunder, and blinding sheets of lightning. He covered his head with the bedclothes and waited in a horror of suspense for his doom; for he had not the shadow of a doubt that all this hubbub was about him. He believed he had taxed the forbearance of the powers above to the extremity of endurance, and that this was the result. It might have seemed to him a waste of pomp and ammunition to kill a bug with a battery of artillery, but there seemed nothing incongruous about the getting up of such an expensive thunder-storm as this to knock the turf from under an insect like himself.

By-and-by the tempest spent itself and died without accomplishing its object. The boy's first impulse was to be grateful and reform. His second was to wait—for there might not be any more storms.

The next day the doctors were back Tom had relapsed. The three weeks he spent on his back this time seemed an entire age. When he got abroad at last he was hardly grateful that he had been spared, remembering how lonely was his estate, how com-panionless and forlorn he was. He drifted listlessly down the street and found Jim Hollis acting as judge in a juvenile court that was trying a cat for murder, in the presence of her victim, a bird. He found Joe Harper and Huck Finn up an alley eating a stolen melon. Poor fellows, they, like Tom, had suffered a relapse.

CHAPTER XXIV

AT last the sleepy atmosphere was stirred, and vigorously. The murder trial came on in the court. It became the absorbing topic of village talk immediately. Tom could not get away from it. Every reference to the murder sent a shudder to his heart, for his troubled conscience and his fears almost persuaded him that these remarks were put forth in his hearing as " feelers " ; he did not see how he could be suspected of knowing anything about the murder, but still he could not be comfortable in the midst of this gossip. It kept him in a cold shiver all the time. He took Huck to a lonely place to have a talk with him. It would be some relief to unseal his tongue for a little while ; to divide his burden of distress with another sufferer. Moreover, he wanted to assure himself that Huck had remained discreet :

" Huck, have you ever told anybody about that ? "

" 'Bout what ? "

" You know what."

" *Oh,* 'course I haven't."

" Never a word ? "

" Never a solitary word, so help me. What makes you ask ? "

" Well, I was afeard."

" Why, Tom Sawyer, we wouldn't be alive two days if that got found out. *You* know that."

Tom felt more comfortable. After a pause :

"Huck, they couldn't anybody get you to tell, could they?"

"Get me to tell? Why, if I wanted that half-breed devil to drownd me they could get me to tell. They ain't no different way."

"Well, that's all right then. I reckon we're safe as long as we keep mum. But let's swear again, anyway. It's more surer."

"I'm agreed."

So they swore again with dread solemnities.

"What is the talk around, Huck? I've heard a power of it."

"Talk? Well, it's just Muff Potter, Muff Potter, Muff Potter all the time. It keeps me in a sweat, constant, so's I want to hide som'ers."

"That's just the same way they go on round me. I reckon he's a goner. Don't you feel sorry for him sometimes?"

"Most always—most always. He ain't no account; but then he ain't ever done anything to hurt anybody. Just fishes a little to get money to get drunk on—and loafs around considerable; but, Lord, we all do that—leastways most of us—preachers and such like. But he's kind of good—he give me half a fish, once, when there wasn't enough for two; and lots of times he's kind of stood by me when I was out of luck."

"Well, he's mended kites for me, Huck, and knitted hooks on to my line. I wish we could get him out of there."

"My! we couldn't get him out, Tom. And besides, 'twouldn't do any good; they'd ketch him again."

"Yes—so they would. But I hate to hear 'em abuse him so like the dickens when he never done—that."

"I do too, Tom. Lord, I hear 'em say he's the bloodiest-looking villain in this country, and they wonder he wasn't ever hung before."

"Yes; they talk like that all the time. I've heard 'em say that if he was to get free they'd lynch him."

"And they'd do it, too."

The boys had a long talk, but it brought them little comfort. As the twilight drew on, they found themselves hanging about the neighbourhood of the little isolated jail, perhaps with an undefined hope that something would happen that might clear away their difficulties. But nothing happened! there seemed to be no angels or fairies interested in this luckless captive.

The boys did as they had often done before—went to the cell grating and gave Potter some tobacco and matches. He was on the ground floor, and there were no guards.

His gratitude for their gifts had always smote their consciences before—it cut deeper than ever, this time. They felt cowardly and treacherous to the last degree when Potter said:

"You've ben mighty good to me, boys—better'n anybody else in this town. And I don't forget it, I don't. Often I says to myself, says I, 'I used to mend all the boys' kites and things, and show 'em where the good fishin' places was, and befriend 'em what I could, and now they've all forgot old Muff when he's in trouble, but Tom don't, and Huck don't—_they_ don't forget him,' says I, 'and I don't forget _them!_' Well, boys, I done an awful thing — drunk and crazy at the time, that's the only way I account for it, and now I got to swing for it, and it's right. Right, and _best_, too, I reckon; hope so, anyway. Well, we won't talk about that. I don't want to make *you* feel bad ; you've befriended me. But what I want to say is, don't *you* ever get drunk, then you won't ever get here. Stand a little furder west ; so, that's it ; it's a prime comfort to see faces that's friendly when a body's in such a muck of trouble, and there don't none come here but yourn. Good friendly faces—good friendly faces. Get up on one another's backs, and let me touch 'em. That's it. Shake hands—yourn'll come through the bars, but mine's too big. Little hands, and weak—but they've helped Muff Potter a power, and they'd help him more if they could."

Tom went home miserable, and his dreams that night were full of horrors. The next day and the day after, he hung about the court-room, drawn by an irresistible impulse to go in, but forcing himself to stay out. Huck was having the same experience. They studiously avoided each other. Each wandered away from time to time, but the same dismal fascination always brought them back presently. Tom kept his ears open when idlers sauntered out of the court-room, but invariably heard distressing news ; the toils were closing more and more relentlessly around poor Peter. At the end of the second day the village talk was to the effect that Injun Joe's evidence stood firm and unshaken, and that there was not the slightest question as to what the jury's verdict would be.

Tom was out late that night, and came to bed through the window. He was in a tremendous state of excitement. It was hours before he got to sleep. All the village flocked to the court-house the next morning, for this was to be the great day. Both sexes were about equally represented in the packed audience. After a long wait the jury filed in and took their places; shortly afterwards, Potter, pale and haggard, timid and hopeless, was brought in with chains upon him, and seated where all the curious eyes could stare at him; no less conspicuous was Injun Joe, stolid as ever. There was another pause, and then the judge arrived, and the sheriff proclaimed the opening of the court. The usual whisperings among the lawyers and gathering together of papers followed. These details and accompanying delays worked up an atmosphere of preparation that was as impressive as it was fascinating.

Now a witness was called who testified that he found Muff Potter washing in the brook at an early hour of the morning that the murder was discovered, and that he immediately sneaked away. After some further questioning, counsel for the prosecution said:

" Take the witness."

The prisoner raised his eyes for a moment, but dropped them again when his own counsel said:

" I have no questions to ask him."

The next witness proved the finding of the knife near the corpse. Counsel for the prosecution said:

" Take the witness."

" I have no questions to ask him," Potter's lawyer replied.

A third witness swore he had often seen the knife in Potter's possession.

" Take the witness."

Counsel for Potter declined to question him.

The faces of the audience began to betray annoyance. Did this attorney mean to throw away his client's life without an effort?

Several witnesses deposed concerning Potter's guilty behaviour when brought to the scene of the murder. They were allowed to leave the stand without being cross-questioned.

Every detail of the damaging circumstances that occurred in the graveyard upon that morning which all present remembered so well was brought out by credible witnesses, but none of them were cross-examined by Potter's lawyer. The perplexity and dissatisfaction of the house expressed itself in murmurs and provoked a reproof from the bench. Counsel for the prosecution now said :

" By the oaths of citizens whose simple word is above suspicion, we have fastened this awful crime beyond all possibility of question upon the unhappy prisoner at the bar. We rest our case here."

A groan escaped from poor Potter, and he put his face in his hands, and rocked his body softly to and fro, while a painful silence reigned in the court-room. Many men were moved, and many women's compassion testified itself in tears. Counsel for the defence rose and said :

" Your Honour—In our remarks at the opening of this trial, we foreshadowed our purpose to prove that our client did this fearful deed while under the influence of a blind and irresponsible delirium produced by drink. We have changed our mind ; we shall not offer that plea. [Then to the clerk.] Call Thomas Sawyer."

A puzzled amazement awoke in every face in the house, not even excepting Potter's. Every eye fastened itself with wondering interest upon Tom as he rose and took his place upon the stand. The boy looked wild enough, for he was badly scared. The oath was administered.

" Thomas Sawyer, where were you on the seven-teenth of June, about the hour of midnight ? "

Tom glanced at Injun Joe's iron face, and his tongue failed him. The audience listened breathless, but the words refused to come. After a few moments, however, the boy got a little of his strength back, and managed to put enough of it into his voice to make part of the house hear :

" In the graveyard ! "

" A little bit louder, please. Don't be afraid. You were——"

" In the graveyard."

A contemptuous smile flitted across Injun Joe's face.

" Were you anywhere near Horse William's grave ? "

" Yes, sir."

" Speak up just a trifle louder. How near were you ? "

" Near as I am to you."

" Were you hidden or not ? "

" I was hid."

" Where ? "

" Behind the elms that's on the edge of the grave."

Injun Joe gave a barely perceptible start.

" Any one with you ? "

" Yes, sir. I went there with——".

" Wait—wait a moment. Never mind mentioning your companion's name. We will produce him at the proper time. Did you carry anything there with you ? "

Tom hesitated and looked confused.

" Speak out, my boy—don't be diffident. The truth is always respectable. What did you take there ? "

" Only a—a—dead cat."

There was a ripple of mirth, which the court checked.

" We will produce the skeleton of that cat. Now, my boy, tell us everything that occurred—tell it in your own way—don't skip anything, and don't be afraid."

Tom began—hesitatingly at first, but, as he warmed to his subject, his words flowed more and more easily ; in a little while every sound ceased but his own voice ; every eye fixed itself upon him ; with parted lips and bated breath the audience hung upon his words, taking no note of time, rapt in the ghastly fascinations of the tale. The strain upon pent emotion reached its climax when the boy said, " And as the doctor fetched the board around and Muff Potter fell, Injun Joe jumped with the knife and——"

Crash ! quick as lightning, the half-breed sprang for a window, tore his way through all opposers, and was gone !

CHAPTER XXV

Tom was a glittering hero once more—the pet of the old, the envy of the young. His name even went into immortal print, for the village paper magnified him. There were some that believed he would be President yet, if he escaped hanging.

As usual, the fickle unreasoning world took Muff Potter to its bosom, and fondled him as lavishly as it had abused him before. But that sort of conduct is to the world's credit ; therefore it is not well to find fault with it.

Tom's days were days of splendour and exultation to him, but his nights were seasons of horror. Injun Joe infested all his dreams, and always with doom in his eye. Hardly any temptation could persuade the boy to stir abroad after nightfall. Poor Huck was in the same state of wretchedness and terror, for Tom had told the whole story to the lawyer the night before the great day of the trial, and Huck was sore afraid that his share in the business might leak out yet, notwithstanding Injun Joe's flight had saved him the suffering of testifying in court. The poor fellow had got the attorney to promise secrecy, but what of that ? Since Tom's harassed conscience had managed to drive him to the lawyer's house by night and wring a dread tale from lips that had been sealed with the dismallest and most formidable of oaths, Huck's confidence in the human race was well-nigh

184

obliterated. Daily Muff Potter's gratitude made Tom glad he had spoken : but nightly he wished he had sealed up his tongue. Half the time Tom was afraid Injun Joe would never be captured ; the other half he was afraid he would be. He felt sure he never could draw a safe breath again until that man was dead and he had seen the corpse.

Rewards had been offered, the country had been scoured, but no Injun Joe was found. One of those omniscient and awe-inspiring marvels, a detective, came from St. Louis, moused around, shook his head, looked wise, and made that sort of astounding success which members of that craft usually achieve. That is to say, "he found a clew." But you can't hang a " clew " for murder, and so after that detective had got through and gone home, Tom felt just as insecure as he was before.

The slow days drifted on, and each left behind it a slightly lightened weight of apprehension.

CHAPTER XXVI

THERE comes a time in every rightly constructed
boy's life when he has a raging desire to go somewhere
and dig for hidden treasure. This desire suddenly
came upon Tom one day. He sallied out to find Joe
Harper, but failed of success. Next he sought Ben
Rogers; he had gone fishing. Presently he stumbled
upon Huck Finn the Red-handed. Huck would
answer. Tom took him to a private place and
opened the matter to him confidentially. Huck was
willing. Huck was always willing to take a hand
in any enterprise that offered entertainment and
required no capital, for he had a troublesome super-
abundance of that sort of time which is *not* money.

" Where'll we dig ? " said Huck.

" Oh, 'most anywhere."

" Why, is it hid all around ? "

" No, indeed it ain't. It's hid in mighty particular
places, Huck—sometimes on Islands, sometimes in
rotten chests under the end of a limb of an old dead
tree, just where the shadow falls at midnight; but
mostly under the floor in ha'nted houses."

" Who hides it ? "

" Why, robbers, of course—who'd you reckon ?
Sunday-school sup'rintendents ? "

" I don't know. If it was mine I wouldn't hide
it : I'd spend it and have a good time."

" So would I ; but robbers don't do that way, they always hide it and leave it there."

" Don't they come after it any more ? "

" No, they think they will, but they generally forget the marks, or else they die. Anyway it lays there a long time and gets rusty ; and by-and-by somebody finds an old yellow paper that tells how to find the marks—a paper that's got to be ciphered over about a week because its mostly signs and hy'rogliphics."

" Hyro—which ? "

" Hy'rogliphics—pictures and things, you know, that don't seem to mean anything."

" Have you got one of them papers, Tom ? "

" No."

" Well, then, how you going to find out the marks ? "

" I don't want any marks. They always bury it under a ha'nted house, or on an Island, or under a dead tree that's got one limb sticking out. Well, we've tried Jackson's Island a little, and we can try it again sometime ; and there's the old ha'nted house up the Still-House branch, and there's lots of dead-limb trees—dead loads of 'em."

" Is it under all of them ? "

" How you talk ! No ! "

" Then how you going to know which one to go for ? "

" Go for all of 'em."

" Why, Tom, it'll take all summer."

" Well, what of that ? Suppose you find a brass pot with a hundred dollars in it, all rusty and gay, or a rotten chest full of di'monds. How's that ? "

Huck's eyes glowed.

" That's bully, plenty bully enough for me.

Just you gimme the hundred dollars, and I don't want no di'monds."

"All right. But I bet you *I* ain't going to throw off on di'monds. Some of 'em's worth twenty dollars apiece. There ain't any, hardly, but's worth six bits or a dollar."

"No! Is that so?"

"Cert'nly—anybody'll tell you so. Hain't you ever seen one, Huck?"

"Not as I remember."

"Oh, kings have slathers of them."

"Well, I don't know no kings, Tom."

"I reckon you don't. But if you was to go to Europe you'd see a raft of 'em hopping around."

"Do they hop?"

"Hop?—your granny! No!"

"Well, what did you say they did for?"

"Shucks! I only meant you'd *see* 'em—not hopping, of course—what do they want to hop for? But I mean you'd just see 'em—scattered around, you know, in a kind of a general way. Like that old hump-backed Richard."

"Richard! What's his other name?"

"He didn't have any other name. Kings don't have any but a given name."

"No?"

"But they don't."

"Well, if they like it, Tom, all right; but I don't want to be a king and have only just a given name, like a nigger. But say—where you going to dig first?"

"Well, I don't know. S'pose we tackle that old dead-limb tree on the hill t'other side of Still-House branch?"

"I'm agreed."

So they got a crippled pick and a shovel, and set out

on their three-mile tramp. They arrived hot and panting, and threw themselves down in the shade of a neighbouring elm to rest and have a smoke.

" I like this," said Tom.

" So do I."

" Say, Huck, if we find a treasure here, what you going to do with your share ? "

" Well, I'll have pie and a glass of soda every day, and I'll go to every circus that comes along. I'll bet I'll have a gay time."

" Well, ain't you going to save any of it ? "

" Save it ? What for ? "

" Why, so as to have something to live on by-and-by."

" Oh, that ain't any use. Pap would come back to thish yer town some day and get his claws on it if I didn't hurry up, and I tell you he'd clean it out pretty quick. What you going to do with yourn, Tom ? "

" I'm going to buy a new drum, and a sure-'nough sword, and a red necktie, and a bull pup, and get married."

" Married ! "

" That's it."

" Tom, you—why you ain't in your right mind."

" Wait—you'll see."

" Well, that's the foolishest thing you could do, Tom. Look at pap and my mother. Fight ! why they used to fight all the time. I remember, mighty well."

" That ain't anything. The girl I'm going to marry won't fight."

" Tom, I reckon they're all alike. They'll all comb a body. Now you better think about this awhile. I tell you you better. What's the name of the gal ? "

" It ain't a gal at all—it's a girl."

" It's all the same, I reckon ; some says gal, some says girl—both's right, like enough. Anyway, what's her name, Tom ? "

" I'll tell you some time—not now."

" All right—that'll do. Only if you get married I'll be more lonesomer than ever."

" No you won't, you'll come and live with me. Now stir out of this, and we'll go to digging."

They worked and sweated for half-an-hour. No result. They toiled another half-hour. Still no result. Huck said :

" Do they always bury it as deep as this ? "

" Sometimes—not always. Not generally. I reckon we haven't got the right place."

So they chose a new spot and began again. The labour dragged a little, but still they made progress. They pegged away in silence for some time. Finally Huck leaned on his shovel, swabbed the beaded drops from his brow with his sleeve, and said :

" Where you going to dig next, after we get this one ? "

" I reckon maybe we'll tackle the old tree that's over yonder on Cardiff Hill, back of the widow's."

" I reckon that'll be a good one. But won't the widow take it away from us, Tom. It's on her land."

" She take it away ! Maybe she'd like to try it once. Whoever finds one of these hid treasures, it belongs to him. It don't make any difference whose land it's on. "

That was satisfactory. The work went on. By-and-by Huck said :

" Blame it, we must be in the wrong place again.
What do you think ? "

" It is mighty curious, Huck. I don't understand
it. Sometimes witches interfere. I reckon maybe
that's what's the trouble now."

" Shucks ! witches ain't got no power in the daytime."

" Well, that's so. I didn't think of that. Oh,
I know what the matter is ! What a blamed lot
of fools we are ! You got to find out where the
shadow of the limb falls at midnight, and that's
where you dig ! "

" Then confound it, we've fooled away all this
work for nothing. Now hang it all, we got to come
back in the night. It's an awful long way. Can
you get out ? "

" I bet I will. We've got to do it to-night, too,
because if somebody sees these holes they'll know
in a minute what's here and they'll go for it."

" Well, I'll come around and meow to-night."

" All right. Let's hide the tools in the bushes."

The boys were there that night about the appointed time. They sat in the shadow waiting. It
was a lonely place, and an hour made solemn by old
traditions. Spirits whispered in the rustling leaves,
ghosts lurked in the murky nooks, the deep baying
of a hound floated up out of the distance, an owl
answered with his sepulchral note. The boys were
subdued by these solemnities, and talked little.
By-and-by they judged that twelve had come ; they
marked where the shadow fell and began to dig.
Their hopes commenced to rise. Their interest grew
stronger, and their industry kept pace with it. The
hole deepened and still deepened, but every time
their hearts jumped to hear the pick strike upon

something, they only suffered a new disappointment. It was only a stone or a chunk. At last Tom
said : " It ain't any use, Huck, we're wrong again."

" Well, but we can't be wrong. We spotted the
shadder to a dot."

" I know it, but then there's another thing."

" What's that ? "

" Why we only guessed at the time. Like enough
it was too late or too early."

Huck dropped his shovel.

" That's it," said he. " That's the very trouble.
We got to give this one up. We can't ever tell the
right time, and besides, this kind of thing's too
awful, here this time of night with witches and
ghosts a-fluttering around so. I feel as if something's behind me all the time ; and I'm afeard to
turn around, becuz maybe there's others in front
a-waiting for a chance. I been creeping all over
ever since I got here."

" Well, I've been pretty much so too, Huck.
They 'most always put in a dead man when they
bury a treasure under a tree, to look out for it."

" Lordy ! "

" Yes they do. I've always heard that."

" Tom, I don't like to fool around much where
there's dead people. A body's bound to get into
trouble with 'em, sure."

" I don't like to stir 'em up, either, Huck. S'pose
this one here was to stick his skull out and say something ! "

" Don't, Tom ! It's awful."

" Well it just is, Huck. I don't feel comfortable
a bit."

" Say, Tom, let's give this place up, and try some
wheres else."

" All right, I reckon we better."

" What'll it be ? "

Tom considered awhile, and then said :

" The ha'nted house. That's it."

" Blame it. I don't like ha'nted houses, Tom. Why, they're a dern sight worse'n dead people. Dead people might talk maybe, but they don't come sliding around in a shroud when you ain't noticing, and peep over your shoulder all of a sudden and grit their teeth the way a ghost does. I couldn't stand such a thing as that, Tom—nobody could."

" Yes ; but, Huck, ghosts don't travel around only at night—they won't hinder us from digging there in the daytime."

" Well, that's so. But you know mighty well people don't go about that ha'nted house in the day nor the night."

" Well, that's mostly because they don't like to go where a man's been murdered, anyway. But nothing's ever been seen around that house in the night—just some blue light slipping by the window —no regular ghosts."

" Well, where you see one of them blue lights flickering around, Tom, you can bet there's a ghost mighty close behind it. It stands to reason. Becuz you know that they don't anybody but ghosts use 'em."

" Yes, that's so. But anyway they don't come around in the daytime, so what's the use of our being afeard ? "

" Well, all right. We'll tackle the ha'nted house if you say so ; but I reckon it's taking chances."

They had started down the hill by this time. There in the middle of the moonlit valley below them stood the " haunted " house, utterly isolated,

its fences gone long ago, rank weeds smothering the
very doorstep, the chimney crumbled to ruin, the
window-sashes vacant, a corner of the roof caved in.
The boys gazed awhile, half expecting to see a blue
light flit past a window ; then talking in a low tone,
as befitted the time and the circumstances, they
struck far off to the right, to give the haunted house
a wide berth, and took their way homeward through
the woods that adorned the rearward side of Cardiff
Hill.

CHAPTER XXVII

ABOUT noon the next day the boys arrived at the dead tree; they had come for their tools. Tom was impatient to go to the haunted house; Huck was measurably so, also, but suddenly said—

" Looky here, Tom, do you know what day it is ? "

Tom mentally ran over the days of the week and then quickly lifted his eyes with a startled look in them—

" My ! I never once thought of it, Huck ! "

" Well, I didn't, neither, but all at once it popped on to me that it was Friday."

" Blame it ; a body can't be too careful, Huck. We might a got into an awful scrape, tackling such a thing on a Friday."

" Might ! Better say we would ! There's some lucky days, maybe, but Friday ain't."

" Any fool knows that. I don't reckon you was the fust that found it out, Huck."

" Well, I never said I was, did I ? And Friday ain't all, neither. I had a rotten bad dream last night—dreamt about rats."

" No ! Sure sign of trouble. Did they fight ? "

" No."

" Well, that's good, Huck. When they don't fight, it's only a sign that there's trouble around, you know. All we got to do is to look mighty

195

sharp and keep out of it. We'll drop this thing for to-day, and play. Do you know Robin Hood, Huck?"

"No. Who's Robin Hood?"

"Why, he was one of the greatest men that was ever in England—and the best. He was a robber."

"Cracky, I wisht I was. Who did he rob?"

"Only sheriffs and bishops and rich people and kings, and such like. But he never bothered the poor. He loved 'em. He always divided up with 'em perfectly square."

"Well, he must a ben a brick."

"I bet you he was, Huck. Oh, he was the noblest man that ever was. They ain't any such men now, I can tell you. He could lick any man in England with one hand tied behind him; and he could take his yew bow and plug a ten-cent piece every time, a mile and a half."

"What's a *yew* bow?"

"I don't know. It's some kind of a bow, of course. And if he hit that dime only on the edge he would set down and cry—and curse. But we'll play Robin Hood—it's noble fun. I'll learn you."

"I'm agreed."

So they played Robin Hood all the afternoon, now and then casting a yearning eye down upon the haunted house and passing a remark about the morrow's prospects and possibilities there. As the sun began to sink into the west, they took their way homeward athwart the long shadows of the trees and soon were buried from sight in the forests of Cardiff Hill.

On Saturday, shortly after noon, the boys were at the dead tree again. They had a smoke and a chat in the shade, and then dug a little in their last hole, not with great hope, but merely because Tom said there were so many cases where people had given up a treasure after getting down within six inches of it, and then somebody else had come along and turned it up with a single thrust of a shovel. The thing failed this time, however, so the boys shouldered their tools and went away, feeling that they had not trifled with fortune, but had fulfilled all the requirements that belong to the business of treasure-hunting.

When they reached the haunted house, there was something so weird and grisly about the dead silence that reigned there under the baking sun, and something so depressing about the loneliness and desolation of the place, that they were afraid, for a moment, to venture in. Then they crept to the door and took a trembling peep. They saw a weed-grown, floorless room, unplastered, an ancient fireplace, vacant windows, a ruinous staircase; and here, there, and everywhere, hung ragged and abandoned cobwebs. They presently entered softly, with quickened pulses, talking in whispers, ears alert to catch the slightest sound, and muscles tense and ready for instant retreat.

In a little while familiarity modified their fears and they gave the place a critical and interested examination, rather admiring their own boldness, and wondering at it, too. Next they wanted to look upstairs. This was something like cutting off retreat, but they got to daring each other, and of course there could be but one result—they threw their tools into a corner and made the ascent. Up there were the same signs of decay. In one corner they found a closet that promised mystery, but the promise was a fraud—there was nothing in it. Their courage was up now, and well in hand. They were about to go down and begin work when—

" *Sht !* " said Tom.

" What is it ? " whispered Huck, blanching with fright.

" *Sh !* There ! Hear it ? "

" Yes ! O my ! Let's run ! "

" Keep still ! Don't you budge ! They're coming right towards the door."

The boys stretched themselves upon the floor with their eyes to knot-holes in the planking, and lay waiting in a misery of fear.

" They've stopped— No—coming— Here they are. Don't whisper another word, Huck. My goodness, I wish I was out of this ! "

Two men entered. Each boy said to himself :

" There's the old deaf and dumb Spaniard that's been about town once or twice lately—never saw t'other man before."

" T'other " was a ragged, unkempt creature, with nothing very pleasant in his face. The Spaniard was wrapped in a *serape;* he had bushy white whiskers, long white hair flowed from under his sombrero, and he wore green goggles. When they came in, " t'other " was talking in a low voice ; they sat down on the ground, facing the door, with their backs to the wall, and the speaker continued his remarks. His manner became less guarded and his words more distinct as he proceeded.

" No," said he, " I've thought it all over, and I don't like it. It's dangerous."

" Dangerous ! " grunted the " deaf and dumb " Spaniard, to the vast surprise of the boys. " Milksop ! "

This voice made the boys gasp and quake. It

was Injun Joe's! There was silence for some time.
Then Joe said :

" What's anymore dangerous than that job up
yonder—but nothing's come of it."

" That's different. Away up the river so, and
not another house about. 'Twon't ever be known
that we tried, anyway, long as we didn't succeed."

" Well, what's more dangerous than coming here
in the daytime ?—anybody would suspicion us that
saw us."

" I know that. But there wasn't any other place
as handy after that fool of a job. I want to quit
this shanty. I wanted to yesterday, only it wasn't
any use trying to stir out of here with those infernal
boys playing over there on the hill right in full
view."

" Those infernal boys " quaked again under the
inspiration of this remark, and thought how lucky
it was that they had remembered it was Friday and
concluded to wait a day. They wished in their
hearts they had waited a year. The two men got
out some food and made a luncheon. After a long
and thoughtful silence, Injun Joe said :

" Look here, lad, you go back up the river where
you belong. Wait there till you hear from me. I'll
take the chances on dropping into this town just
once more, for a look. We'll do that ' dangerous '
job after I've spied around a little and think things
look well for it. Then for Texas! We'll leg it
together! "

This was satisfactory. Both men presently fell to
yawning, and Injun Joe said :

" I'm dead for sleep! It's your turn to watch."

He curled down in the weeds and soon began to
snore. His comrade stirred him once or twice, and

he became quiet. Presently the watcher began to nod; his head drooped lower and lower; both men began to snore now.

The boys drew a long grateful breath. Tom whispered—

"Now's our chance—come!"

Huck said: "I can't—I'd die if they was to wake."

Tom urged—Huck held back. At last Tom rose slowly and softly, and started alone. But the first step he made wrung such a hideous creak from the crazy floor that he sank down almost dead with fright. He never made a second attempt. The boys lay there counting the dragging moments till it seemed to them that time must be done and eternity growing grey; and then they were grateful to note that at last the sun was setting.

Now one snore ceased. Injun Joe sat up, stared around—smiled grimly upon his comrade, whose head was drooping upon his knees—stirred him up with his foot and said—

"Here! You're a watchman, ain't you!"

"All right, though—nothing's happened."

"My! Have I been asleep?"

"Oh, partly, partly. Nearly time for us to be moving, pard. What'll we do with what little swag we've got left?"

"I don't know—leave it here as we've always done, I reckon. No use to take it away till we start south. Six hundred and fifty in silver's something to carry."

"Well—all right—it won't matter to come here again."

"No—but I'd say come in the night as we used to do—it's better."

"Yes, but look here; it may be a good while

before I get the right chance at that job; accidents might happen, 'taint in such a very good place; we'll just regularly bury it—and bury it deep."

" Good idea," said the comrade, who walked across the room, knelt down, raised one of the rearward hearthstones and took out a bag that jingled pleasantly. He subtracted from it twenty or thirty dollars for himself and as much for Injun Joe, and passed the bag to the latter, who was on his knees in the corner, now, digging with his bowie-knife.

The boys forgot all their fears, all their miseries in an instant. With gloating eyes they watched every movement. Luck!—the splendour of it was beyond all imagination! Six hundred dollars was money enough to make half a dozen boys rich! Here was treasure-hunting under the happiest auspices—there would not be any bothersome uncertainty as to where to dig. They nudged each other every moment—eloquent nudges and easily understood, for they simply meant, " Oh, but ain't you glad now we're here !"

Joe's knife struck upon something.

" Hello !" said he.

" What is it ? " said his comrade.

" Half-rotten plank—no, it's a box, I believe. Here, bear a hand, and we'll see what it's here for. Never mind, I've broke a hole."

He reached his hand in and drew it out.

" Man, it's money !"

The two men examined the handful of coins. They were gold. The boys above were as excited as themselves, and as delighted.

Joe's comrade said :

" We'll make quick work of this. There's an old rusty pick over amongst the weeds in the corner, the other side of the fireplace—I saw it a minute ago."

He ran and brought the boys' pick and shovel. Injun Joe took the pick, looked it over critically, shook his head, muttered something to himself, and then began to use it.

The box was soon unearthed. It was not very large; it was iron-bound and had been very strong before the slow years had injured it. The men contemplated the treasure awhile in blissful silence.

"Pard, there's thousands of dollars here," said Injun Joe.

"'Twas always said that Murrel's gang used around here one summer," the stranger observed.

"I know it," said Injun Joe; "and this looks like it, I should say."

"Now you won't need to do that job."

The half-breed frowned. Said he:

"You don't know me. Least you don't know all about that thing. 'Tain't robbery altogether—it's revenge!" and a wicked light flamed in his eyes. "I'll need your help in it. When it's finished—then Texas. Go home to your Nance and your kids, and stand by till you hear from me."

"Well, if you say so. What'll we do with this—bury it again?"

"Yes" [ravishing delight overhead]. "No! by the great Sachem, no!" [profound distress overhead]. "I'd nearly forgot. That pick had fresh earth on it!" [The boys were sick with terror in a moment.] "What business has a pick and a shovel here? What business with fresh earth on them? Who brought them here—and where are they gone? Have you heard anybody?—seen anybody? What! bury it again and leave them to come and see the ground disturbed ? Not exactly—not exactly. We'll take it to my den."

" Why, of course ! Might have thought of that before. You mean number one ? "

" No—number two—under the cross. The other place is bad—too common."

" All right. It's nearly dark enough to start."

Injun Joe got up and went about from window to window, cautiously peeping out. Presently he said :

" Who could have brought those tools here ? Do you reckon they can be upstairs ? "

The boys' breath forsook them. Injun Joe put his hand on his knife, halted a moment, undecided, and then turned towards the stairway. The boys thought of the closet, but their strength was gone. The steps came creaking up the stairs—the intolerable distress of the situation woke the stricken resolution of the lads—they were about to spring for the closet, when there was a crash of rotten timbers, and Injun Joe landed on the ground amid the débris of the ruined stairway. He gathered himself up cursing, and his comrade said :

" Now what's the use of all that ? If it's anybody, and they're up there, let them stay there— who cares ? If they want to jump down, now, and get into trouble, who objects ? It will be dark in fifteen minutes—and then let them follow us if they want to ; I'm willing. In my opinion, whoever hove those things in here caught a sight of us, and took us for ghosts or devils or something. I'll bet they're running yet."

Joe grumbled awhile ; then he agreed with his friend that what daylight was left ought to be economised in getting things ready for leaving. Shortly afterwards they slipped out of the house in

the deepening twilight, and moved towards the
river with their precious box.

Tom and Huck rose up, weak but vastly relieved,
and stared after them through the chinks between
the logs of the house. Follow? Not they—they
were content to reach the ground again without
broken necks, and take the townward track over
the hill. They did not talk much, they were too
much absorbed in hating themselves—hating the
ill-luck that made them take the spade and the
pick there. But for that, Injun Joe never would
have suspected. He would have hidden the silver
with the gold to wait there till his "revenge" was
satisfied, and then he would have had the misfortune
to find that money turn up missing. Bitter, bitter
luck that the tools were ever brought there! They
resolved to keep a look-out for that Spaniard when
he should come to town spying out for chances to
do his revengeful job, and follow him to "number
two," wherever that might be. Then a ghastly
thought occurred to Tom:

"Revenge? What if he means *us*, Huck!"

"Oh, don't," said Huck, nearly fainting.

They talked it all over, and as they entered town
they agreed to believe that he might possibly mean
somebody else—at least that he might at least
mean nobody but Tom, since only Tom had testified.

Very, very small comfort it was to Tom to be
alone in danger! Company would be a palpable
improvement, he thought.

CHAPTER XXVIII

THE adventure of the day mightily tormented Tom's dreams that night. Four times he had his hands on that rich treasure, and four times it wasted to nothingness in his fingers as sleep forsook him, and wakefulness brought back the hard reality of his misfortune. As he lay in the early morning recalling the incidents of his great adventure, he noticed that they seemed curiously subdued and far away, somewhat as if they had happened in another world, or in a time long gone by. Then it occurred to him that the great adventure itself must be a dream! There was one very strong argument in favour of this idea, namely, that the quantity of coin he had seen was too vast to be real. He had never seen as much as fifty dollars in one mass before, and he was like all boys of his age and station in life, in that he imagined that all references to "hundreds" and "thousands" were mere fanciful forms of speech, and that no such sums existed in the world. He never had supposed for a moment that so large a sum as a hundred dollars was to be found in actual money in any one's possession. If his notions of hidden treasure had been analysed, they would have been found to consist of a handful of real dimes, and a bushel of vague, splendid, ungraspable ones.

But the incidents of his adventure grew sensibly

sharper and clearer under the attrition of thinking them over, and so he presently found himself leaning to the impression that the thing might not have been a dream after all. This uncertainty must be swept away. He would snatch a hurried breakfast, and go and find Huck.

Huck was sitting on the gunwale of a flat boat, listlessly dangling his feet in the water, and looking very melancholy. Tom concluded to let Huck lead up to the subject. If he did not do it, then the adventure would be proved to have been only a dream.

" Hello, Huck ! ""

" Hello yourself.""

Silence for a minute.

" Tom, if we'd a left the blame tools at the dead tree we'd a got the money. Oh, ain't it awful ! "

" 'Tain't a dream, then, 'tain't a dream ! Somehow I 'most wish it was. Dog'd if I don't.''

" What ain't a dream ? "

" Oh, that thing yesterday. I ben half thinking it was.''

" Dream ! If them stairs hadn't broke down you'd a seen how much dream it was ! I've had dreams enough all night, with that patch-eyed Spanish devil going for us all through 'em, rot him ! "

" No, not rot him. Find him ! Track the money ! "

" Tom, we'll never find him. A feller don't only have one chance for such a pile, and that one's lost. I'd feel mighty shaky if I was to see him, anyway.''

" Well, so'd I ; but I'd like to see him anyway, and track him out—to his number two.''

" Number two ; yes, that's it. I ben thinking

'bout that. But I can't make nothing out of it. What do you reckon it is?"

"I dono. It's too deep. Say, Huck—maybe it's the number of a house!"

"Goody!—No, Tom, that ain't it If it is, it ain't in this one-horse town. They ain't no numbers here."

"Well, that's so. Lemme think a minute. Here —it's the number of a room—in a tavern, you know!"

"Oh, that's the trick! They ain't only two taverns. We can find out quick."

"You stay here, Huck, till I come."

Tom was off at once. He did not care to have Huck's company in public places. He was gone half-an-hour. He found that in the best tavern, number two had long been occupied by a young lawyer, and was still so occupied. In the less ostentatious house number two was a mystery. The tavern-keeper's young son said it was kept locked all the time, and he never saw anybody go into it or come out of it except at night; he did not know any particular reason for this state of things; had had some little curiosity but it was rather feeble; had made the most of the mystery by entertaining himself with the idea that that room was "ha'nted"; had noticed that there was a light in there the night before.

"That's what I've found out, Huck. I reckon that's the very number two we're after."

"I reckon it is, Tom. Now what you going to do?"

"Lemme think."

Tom thought for a long time. Then he said:

"I'll tell you. The back door of that number

two is the door that comes out into that little close alley between the tavern and the old rattle-trap of a brick store.   Now you get hold of all the doorkeys you can find and I'll nip all of auntie's, and the first dark night we'll go there and try 'em.   And mind you keep a look-out for Injun Joe, because he said he was going to drop into town and spy around once more for a chance to get his revenge.   If you see him, you just follow him ; and if he don't go to that number two, that ain't the place."

"Lordy, I don't want to foller him by myself ! "

"Why, it'll be night, sure.   He mightn't ever see you—and if he did, maybe he'd never think anything."

"Well, if it's pretty dark I reckon I'll track him. I dono—I dono.   I'll try."

"You bet I'll follow him if it's dark, Huck ! Why, he might afound out he couldn't get his revenge, and be going right after that money."

"It's so, Tom, it's so.   I'll foller him ; I will, by jingoes ! "

"Now you're talking !   Don't you ever weaken, Huck, and I won't."

CHAPTER XXIX

THAT night Tom and Huck were ready for their adventure. They hung about the neighbourhood of the tavern until after nine, one watching the alley at a distance and the other the tavern door. Nobody entered the alley or left it ; nobody resembling the Spaniard entered or left the tavern door. The night promised to be a fair one ; so Tom went home, with the understanding that if a considerable degree of darkness came on, Huck was to come and " meow," whereupon he would slip out and try the keys. But the night remained clear, and Huck closed his watch and retired to bed in an empty sugar hogshead about twelve.

Tuesday the boys had the same ill-luck. Also Wednesday. But Thursday night promised better. Tom slipped out in good season with his aunt's old tin lantern, and a large towel to blindfold it with. He hid the lantern in Huck's sugar hogshead and the watch began. An hour before midnight the tavern closed up, and its lights (the only ones thereabouts) were put out. No Spaniard had been seen. Nobody had entered or left the alley. Everything was auspicious. The blackness of darkness reigned, the perfect stillness was interrupted only by occasional mutterings of distant thunder.

Tom got his lantern, lit it in the hogshead, wrapped it closely in the towel, and the two adventurers crept in the gloom towards the tavern. Huck stood sentry and Tom felt his way into the alley. Then there was a season of waiting anxiety that weighed upon Huck's spirits like a mountain. He began to wish he could see a flash from the lantern—it would frighten him, but it would at least tell him that Tom was alive yet.

It seemed hours since Tom had disappeared. Surely he must have fainted; maybe he was dead; maybe his heart had burst under terror and excitement. In his uneasiness Huck found himself drawing closer and closer to the alley, fearing all sorts of dreadful things, and momentarily expecting some catastrophe to happen that would take away his breath. There was not much to take away, for he seemed only able to inhale it by thimblefuls, and his heart would soon wear itself out, the way it was beating. Suddenly there was a flash of light, and Tom came tearing by him:

"Run!" said he; "run for your life!"

He needn't have repeated it; once was enough; Huck was making thirty or forty miles an hour before the repetition was uttered. The boys never stopped till they reached the shed of a deserted slaughter-house at the lower end of the village. Just as they got within its shelter the storm burst and the rain poured down. As soon as Tom got his breath he said:

"Huck, it was awful! I tried two of the keys just as soft as I could; but they seemed to make such a power of racket that I couldn't hardly get my breath, I was so scared. They wouldn't turn in the lock either. Well, without noticing what I was doing, I took hold of the knob, and open comes the door! It wasn't locked! I hopped in and shook off the towel, and *great Cæsar's ghost!*"

" What !—what'd you see, Tom ? "

" Huck, I most stepped on to Injun Joe's hand ! "

" No ! "

" Yes. He was laying there, sound asleep on the floor, with his old patch on his eye and his arms spread out."

" Lordy, what did you do ? Did he wake up ? "

" No, never budged. Drunk, I reckon. I just grabbed that towel and started ! "

" I'd never a thought of the towel, I bet ! "

" Well, I would. My aunt would make me mighty sick if I lost it."

" Say, Tom, did you see that box ? "

" Huck, I didn't wait to look around. I didn't see the box, I didn't see the cross. I didn't see anything but a bottle and a tin cup on the floor by Injun Joe ! Yes, and I saw two barrels and lots more bottles in the room. Don't you see, now, what's the matter with that ha'nted room ? "

" How ? "

" Why, it's ha'nted with whisky ! Maybe all the Temperance Taverns have got a ha'nted room, hey, Huck ? "

" Well, I reckon maybe that's so. Who'd a thought such a thing ? But say, Tom, now's a mighty good time to get that box, if Injun Joe's drunk."

" It is that ! You try it ! "

Huck shuddered.

" Well, no—I reckon not."

" And I reckon not, Huck. Only one bottle along-side of Injun Joe ain't enough. If there'd been three he'd be drunk enough and I'd do it.'

There was a long pause for reflection, and then Tom said :

" Looky here, Huck, less not try that thing any more till we know Injun Joe's not in there. It's too scary. Now if we watch every night, we'll be dead sure to see him go out some time or other, then we'll snatch that box quicker'n lightning."

" Well, I'm agreed. I'll watch the whole night long, and I'll do it every night, too, if you'll do the other part of the job."

" All right, I will. All you got to do is to trot up Hooper Street a block and meow—and if I'm asleep, you throw some gravel at the window and that'll fetch me."

" Agreed, and good as wheat ! "

" Now, Huck, the storm's over, and I'll go home. It'll begin to be daylight in a couple of hours. You go back and watch that long, will you ? "

" I said I would, Tom, and I will. I'll ha'nt that tavern every night for a year. I'll sleep all day and I'll stand watch all night."

" That's all right. Now where are you going to sleep ? '

" In Ben Rogers's hay-loft. He lets me, and so does his pap's nigger man, Uncle Jake. I tote water for Uncle Jake whenever he wants me to, and any time I ask him he gives me a little something to eat if he can spare it. That's a mighty good nigger, Tom. He likes me, becuz I don't ever act as if I was above him. Sometimes I've set right down and eat with him. But you needn't tell that A body's got to do things when he's awful hungry he wouldn't want to do as a steady thing."

" Well, if I don't want you in the daytime, Huck, I'll let you sleep. I won't come bothering around. Any time you see something's up in the night, just skip right around and meow."

CHAPTER XXX

THE first thing Tom heard on Friday morning was a glad piece of news—Judge Thatcher's family had come back to town the night before. Both Injun Joe and the treasure sunk into secondary importance for a moment, and Becky took the chief place in the boy's interest. He saw her, and they had an exhausting good time playing "hi-spy" and "gully-keeper" with a crowd of their schoolmates. The day was completed and crowned in a peculiarly satisfactory way: Becky teased her mother to appoint the next day for the long-promised and long-delayed picnic, and she consented. The child's delight was boundless, and Tom's not more moderate. The invitations were sent out before sunset, and straightway the young folks of the village were thrown into a fever of preparation and pleasurable anticipation. Tom's excitement enabled him to keep awake until a pretty late hour, and he had good hopes of hearing Huck's "meow" and of having his treasure to astonish Becky and the picnickers with, next day; but he was disappointed. No signal came that night.

Morning came eventually, and by ten or eleven o'clock, a giddy and rollicking company were gathered at Judge Thatcher's, and everything was ready for a start. It was not the custom for elderly people to mar picnics with their presence. The

children were considered safe enough under the wings
of a few young ladies of eighteen and a few young
gentlemen of twenty-three or thereabouts. The
old steam ferryboat was chartered for the occasion:
presently the gay throng filed up the main street
laden with provision-baskets. Sid was sick and had
to miss the fun; Mary remained at home to enter-
tain him. The last thing Mrs. Thatcher said to
Becky was:

"You'll not get back till late. Perhaps you'd
better stay all night with some of the girls that live
near the ferry landing, child!"

"Then I'll stay with Susy Harper, mamma."

"Very well. And mind and behave yourself, and
don't be any trouble."

Presently, as they tripped along, Tom said to
Becky:

"Say—I'll tell you what we'll do. 'Stead of going
to Joe Harper's, we'll climb right up the hill and stop
at Widow Douglas's. She'll have ice-cream! She has
it 'most every day—dead loads of it. And she'll be
awful glad to have us."

"Oh, that will be fun!"

Then Becky reflected a moment, and said:

"But what will mamma say?"

"How'll she ever know?"

The girl turned the idea over in her mind, and said
reluctantly:

"I reckon it's wrong—but——"

"But; shucks! Your mother won't know, and
so what's the harm? All she wants is that you'll
be safe; and I bet you she'd a said go there if she'd
a thought of it. I know she would!"

The Widow Douglas's splendid hospitality was a
tempting bait. It and Tom's persuasions presently

carried the day. So it was decided to say nothing to anybody about the night's programme.

Presently it occurred to Tom that maybe Huck might come this very night and give the signal. The thought took a deal of the spirit out of his anticipations. Still he could not bear to give up the fun at Widow Douglas's. And why should he give it up, he reasoned—the signal did not come the night before, so why should it be any more likely to come to-night? The sure fun of the evening outweighed the uncertain treasure; and, boy-like, he determined to yield to the stronger inclination and not allow himself to think of the box of money another time that day.

Three miles below town the ferryboat stopped at the mouth of a woody hollow and tied up. The crowd swarmed ashore, and soon the forest distances and craggy heights echoed far and near with shoutings and laughter. All the different ways of getting hot and tired were gone through with, and by-and-by the rovers straggled back to camp fortified with responsible appetites, and then the destruction of the good things began. After the feast there was a refreshing season of rest and chat in the shade of spreading oaks. By-and-by somebody shouted:

" Who's ready for the cave ? "

Everybody was. Bundles of candles were produced, and straightway there was a general scamper up the hill. The mouth of the cave was high up the hillside, an opening shaped like the letter A. Its massive oaken door stood unbarred. Within was a small chamber, chilly as an ice-house, and walled by Nature with solid limestone that was dewy with a cold sweat. It was romantic and mysterious to stand here in the deep gloom and look out upon the green valley shining in the sun. But the impressiveness of the situation quickly wore off, and the romping began again. The moment a candle was lighted, there was a general rush upon the owner of it ; a struggle and a gallant defence followed, but the candle was soon knocked down or blown out, and then there was a glad clamour of laughter and a new chase. But all things have an end. By-and-by the procession went filing down the steep descent of the main avenue, the flickering rank of lights dimly revealing the lofty walls of rock almost to their point of junction sixty feet overhead. This main avenue was not more than eight or ten feet wide. Every few steps, other lofty and still narrower crevices branched from it on either hand, for McDougal's cave was but a vast labyrinth of crooked aisles that ran into each other and out again and led nowhere. It was said that one might wander days and nights together through its intricate tangle of rifts and chasms, and never find the end of the cave ; and that he might go down and down, and still down into the earth, and it was just the same—labyrinth underneath labyrinth, and no end to any of them. No man "knew" the cave. That was an impossible thing. Most of the young men knew a portion of it, and it was not customary to venture much beyond this known portion. Tom Sawyer knew as much of the cave as any one.

The procession moved along the main avenue some three-quarters of a mile, and then groups and couples began to slip aside into branch avenues, fly along the dismal corridors, and take each other by surprise at points where the corridors joined again. Parties were able to elude each other for the space of half-an-hour without going beyond the " known " ground.

By-and-by, one group after another came straggling back to the mouth of the cave, panting, hilarious,
smeared from head to foot with tallow drippings,
daubed with clay, and entirely delighted with the
success of the day. Then they were astonished to
find that they had been taking no note of time, and
that night was about at hand. The clanging bell
had been calling for half-an-hour. However, this
sort of close to the day's adventures was romantic
and therefore satisfactory. When the ferryboat
with her wild freight pushed into the stream, nobody
cared sixpence for the wasted time but the captain
of the craft.

Huck was already upon his watch when the ferry-
boat's lights went glinting past the wharf. He
heard no noise on board, for the young people were
as subdued and still as people usually are who are
nearly tired to death. He wondered what boat it
was, and why she did not stop at the wharf—and
then he dropped her out of his mind and put his attention upon his business. The night was growing
cloudy and dark. Ten o'clock came, and the noise
of vehicles ceased, scattered lights began to wink
out, all straggling foot-passengers disappeared, the
village betook itself to its slumbers and left the
small watcher alone with the silence and the ghosts.
Eleven o'clock came, and the tavern lights were put
out; darkness everywhere, now. Huck waited
what seemed a weary long time, but nothing happened. His faith was weakening. Was there any
use? Was there really any use? Why not give it
up and turn in?

A noise fell upon his ear. He was all attention in
an instant. The alley door closed softly. He sprang
to the corner of the brick store. The next moment

two men brushed by him, and one seemed to have
something under his arm. It must be that box!
So they were going to remove the treasure. Why
call Tom now? It would be absurd—the men
would get away with the box and never be found
again. No, he would stick to their wake and follow
them ; he would trust to the darkness for security
from discovery. So communing with himself, Huck
stepped out and glided along behind the men, catlike, with bare feet, allowing them to keep just far
enough ahead not to be invisible.

They moved up the river street three blocks, then
turned to the left up a cross street. They went
straight ahead, then, until they came to the path
that led up Cardiff Hill ; this they took. They
passed by the old Welshman's house, half-way up
the hill, without hesitation, and still climbed upward. Good, thought Huck, they will bury it in the
old quarry. But they never stopped at the quarry.
They passed on, up the summit. They plunged into
the narrow path between the tall sumach bushes,
and were at once hidden in the gloom. Huck closed
up and shortened his distance, now, for they would
never be able to see him. He trotted along a while ;
then slackened his pace, fearing he was gaining too
fast ; moved on a piece, then stopped altogether;
listened ; no sound ; none, save that he seemed to
hear the beating of his own heart. The hooting of
an owl came from over the hill—ominous sound !
But no footsteps. Heavens, was everything lost ?
He was about to spring with winged feet, when a
man cleared his throat, not four feet from him !
Huck's heart shot into his throat, but he swallowed
it again ; and then he stood there shaking as if a
dozen agues had taken charge of him at once, and

so weak that he thought he must surely fall to the ground. He knew where he was. He knew he was within five steps of the stile leading into Widow Douglas's grounds. "Very well," he thought, "let them bury it there; it won't be hard to find."

Now there was a low voice—a very low voice— Injun Joe's:

"Damn her, maybe she's got company—there's lights, late as it is."

"I can't see any."

This was that stranger's voice—the stranger of the haunted house. A deadly chill went to Huck's heart—this, then, was the "revenge" job! His thought was to fly. Then he remembered that the Widow Douglas had been kind to him more than once, and maybe these men were going to murder her. He wished he dared venture to warn her; but he knew he didn't dare—they might come and catch him. He thought all this and more in the moment that elapsed between the stranger's remark and Injun Joe's next—which was:

"Because the bush is in your way. Now—this way—now you see, don't you?"

"Yes. Well, there is company there, I reckon. Better give it up."

"Give it up, and I just leaving this country for ever! Give it up, and maybe never have another chance. I tell you again, as I've told you before, I don't care for her swag—you may have it. But her husband was rough on me—many times he was rough on me—and mainly he was the justice of the peace that jugged me for a vagrant. And that ain't all! It ain't the millionth part of it? He had me horsewhipped!—horsewhipped in front of the jail, like a nigger!—with all the town looking on!

Horsewhipped!—do you understand? He took advantage of me and died. But I'll take it out of her!"

"Oh, don't kill her! Don't do that!"

"Kill? Who said anything about killing? I would kill him if he was here; but not her. When you want to get revenge on a woman you don't kill her—bosh! you go for her looks. You slit her nostrils—you notch her ears like a sow's!"

"By God, that's—"

"Keep your opinion to yourself! It will be safest for you. I'll tie her to the bed. If she bleeds to death, is that my fault? I'll not cry if she does. My friend, you'll help me in this thing—for my sake—that's why you're here—I mightn't be able alone. If you flinch, I'll kill you! Do you understand that? And if I have to kill you, I'll kill her—and then I reckon nobody'll ever know much about who done this business."

"Well, if it's got to be done, let's get at it. The quicker the better—I'm all in a shiver."

"Do it now?—and company there? Look here—I'll get suspicious of you, first thing, you know. No —we'll wait till the lights are out—there's no hurry."

Huck felt that a silence was going to ensue—a thing still more awful than any amount of murderous talk; so he held his breath and stepped gingerly back; planted his foot carefully and firmly, after balancing, one-legged, in a precarious way and almost toppling over, first on one side and then on the other. He took another step back with the same elaboration and the same risks; then another and another, and a twig snapped under his foot! His breath stopped and he listened. There was no sound—the stillness was perfect. His gratitude was measureless. Now he turned in his tracks between the walls of sumach bushes—turned himself as carefully as if he were a ship—and then stepped quickly but cautiously along. When he emerged at the quarry he felt secure, so he picked up his nimble heels and flew. Down, down he sped till he reached the Welshman's. He banged at the door, and presently the heads of the old man and his two stalwart sons were thrust from windows.

"What's the row there? Who's banging? What do you want?"

"Let me in—quick! I'll tell everything."

"Why, who are you?"

"Huckleberry Finn—quick, let me in!"

"Huckleberry Finn, indeed! It ain't a name to open many doors, I judge! But let him in, lads, and let's see what's the trouble."

"Please don't ever tell I told you," were Huck's first words when he got in. "Please don't—I'd be killed sure—but the widow's been good friend to me sometimes, and I want to tell—I will tell if you'll promise you won't ever say it was me."

"By George he has got something to tell, or he wouldn't act so!" exclaimed the old man. "Out with it, and nobody here'll ever tell, lad."

Three minutes later the old man and his sons, well-armed, were up the hill, and just entering the sumach path on tip-toe, their weapons in their hands. Huck accompanied them no further. He hid behind a great boulder and fell to listening. There was a lagging, anxious silence, and then all of a sudden there was an explosion of fire-arms and a cry. Huck waited for no particulars. He sprang away and sped down the hill as fast as his legs would carry him.

CHAPTER XXXI

As the earliest suspicion of dawn appeared on Sunday morning, Huck came groping up the hill and rapped gently at the old Welshman's door. The inmates were asleep, but it was a sleep that was set on a hair-trigger, on account of the exciting episode of the night. A call came from a window:

"Who's there?"

Huck's scared voice answered in a low tone:

"Do please let me in! It's only Huck Finn!"

"It's a name that can open this door night or day, lad!—and welcome!"

These were strange words to the vagabond boy's ears, and the pleasantest he had ever heard. He could not recollect that the closing word had ever been applied in his case before.

The door was quickly unlocked and he entered. Huck was given a seat, and the old man and his brace of tall sons speedily dressed themselves.

"Now, my boy, I hope you're good and hungry, because breakfast will be ready as soon as the sun's up, and we'll have a piping hot one, too—make yourself easy about that. I and the boys hoped you'd turn up and stop here last night."

"I was awful scared," said Huck, "and I run. I took out when the pistols went off, and I didn't stop for three mile. I've come now becuz I wanted to know about it, you know; and I come before day-

222

light becuz I didn't want to run across them devils, even if they was dead."

"Well, poor chap, you do look as if you'd had a hard night of it—but there's a bed here for you when you've had your breakfast. No, they ain't dead, lad —we are sorry enough for that. You see we knew right where to put our hands on them, by your description; so we crept along on tip-toe till we got within fifteen feet of them—dark as a cellar that sumach path was—and just then I found I was going to sneeze. It was the meanest kind of luck! I tried to keep it back, but no use—'twas bound to come, and it did come! I was in the lead, with my pistol raised, and when the sneeze started those scoundrels a-rustling to get out of the path, I sang out "Fire, boys!" and blazed away at the place where the rustling was. So did the boys. But they were off in a jiffy, those villains, and we after them, down through the woods. I judge we never touched them. They fired a shot apiece as they started, but their bullets whizzed by and didn't do us any harm. As soon as we lost the sound of their feet we quit chasing, and went down and stirred up the constables. They got a posse together, and went off to guard the river bank, and as soon as it is light the sheriff and a gang are going to beat up the woods. My boys will be with them presently. I wish we had some sort of a description of those rascals—'twould help a good deal. But you couldn't see what they were like in the dark, lad, I suppose?"

"Oh yes, I saw them down town, and follered them."

"Splendid! Describe them—describe them, my boy!"

"One's the old deaf and dumb Spaniard that's

been around here once or twice, and t'other's a mean-looking, ragged——"

" That's enough, lad, we know the men ! Happened on them in the woods back of the widow's one day, and they slunk away. Off with you, boys, and tell the sheriff—get your breakfast to-morrow morning ! "

The Welshman's sons departed at once. As they were leaving the room Huck sprang up and exclaimed:

" Oh, please don't tell anybody it was me that blowed on them ! Oh, please ! "

" All right if you say it, Huck, but you ought to have the credit of what you did."

" Oh no, no ! Please don't tell ! "

When the young men were gone, the old Welshman said :

" They won't tell—and I won't. But why don't you want it known ? "

Huck would not explain further than to say that he already knew too much about one of those men and would not have the man know that he knew anything against him for the whole world—he would be killed for knowing it, sure.

The old man promised secrecy once more, and said:

" How did you come to follow these fellows, lad ? Were they looking suspicious ? "

Huck was silent, while he framed a duly cautious reply. Then he said :

" Well, you see, I'm a kind of a hard lot—least everybody says so, and I don't see nothing agin it— and sometimes I can't sleep much, on accounts of thinking about it, and sort of trying to strike out a new way of doing. That was the way of it last night. I couldn't sleep, and so I come along up street 'bout midnight a-turning it all over, and when I got to that

old shackly brick-store by the Temperance Tavern,
I backed up agin the wall to have another think.
Well, just then along comes these two chaps slipping
along close by me, with something under their arm,
and I reckoned they'd stole it. One was a-smoking,
and t'other one wanted a light ; so they stopped right
before me, and the cigars lit up their faces, and I see
that the big one was the deaf and dumb Spaniard,
by his white whiskers and the patch on his eye, and
t'other one was a rusty, ragged-looking devil."

" Could you see the rags by the light of the cigars ? "

This staggered Huck for a moment. Then he said :

" Well, I don't know—but somehow it seems as
if I did."

" Then they went on, and you——"

" Followed 'em—yes. That was it. I wanted to
see what was up—they sneaked along so. I dogged
'em to the widder's stile, and stood in the dark, and
heard the ragged one beg for the widder, and the
Spaniard swear he'd spile her looks, just as I told you
and your two——"

" What ! the deaf and dumb man said all that ! "

Huck had made another terrible mistake ! He
was trying his best to keep the old man from getting
the faintest hint of who the Spaniard might be, and
yet his tongue seemed determined to get him into
trouble in spite of all he could do. He made several
efforts to creep out of his scrape, but the old man's
eye was upon him, and he made blunder after blunder.
Presently the Welshman said :

" My boy, don't be afraid of me, I wouldn't hurt a
hair of your head for all the world. No—I'd protect you—I'd protect you. This Spaniard is not deaf
and dumb ; you've let that slip without intending it ;
you can't cover that up now. You know something

about that Spaniard that you want to keep dark.
Now trust me—tell me what it is, and trust me—I
won't betray you."

Huck looked into the old man's honest eyes a
moment, and then bent over and whispered in his ear:

"'Tain't a Spaniard—it's Injun Joe!'"

The Welshman almost jumped out of his chair.
In a moment he said :

"It's all plain enough now. When you talked
about notching ears and slitting noses, I judged
that that was your own embellishment, because
white men don't take that sort of revenge. But an
Injun! That's a different matter altogether."

During breakfast the talk went on, and in the
course of it the old man said that the last thing which
he and his sons had done, before going to bed, was
to get a lantern and examine the stile and its vicinity
for marks of blood. They found none, but captured
a bulky bundle of——

"Of WHAT!"

If the words had been lightning, they could not
have leaped with a more stunning suddenness from
Huck's blanched lips. His eyes were staring wide,
now, and his breath suspended—waiting for the
answer. The Welshman started—stared in return—
three seconds—five seconds—ten—then replied :

"Of burglar's tools."

"Why, what's the matter with you ?"

Huck sank back, panting gently, but deeply,
unutterably grateful. The Welshman eyed him
gravely, curiously—and presently said :

"Yes, burglar's tools. That appears to relieve you
a great deal. But what did give you that turn ?
What were you expecting we'd found ?"

Huck was in a close place ; the inquiring eye

was upon him—he would have given anything for material for a plausible answer. Nothing suggested itself ; the inquiring eye was boring deeper and deeper—a senseless reply offered—there was no time to weigh it, so at a venture he uttered it feebly :

" Sunday-school books, maybe."

Poor Huck was too distressed to smile, but the old man laughed loud and joyously, shook up the details of his anatomy from head to foot, and ended by saying that such a laugh was money in a man's pocket, because it cut down the doctor's bills like everything. Then he added :

" Poor old chap, you're white and jaded ; you ain't well a bit. No wonder you're a little flighty and off your balance. But you'll come out of it. Rest and sleep will fetch you all right, I hope."

Huck was irritated to think he had been such a goose and betrayed such a suspicious excitement, for he had dropped the idea that the parcel brought from the tavern was the treasure as soon as he had heard the talk at the widow's stile. He had only thought it was not the treasure, however, he had not known that it wasn't ; and so the suggestion of a captured bundle was too much for his self-possession. But on the whole he felt glad the little episode had happened, for now he knew beyond all question that that bundle was not *the* bundle, and so his mind was at rest and exceedingly comfortable. In fact everything seemed to be drifting just in the right direction, now ; the treasure must be still in number two, the men would be captured and jailed that day, and he and Tom could seize the gold that night without any trouble or any fear of interruption.

Just as breakfast was completed there was a knock at the door. Huck jumped for a hiding-place, for he had no mind to be connected even remotely with the late event. The Welshman admitted several ladies and gentlemen, among them the Widow Douglas, and noticed that groups of citizens were climbing the hill to stare at the stile. So the news had spread.

The Welshman had to tell the story of the night to the visitors. The widow's gratitude for her preservation was outspoken.

"Don't say a word about it, madam. There's another that you're more beholden to than you are to me and my boys maybe, but he don't allow me to tell his name. We wouldn't ever have been there but for him."

Of course this excited a curiosity so vast that it almost belittled the main matter ; but the Welshman allowed it to eat into the vitals of his visitors, and through them he transmitted it to the whole town, for he refused to part with his secret. When all else had been learned the widow said :

"I went to sleep reading in bed, and slept straight through all that noise. Why didn't you come and wake me ? "

"We judged it wasn't worth while. Those fellows weren't likely to come again ; they hadn't any tools left to work with, and what was the use of waking you up and scaring you to death ? My three negro men stood guard at your house all the rest of the night. They've just come back."

More visitors came, and the story had to be told and retold for a couple of hours more.

There was no Sabbath-school during day-school vacation, but everybody was early at church. The stirring event was well canvassed. News came that not a sign of the villains had been yet discovered.

When the sermon was finished Judge Thatcher's wife dropped alongside of Mrs. Harper as she moved down the aisle with the crowd, and said :

"Is my Becky going to sleep all day? I just expected she would be tired to death."

"Your Becky?"

"Yes," with a startled look. "Didn't she stay with you last night?"

"Why, no."

Mrs. Thatcher turned pale, and sank into a pew just as Aunt Polly, talking briskly with a friend, passed by. Aunt Polly said :

"Good morning, Mrs. Thatcher. Good morning, Mrs. Harper. I've got a boy that's turned up missing. I reckon my Tom stayed at your house last night—one of you. And now he's afraid to come to church. I've got to settle with him."

Mrs. Thatcher shook her head feebly and turned paler than ever.

"He didn't stay with us," said Mrs. Harper, beginning to look uneasy. A marked anxiety came into Aunt Polly's face.

"Joe Harper, have you seen my Tom this morning?"

"No'm."

"When did you see him last?"

Joe tried to remember, but was not sure he could say. The people had stopped moving out of church. Whispers passed along, and a brooding uneasiness took possession of every countenance. Children were anxiously questioned, and young teachers. They all said they had not noticed whether Tom and Becky were on board the ferryboat on the homeward trip; it was dark; no one thought of inquiring if any one was missing. One young man finally

blurted out his fear that they were still in the cave!
Mrs. Thatcher swooned away; Aunt Polly fell to
crying and wringing her hands.

The alarm swept from lip to lip, from group to
group, from street to street; and within five minutes
the bells were wildly clanging, and the whole town
was up! The Cardiff Hill episode sank into instant
insignificance, the burglars were forgotten, horses
were saddled, skiffs were manned, the ferryboat
ordered out, and before the horror was half-an-hour
old two hundred men were pouring down high-road
and river toward the cave.

All the long afternoon the village seemed empty
and dead. Many women visited Aunt Polly and
Mrs. Thatcher, and tried to comfort them. They
cried with them, too, and that was still better than
words.

All the tedious night the town waited for news;
but when the morning dawned at last, all the word
that came was, "Send more candles, and send food."
Mrs. Thatcher was almost crazed, and Aunt Polly
also. Judge Thatcher sent messages of hope and
encouragement from the cave, but they conveyed
no real cheer.

The old Welshman came home towards daylight,
spattered with candle-grease, smeared with clay,
and almost worn out. He found Huck still in the
bed that had been provided for him, and delirious
with fever. The physicians were all at the cave,
so the Widow Douglas came and took charge of the
patient. She said she would do her best by him,
because, whether he was good, bad, or indifferent,
he was the Lord's, and nothing that was the Lord's
was a thing to be neglected. The Welshman said
Huck had good spots in him, and the widow said:

" You can depend on it. That's the Lord's mark. He don't leave it off. He never does. Puts it somewhere on every creature that comes from His hands."

Early in the forenoon parties of jaded men began to straggle into the village, but the strongest of the citizens continued searching. All the news that could be gained was that remotenesses of the cavern were being ransacked that had never been visited before ; that every corner and crevice was going to be thoroughly searched ; that wherever one wandered through the maze of passages, lights were to be seen flitting hither and thither in the distance, and shoutings and pistol-shots sent their hollow reverberations to the ear down the sombre aisles. In one place, far from the section usually traversed by tourists, the names " BECKY " and " TOM " had been found traced upon the rocky wall with candle smoke, and near at hand a grease-soiled bit of ribbon. Mrs. Thatcher recognised the ribbon and cried over it. She said it was the last relic she should ever have of her child ; and that no other memorial of her could ever be so precious, because this one parted latest from the living body before the awful death came. Some said that now and then in the cave a far-away speck of light would glimmer, and then a glorious shout would burst forth and a score of men go trooping down the echoing aisle—and then a sickening disappointment always followed ; the children were not there ; it was only a searcher's light.

Three dreadful days and nights dragged their tedious hours along, and the village sank into a hopeless stupor. No one had heart for anything. The accidental discovery, just made, that the proprietor of the Temperance Tavern kept liquor on his premises, scarcely fluttered the public pulse, tremendous as the fact was. In a lucid interval, Huck feebly led up to the subject of taverns and finally asked, dimly dreading the worst, if anything had been discovered at the Temperance Tavern since he had been ill?

"Yes," said the widow.

Huck started up in bed wild-eyed:

"What! What was it?"

"Liquor!—and the place has been shut up. Lie down, child—what a turn you did give me!"

"Only tell me one thing—only just one—please! Was it Tom Sawyer that found it?"

The widow burst into tears.

"Hush, hush, child, hush! I've told you before, you must *not* talk. You are very, very sick!"

Then nothing but liquor had been found; there would have been a great pow-wow if it had been the gold. So the treasure was gone for ever—gone for ever. But what could she be crying about? Curious that she should cry.

These thoughts worked their dim way through Huck's mind, and under the weariness they gave him he fell asleep. The widow said to herself:

"There—he's asleep, poor wreck. Tom Sawyer find it! Pity but somebody could find Tom Sawyer! Ah, there ain't many left, now, that's got hope enough, or strength either, to go on searching."

CHAPTER XXXII

Now to return to Tom and Becky's share in the picnic. They tripped along the murky aisles with the rest of the company, visiting the familiar wonders of the cave—wonders dubbed with rather over-descriptive names, such as " The Drawing Room," " The Cathedral," " Aladdin's Palace," and so on. Presently the hide-and-seek frolicking began, and Tom and Becky engaged in it with zeal until the exertion began to grow a trifle wearisome ; then they wandered down a sinuous avenue, holding their candles aloft and reading the tangled web-work of names, dates, post-office addresses, and mottoes with which the rocky walls had been frescoed (in candle smoke). Still drifting along and talking, they scarcely noticed that they were now in a part of the cave whose walls were not frescoed. They smoked their own names under an overhanging shelf and moved on. Presently they came to a place where a little stream of water, trickling over a ledge and carrying a lime-stone sediment with it, had, in the slow dragging ages, formed a laced and ruffled Niagara in gleaming and imperishable stone. Tom squeezed his small body behind it in order to illuminate it for Becky's gratification. He found that it curtained a sort of steep natural stairway which was enclosed between narrow walls, and at once the ambition to be

a discoverer seized him. Becky responded to his call,
and they made a smoke mark for future guidance
and started upon their quest. They wound this way
and that, far down into the secret depths of the cave,
made another mark, and branched off in search of
novelties to tell the upper world about. In one
place they found a spacious cavern, from whose
ceiling depended a multitude of shining stalactites
of the length and circumference of a man's leg; they
walked all about it, wondering and admiring, and
presently left it by one of the numerous passages
that opened into it. This shortly brought them to
a bewitching spring, whose basin was encrusted
with a frost-work of glittering crystals; it was in
the midst of a cavern whose walls were supported
by many fantastic pillars which had been formed by
the joining of great stalactites and stalagmites
together, the result of the ceaseless water drip of
centuries. Under the roof vast knots of bats had
packed themselves together, thousands in a bunch;
the lights disturbed the creatures, and they came
flocking down by hundreds, squeaking and darting
furiously at the candles. Tom knew their ways,
and the danger of this sort of conduct. He seized
Becky's hand and hurried her into the first corridor
that offered; and none too soon, for a bat struck
Becky's light out with its wing while she was passing
out of the cavern. The bats chased the children a
good distance; but the fugitives plunged into every
new passage that offered, and at last got rid of the
perilous things. Tom found a subterranean lake,
shortly, which stretched its dim length away until
its shape was lost in the shadows. He wanted to
explore its borders, but concluded that it would
be best to sit down and rest a while first. Now for

the first time the deep stillness of the place laid a clammy hand upon the spirits of the children. Becky said:

" Why, I didn't notice, but it seems ever so long since I heard any of the others."

" Come to think, Becky, we are away down below them, and I don't know how far away north, or south, or east, or whichever it is. We couldn't hear them here."

Becky grew apprehensive.

" I wonder how long we've been down here, Tom? We better start back."

" Yes, I reckon we better. P'raps we better."

" Can you find the way, Tom? It's all a mixed-up crookedness to me."

" I reckon I could find it, but then the bats. If they put both our candles out it will be an awful fix. Let's try some other way, so as not to go through there."

" Well, but I hope we won't get lost. It would be so awful!" and the child shuddered at the thought of the dreadful possibilities.

They started through a corridor, and traversed it in silence a long way, glancing at each new opening, to see if there was anything familiar about the look of it; but they were all strange. Every time Tom made an examination, Becky would watch his face for an encouraging sign, and he would say cheerily:

" Oh, it's all right. This ain't the one, but we'll come to it right away! But he felt less and less hopeful with each failure, and presently began to turn off into diverging avenues at sheer random in the desperate hope of finding the one that was wanted. He still said it was " All right," but there was such a

leaden dread at his heart, that the words had lost
their ring, and sounded as if he had said, "All is
lost!" Becky clung to his side in an anguish of
fear, and tried hard to keep back the tears, but they
would come. At last she said:

"Oh, Tom, never mind the bats; let's go back
that way! We seem to get worse and worse off all
the time."

Tom stopped.

"Listen!" said he.

Profound silence; silence so deep that even their
breathings were conspicuous in the hush. Tom
shouted. The call went echoing down the empty
aisles, and died out in the distance in a faint sound
that resembled a ripple of mocking laughter.

"Oh, don't do it again, Tom, it is too horrid,"
said Becky.

"It is horrid, but I better, Becky; they *might*
hear us, you know," and he shouted again.

The "might" was even a chillier horror than
the ghostly laughter, it so confessed a perishing hope.
The children stood still and listened; but there was
no result. Tom turned upon the back track at
once, and hurried his steps. It was but a little
while before a certain indecision in his manner
revealed another fearful fact to Becky; he could
not find his way back!

"Oh, Tom, you didn't make any marks!"

"Becky, I was such a fool! such a fool! I never
thought we might want to come back! No, I can't
find the way. It's all mixed up."

"Tom, Tom, we're lost! we're lost! We never,
never can get out of this awful place! Oh, why did
we ever leave the others?"

She sank to the ground, and burst into such a

frenzy of crying that Tom was appalled with the idea that she might die, or lose her reason. He sat down by her and put his arms around her; she buried her face in his bosom, she clung to him, she poured out her terrors, her unavailing regrets, and the far echoes turned them all to jeering laughter. Tom begged her to pluck up hope again, and she said she could not. He fell to blaming and abusing himself for getting her into this miserable situation; this had a better effect. She said she would try to hope again, she would get up and follow wherever he might lead, if only he would not talk like that any more. For he was no more to blame than she, she said.

So they moved on again—aimlessly—simply at random—all they could do was to move, keep moving. For a little while, hope made a show of reviving—not with any reason to back it, but only because it is its nature to revive when the spring has not been taken out of it by age and familiarity with failure.

By-and-by Tom took Becky's candle and blew it out. This economy meant so much. Words were not needed. Becky understood, and her hope died again. She knew that Tom had a whole candle and three or four pieces in his pocket—yet he must economise.

By-and-by, fatigue began to assert its claims; the children tried to pay no attention, for it was dreadful to think of sitting down when time was grown to be so precious; moving, in some direction, in any direction, was at least progress and might bear fruit; but to sit down was to invite death and shorten its pursuit.

At last Becky's frail limbs refused to carry her

farther. She sat down. Tom rested with her, and
they talked of home, and the friends there, and the
comfortable beds, and above all, the light! Becky
cried, and Tom tried to think of some way of com-
forting her, but all his encouragements were grown
threadbare with use, and sounded like sarcasms.
Fatigue bore so heavily upon Becky that she drowsed
off to sleep. Tom was grateful. He sat looking
into her drawn face and saw it grow smooth and
natural under the influence of pleasant dreams;
and by-and-by a smile dawned and rested there.
The peaceful face reflected somewhat of peace and
healing into his own spirit, and his thoughts wandered
away to bygone times and dreamy memories.
While he was deep in his musings, Becky woke up
with a breezy little laugh: but it was stricken dead
upon her lips, and a groan followed it.

"Oh, how *could* I sleep! I wish I never, never
had waked! No, no, I don't, Tom! Don't look so!
I won't say it again."

"I'm glad you slept, Becky; you'll feel rested,
now, and we'll find the way out."

"We can try, Tom; but I've seen such a beautiful
country in my dream. I reckon we are going there."

"Maybe not, maybe not. Cheer up, Becky, and
let's go on trying."

They rose up and wandered along, hand in hand
and hopeless. They tried to estimate how long they
had been in the cave, but all they knew was that it
seemed days and weeks, and yet it was plain that this
could not be, for their candles were not gone yet.

A long time after this—they could not tell how
long—Tom said they must go softly and listen for
dripping water—they must find a spring. They
found one presently, and Tom said it was time to

rest again. Both were cruelly tired, yet Becky said she thought she could go a little farther. She was surprised to hear Tom dissent. She could not understand it. They sat down, and Tom fastened his candle to the wall in front of them with some clay. Thought was soon busy; nothing was said for some time. Then Becky broke the silence :

" Tom, I am so hungry ! "

Tom took something out of his pocket.

" Do you remember this ? " said he.

Becky almost smiled.

" It's our wedding cake, Tom."

" Yes—I wish it was as big as a barrel, for it's all we've got."

" I saved it from the picnic for us to dream on, Tom, the way grown-up people do with wedding cake—but it'll be our——"

She dropped the sentence where it was. Tom divided the cake, and Becky ate with good appetite, while Tom nibbled at his moiety. There was abundance of cold water to finish the feast with. By-and-by Becky suggested that they move on again. Tom was silent a moment. Then he said :

" Becky, can you bear it if I tell you something ? "

Becky's face paled, but she said she thought she could.

" Well then, Becky, we must stay here, where there's water to drink. That little piece is our last candle ! "

Becky gave loose to tears and wailings. Tom did what he could to comfort her, but with little effect. At length Becky said :

" Tom ! "

" Well, Becky ? "

" They'll miss us and hunt for us ! "

" Yes, they will ! Certainly they will ! "

" Maybe they're hunting for us now, Tom ? "

" Why, I reckon maybe they are ! I hope they are."

" When would they miss us, Tom ? "

" When they get back to the boat, I reckon."

" Tom, it might be dark, then—would they notice we hadn't come ? "

" I don't know. But anyway, your mother would miss you as soon as they got home."

A frightened look in Becky's face brought Tom to his senses, and he saw that he had made a blunder. Becky was not to have gone home that night ! The children became silent and thoughtful. In a moment a new burst of grief from Becky showed Tom that the thing in his mind had struck hers also—that the Sabbath morning might be half spent before Mrs. Thatcher discovered that Becky was not at Mrs. Harper's. The children fastened their eyes upon their bit of candle and watched it melt slowly and pitilessly away ; saw the half-inch of wick stand alone at last : saw the feeble flame rise and fall, rise and fall, climb the thin column of smoke, linger at its top a moment, and then—the horror of utter darkness reigned.

How long afterwards it was that Becky came to a slow consciousness that she was crying in Tom's arms, neither could tell. All that they knew was, that after what seemed a mighty stretch of time, both awoke out of a dead stupor of sleep, and resumed their miseries once more. Tom said it might be Sunday now—maybe Monday. He tried to get Becky to talk, but her sorrows were too oppressive, all her hopes were gone. Tom said that they must have been missed long ago, and no doubt the search was going on. He would shout, and maybe some one would come. He tried it ; but in the darkness the distant echoes sounded so hideously that he tried it no more.

The hours wasted away, and hunger came to torment the captives again. A portion of Tom's half of the cake was left ; they divided and ate it. But they seemed hungrier than before. The poor morsel of food only whetted desire.

By-and-by Tom said :

"*Sh !* Did you hear that ? "

Both held their breath and listened. There was a sound like the faintest far-off shout. Instantly Tom answered it, and leading Becky by the hand, started groping down the corridor in its direction. Presently he listened again ; again the sound was heard, and apparently a little nearer.

"It's them !" said Tom ; "they're coming ! Come along, Becky—we're all right now ! "

The joy of the prisoners was almost overwhelming. Their speed was slow, however, because pitfalls were somewhat common, and had to be guarded against. They shortly came to one, and had to stop. It might be three feet deep, it might be a hundred—there was no passing it, at any rate. Tom got down on his breast, and reached as far down as he could. No bottom. They must stay there and wait until the searchers came. They listened ; evidently the distant shoutings were growing more distant ! A moment or two more, and they had gone altogether. The heart-sinking misery of it ! Tom whooped until he was hoarse, but it was of no use. He talked hopefully to Becky ; but an age of anxious waiting passed and no sound came again.

The children groped their way back to the spring.

The weary time dragged on; they slept again, and awoke famished and woe-stricken. Tom believed it must be Tuesday by this time.

Now an idea struck him. There were some side-passages near at hand. It would be better to explore some of these than bear the weight of the heavy time in idleness. He took a kite-line from his pocket, tied it to a projection, and he and Becky started, Tom in the lead, unwinding the line as he groped along. At the end of twenty steps the corridor ended in a " jumping-off place." Tom got down on his knees and felt below, and then as far around the corner as he could reach with his hands conveniently; he made an effort to stretch yet a little further to the right, and at that moment, not twenty yards away, a human hand, holding a candle, appeared from behind a rock! Tom lifted up a glorious shout, and instantly that hand was followed by the body it belonged to—Injun Joe's! Tom was paralysed; he could not move. He was vastly gratified the next moment to see the " Spaniard " take to his heels and get himself out of sight. Tom wondered that Joe had not recognised his voice and come over and killed him for testifying in court. But the echoes must have disguised the voice. Without doubt that was it, he reasoned. Tom's fright weakened every muscle in his body. He said to himself that if he had strength enough to get back to the spring he would stay there, and nothing should tempt him to run the risk of meeting Injun Joe again. He was careful to keep from Becky what it was he had seen. He told her he had only shouted ' for luck."

But hunger and wretchedness rise superior to fears in the long run. Another tedious wait at the

spring, and another long sleep brought changes.
The children awoke, tortured with a raging hunger.
Tom believed it must be Wednesday or Thursday,
or even Friday or Saturday, now, and that the
search had been given over. He proposed to explore another passage. He felt willing to risk
Injun Joe and all other terrors. But Becky was
very weak. She had sunk into a dreary apathy,
and would not be roused. She said she would wait,
now, where she was, and die—it would not be long.
She told Tom to go with the kite-line and explore
if he chose; but she implored him to come back
every little while and speak to her; and she made
him promise that when the awful time came, he
would stay by her and hold her hand until all was
over. Tom kissed her, with a choking sensation in
his throat, and made a show of being confident of
finding the searchers or an escape from the cave;
then he took the kite-line in his hand and went
groping down one of the passages on his hands
and knees, distressed with hunger and sick with
bodings of coming doom.

CHAPTER XXXIII

TUESDAY afternoon came, and waned to the twilight.
The village of St. Petersburg still mourned. The
lost children had not been found. Public prayers
had been offered up for them, and many and many
a private prayer that had the petitioner's whole
heart in it ; but still no good news came from the
cave. The majority of the searchers had given up
the quest and gone back to their daily avocations,
saying that it was plain the children could never be
found. Mrs. Thatcher was very ill, and a great part
of the time delirious. People said it was heart-
breaking to hear her call her child, and raise her head
and listen a whole minute at a time, then lay it
wearily down again with a moan. Aunt Polly had
drooped into a settled melancholy, and her grey
hair had grown almost white. The village went to
its rest on Tuesday night, sad and forlorn.

Away in the middle of the night a wild peal burst
from the village bells, and in a moment the streets
were swarming with frantic half-clad people, who
shouted, " Turn out ! turn out ! they're found !
they're found ! " Tin pans and horns were added
to the din, the population massed itself and moved
towards the river, met the children coming in an
open carriage drawn by shouting citizens, thronged
around it, joined its homeward march, and swept

magnificently up the main street roaring huzza after huzza !

The village was illuminated ; nobody went to bed again ; it was the greatest night the little town had ever seen. During the first half-hour a procession of villagers filed through Judge Thatcher's house, seized the saved ones and kissed them, squeezed Mrs. Thatcher's hand, tried to speak but couldn't, and drifted out raining tears all over the place.

Aunt Polly's happiness was complete, and Mrs. Thatcher's nearly so. It would be complete, however, as soon as the messenger despatched with the great news to the cave should get the word to her husband.

Tom lay upon a sofa with an eager auditory about him, and told the history of the wonderful adventure, putting in many striking additions to adorn it withal ; and closed with a description of how he left Becky and went on an exploring expedition ; how he followed two avenues as far as his kite-line would reach ; how he followed a third to the fullest stretch of the kite-line, and was about to turn back when he glimpsed a far-off speck that looked like daylight ; dropped the line and groped towards it, pushed his head and shoulders through a small hole and saw the broad Mississippi rolling by ! And if it had only happened to be night he would not have seen that speck of daylight, and would not have explored that passage any more ! He told how he went back for Becky and broke the good news, and she told him not to fret her with such stuff, for she was tired, and knew she was going to die, and wanted to. He described how he laboured with her and convinced her, and how she almost died for joy when she had groped to where she actually saw the blue speck of daylight ; how he pushed his way out of the hole and then helped her out ; how they sat there and cried for gladness ; how some men came along in a skiff, and Tom hailed them and told them their situation and their famished condition ; how the men didn't believe the wild tale at first, " because," said they, " you are five miles down the river below the valley the cave is in ; " then took them aboard, rowed to a house, gave them supper, made them rest till two or three hours after dark, and then brought them home.

Before day-dawn Judge Thatcher and the handful of searchers with him were tracked out in the cave by the twine clews they had strung behind them, and informed of the great news.

Three days and nights of toil and hunger in the cave were not to be shaken off at once, as Tom and Becky soon discovered. They were bedridden all of Wednesday and Thursday, and seemed to grow more and more tired and worn all the time. Tom got about a little on Thursday, was down town on Friday, and nearly as whole as ever Saturday ; but Becky did not leave her room until Sunday, and then she looked as if she had passed through a wasting illness.

Tom learned of Huck's sickness, and went to see him on Friday, but could not be admitted to the bedroom ; neither could he on Saturday or Sunday. He was admitted daily after that, but was warned to keep still about his adventure and introduce no exciting topic. The Widow Douglas stayed by to see that he obeyed. At home Tom learned of the Cardiff Hill event ; also that the ragged man's body had eventually been found in the river near the ferry landing; he had been drowned while trying to escape perhaps.

About a fortnight after Tom's rescue from the cave he started off to visit Huck, who had grown plenty strong enough, now, to hear exciting talk, and Tom had some that would interest him, he thought. Judge Thatcher's house was on Tom's way, and he stopped to see Becky. The Judge and some friends set Tom to talking, and some one asked him ironically if he wouldn't like to go to the cave again. Tom said yes, he thought he wouldn't mind it.

The Judge said :

" Well, there are others just like you, Tom, I've not the least doubt. But we have taken care of that. Nobody will get lost in that cave any more."

" Why ? "

" Because I had its big door sheathed with boiler iron two weeks ago, and triple locked ; and I've got the keys."

Tom turned as white as a sheet.

" What's the matter, boy ? Here, run, somebody ! Fetch a glass of water ! "

The water was brought and thrown into Tom's face.

" Ah, now you're all right. What was the matter with you, Tom ? "

" Oh, Judge, Injun Joe's in the cave ! "

CHAPTER XXXIV

WITHIN a few minutes the news had spread, and a dozen skiff-loads of men were on their way to McDougal's cave, and the ferryboat, well filled with passengers, soon followed. Tom Sawyer was in the skiff that bore Judge Thatcher. When the cave door was unlocked, a sorrowful sight presented itself in the dim twilight of the place. Injun Joe lay stretched upon the ground, dead, with his face close to the crack of the door, as if his longing eyes had been fixed to the latest moment upon the light and the cheer of the free world outside. Tom was touched, for he knew by his own experience how this wretch had suffered. His pity was moved, but nevertheless he felt an abounding sense of relief and security, now, which revealed to him, in a degree which he had not fully appreciated before, how vast a weight of dread had been lying upon him since the day he lifted his voice against this bloody-minded outcast.

Injun Joe's bowie-knife lay close by, its blade broken in two. The great foundation-beam of the door had been chipped and hacked through with tedious labour ; useless labour, too, it was, for the native rock formed a sill outside it, and upon that stubborn material the knife had wrought no effect ; the only damage done was to the knife itself. But if there had been no stony obstruction there, labour would have been useless still, for if the beam had been wholly cut away Injun Joe could not have squeezed his body under the door, and he knew it. So he had only hacked that place in order to be doing something—in order to pass the weary time—in order to employ his tortured faculties. Ordinarily one could find half-a-dozen bits of candle stuck around in the crevices of this vestibule, left by tourists; but there were none, now. The prisoner had searched them out and eaten them. He had also contrived to catch a few bats, and these, also, he had eaten, leaving only their claws. The poor unfortunate had starved to death. In one place near at hand, a stalagmite had been slowly growing up from the ground for ages, builded by the water-drip from a stalactite overhead. The captive had broken off the stalagmite, and upon the stump had placed a stone wherein he had scooped a shallow hollow to catch the precious drop that fell once in every twenty minutes with the dreary regularity of a clock-tick—a dessert-spoonful once in four-and-twenty hours. That drop was falling when the Pyramids were new; when Troy fell; when the foundations of Rome were laid; when Christ was crucified; when the Conqueror created the British Empire; when Columbus sailed, when the massacre at Lexington was " news." It is falling now; it will still be falling when all these things shall have sunk down the afternoon of history and the twilight of tradition, and been swallowed up in the thick night of oblivion. Has everything a purpose and a mission? Did this drop fall patiently during five thousand years to be ready for this flitting human insect's need, and has it another important object to accomplish ten thousand years to come? No matter. It is many and many a year since the hapless half-breed scooped out the stone to catch the priceless drops, but to this day the tourist stares longest at that pathetic stone and that slow-dropping water when he comes to see the wonders of McDougal's cave. Injun Joe's cup stands first in the list of the cavern's marvels; even " Aladdin's Palace " cannot rival it.

Injun Joe was buried near the mouth of the cave; and people flocked there in boats and waggons from the town and from all the farms and hamlets for seven miles around; they brought their children, and all sorts of provisions, and confessed that they had had almost as satisfactory a time at the funeral as they could have had at the hanging.

This funeral stopped the further growth of one thing—the petition to the Governor for Injun Joe's pardon. The petition had been largely signed; many tearful and eloquent meetings had been held, and a committee of sappy women appointed to go in deep mourning and wail around the Governor, and implore him to be a merciful ass, and trample his duty under foot. Injun Joe was believed to have killed five citizens of the village, but what of that? If he had been Satan himself, there would have been plenty of weaklings ready to scribble their names to a pardon-petition, and drip a tear on it from their permanently impaired and leaky waterworks.

The morning after the funeral, Tom took Huck to a private place to have an important talk. Huck had learned all about Tom's adventure from the Welshman and the Widow Douglas by this time, but Tom said he reckoned there was one thing they had not told him; that thing was what he wanted to talk about now. Huck's face saddened. He said:

"I know what it is. You got into number two, and never found anything but whisky. Nobody told me it was you, but I just knowed it must a ben you, soon as I heard 'bout that whisky business; and I knowed you hadn't got the money becuz you'd a got at me some way or other, and told me, even if you was mum to everybody else. Tom, something's always told me we'd never get holt of that swag."

"Why, Huck, I never told on that tavern-keeper. You know his tavern was all right the Saturday I went to the picnic. Don't you remember you was to watch there that night?"

"Oh yes! Why, it seems 'bout a year ago. It was that very night that I follered Injun Joe to the widder's."

"You followed him?"

"Yes—but you keep mum. I reckon Injun Joe's left friends behind him. I don't want 'em souring on me, and doing me mean tricks. If it hadn't been for me he'd be down in Texas now, all right."

Then Huck told his entire adventure in confidence to Tom, who had only heard of the Welshman's part of it before.

"Well," said Huck presently, coming back to the main question, "whoever nipped the whisky in number two nipped the money too, I reckon—anyways it's a goner for us, Tom."

"Huck, that money wasn't ever in number two!"

"What!" Huck searched his comrade's face keenly. "Tom, have you got on the track of that money again?"

"Huck, it's in the cave!"

Huck's eyes blazed.

"Say it again, Tom!"

" The money's in the cave ! "

" Tom—honest injun, now—is it fun or earnest ? "

" Earnest, Huck—just as earnest as ever I was in my life. Will you go in there with me and help get it out ? "

" I bet I will ! I will if it's where we can blaze our way to it and not get lost."

" Huck, we can do that without the least little bit of trouble in the world."

" Good as wheat ! What makes you think the money's——"

" Huck, you just wait till we get in there. If we don't find it, I'll agree to give you my drum and everything I've got in the world. I will, by jings."

" All right—it's a whiz. When do you say ? "

" Right now, if you say it. Are you strong enough ? "

" Is it far in the cave ? I ben on my pins a little three or four days, now, but I can't walk more'n a mile, Tom—least I don't think I could."

" It's about five miles into there the way anybody but me would go, Huck, but there's a mighty short cut that they don't anybody but me know about. Huck, I'll take you right to it in a skiff. I'll float the skiff down there, and I'll pull it back again, all by myself. You needn't ever turn your hand over."

" Less start right off, Tom."

" All right. We want some bread and meat, and our pipes, and a little bag or two, and two or three kite-strings, and some of those newfangled things they call lucifer-matches. I tell you many's the time I wished I had some when I was in there before."

A trifle after noon the boys borrowed a small skiff

from a citizen who was absent, and got under way at once. When they were several miles below " Cave Hollow," Tom said :

" Now you see this bluff here looks all alike all the way down from the cave hollow—no houses, no wood-yards, bushes all alike. But do you see that white place up yonder where there's been a land-slide ? Well, that's one of my marks. We'll get ashore now."

They landed.

" Now, Huck, where we're a standing you could touch that hole I got out of with a fishing-pole. See if you can find it."

Huck searched all the place about, and found nothing. Tom proudly marched into a thick clump of sumach bushes and said :

" Here you are ! Look at it, Huck ; it's the snuggest hole in this country. You just keep mum about it. All along I've been wanting to be a robber, but I knew I'd got to have a thing like this, and where to run across it was the bother. We've got it now, and we'll keep it quiet, only we'll let Joe Harper and Ben Rogers in—because of course there's got to be a gang, or else there wouldn't be any style about it. Tom Sawyer's Gang—it sounds splendid, don't it, Huck ? "

" Well, it just does, Tom. And who'll we rob ? "

" Oh, 'most anybody. Waylay people—that's mostly the way."

" And kill them."

" No—not always. Hive them in the cave till they raise a ransom ! "

" What's a ransom ? "

" Money. You make them raise all they can off'n their friends, and after you've kept them a year, if it ain't raised then you kill them. That's the general way. Only you don't kill the women. You shut up the women, but you don't kill them. They're always beautiful and rich, and awfully scared. You take their watches and things, but you always take your hat off and talk polite. They ain't anybody as polite as robbers—you'll see that in any book. Well, the women get to loving you, and after they've been in the cave a week or two weeks they stop crying, and after that you couldn't get them to leave. If you drove them out, they'd turn right around and come back. It's so in all the books."

"Why, it's real bully, Tom. I b'lieve it's better'n to be a pirate."

"Yes, it's better in some ways, because it's close to home, and circuses, and all that."

By this time everything was ready and the boys entered the hole, Tom in the lead. They toiled their way to the farther end of the tunnel, then made their spliced kite-strings fast and moved on. A few steps brought them to the spring, and Tom felt a shudder quiver all through him. He showed Huck the fragment of candle-wick perched on a lump of clay against the wall, and described how he and Becky had watched the flame struggle and expire.

The boys began to quiet down to whispers, now, for the stillness and gloom of the place oppressed their spirits. They went on, and presently entered and followed Tom's other corridor until they reached the "jumping-off place." The candles revealed the fact that it was not really a precipice, but only a steep clay hill, twenty or thirty feet high. Tom whispered:

"Now I'll show you something, Huck."

He held his candle aloft and said:

" Look as far around the corner as you can. Do you see that? There—on the big rock over yonder —done with candle smoke."

" Tom, it's a *cross*!"

" Now where's your number two? '*Under the cross*,' hey? Right yonder's where I saw Injun Joe poke up his candle, Huck!"

Huck stared at the mystic sign a while, and then said with a shaky voice:

" Tom, less git out of here!"

" What! and leave the treasure?"

" Yes—leave it. Injun Joe's ghost is round about there, certain."

" No it ain't, Huck, no it ain't. It would ha'nt the place where he died—away out at the mouth of the cave—five mile from here."

" No, Tom, it wouldn't. It would hang round the money. I know the ways of ghosts, and so do you."

Tom began to fear that Huck was right. Misgivings gathered in his mind. But presently an idea occurred to him.

" Looky here, Huck, what fools we're making of ourselves! Injun Joe's ghost ain't a going to come around where there's a cross!"

The point was well taken. It had its effect.

" Tom, I didn't think of that. But that's so. It's luck for us, that cross is. I reckon we'll climb down there, and have a hunt for that box."

Tom went first, cutting rude steps in the clay hill as he descended. Huck followed. Four avenues opened out of the small cavern which the great rock stood in. The boys examined three of them with no result. They found a small recess in the one nearest the base of the rock, with a pallet of blankets spread down in it; also an old suspender, some bacon rind, and the well-gnawed bones of two or three fowls. But there was no money-box. The lads searched and re-searched this place, but in vain. Tom said:

"He said *under* the cross. Well, this comes nearest to being under the cross. It can't be under the rock itself, because that sets solid on the ground."

They searched everywhere once more, and then sat down discouraged. Huck could suggest nothing. By-and-by Tom said:

"Looky here, Huck; there's footprints and some candle-grease on the clay about one side of this rock, but not on the other sides. Now, what's that for. I bet you the money *is* under the rock. I'm going to dig in the clay."

"That ain't no bad notion, Tom!" said Huck, with animation.

Tom's "real Barlow" was out at once, and he had not dug four inches before he struck wood.

"Hey, Huck! you hear that?"

Huck began to dig and scratch now. Some boards were soon uncovered and removed. They had concealed a natural chasm which led under the rock. Tom got into this and held his candle as far under the rock as he could, but said he could not see to the end of the rift. He proposed to explore. He stooped and passed under; the narrow way descended gradually. He followed its winding course, first to the right, then to the left, Huck at his heels. Tom turned a short curve by-and-by, and exclaimed:

"My goodness, Huck, looky here!"

It was the treasure-box, sure enough, occupying a snug little cavern, along with an empty powderkeg, a couple of guns in leather cases, two or three pairs of old moccasins, a leather belt, and some other rubbish well soaked with the water-drip.

" Got it at last ! " said Huck, ploughing among the tarnished coins with his hand. " My, but we're rich, Tom ! "

" Huck, I always reckoned we'd get it. It's just too good to believe, but we *have* got it, sure ! Say, let's not fool around here, let's snake it out. Lemme see if I can lift the box."

It weighed about fifty pounds. Tom could lift it after an awkward fashion, but could not carry it conveniently.

" I thought so," he said ; " they carried it like it was heavy that day at the ha'nted house—I noticed that. I reckon I was right to think of fetching the little bags along."

The money was soon in the bags, and the boys took it up to the cross rock.

" Now let's fetch the guns and things," said Huck.

" No, Huck, leave them there. They're just the tricks to have when we go to robbing. We'll keep them there all the time, and we'll hold our orgies there, too. It's an awful snug place for orgies."

" What's orgies ? "

" I donno. But robbers always have orgies, and of course we've got to have them too. Come along, Huck, we've been in here a long time. It's getting late, I reckon. I'm hungry, too. We'll eat and smoke when we get to the skiff."

They presently emerged into the clump of sumach bushes, looked warily out, found the coast clear, and were soon lunching and smoking in the skiff. As the sun dipped towards the horizon they pushed out and got under way. Tom skimmed up the shore through the long twilight, chatting cheerily with Huck, and landed shortly after dark.

" Now, Huck," said Tom, " we'll hide the money in the loft of the widow's wood-shed, and I'll come up in the morning and we'll count and divide, and then we'll hunt up a place out in the woods for it where it will be safe. Just you lay quiet here and watch the stuff till I run and hook Benny Taylor's little waggon. I won't be gone a minute."

He disappeared, and presently returned with the waggon, put the two small sacks into it, threw some old rags on top of them, and started off, dragging his cargo behind him. When the boys reached the Welshman's house they stopped to rest. Just as they were about to move on, the Welshman stepped out and said :

" Hullo, who's that ? "

" Huck and Tom Sawyer."

" Good ! Come along with me, boys, you are keeping everybody waiting. Here, hurry up, trot ahead ; I'll haul the waggon for you Why, it's not as light as it might be. Got bricks in it, or old metal ? "

" Old metal," said Tom.

" I judged so ; the boys in this town will take more trouble and fool away more time hunting up six bits' worth of old iron to sell to the foundry, than they would to make twice the money at regular work. But that's human nature. Hurry along, hurry along ! "

The boys wanted to know what the hurry was about.

" Never mind ; you'll see when we get to the Widow Douglas's."

Huck said with some apprehension, for he was long used to being falsely accused :

"Mr. Jones, we haven't been doing nothing."

The Welshman laughed.

"Well, I don't know, Huck, my boy. I don't know about that. Ain't you and the widow good friends ? "

"Yes. Well, she's been a good friend to me, any ways."

"All right, then. What do you want to be afraid for ? "

This question was not entirely answered in Huck's slow mind before he found himself pushed, along with Tom, into Mrs. Douglas's drawing-room. Mr. Jones left the waggon near the door and followed.

The place was grandly lighted, and everybody that was of any consequence in the village was there. The Thatchers were there, the Harpers, the Rogerses, Aunt Polly, Sid, Mary, the minister, the editor, and a great many more, and all dressed in their best. The widow received the boys as heartily as any one could well receive two such looking beings. They were covered with clay and candle-grease. Aunt Polly blushed crimson with humiliation, and frowned and shook her head at Tom. Nobody suffered half as much as the two boys did, however. Mr. Jones said :

"Tom wasn't at home, yet, so I gave him up ; but I stumbled on him and Huck right at my door, and so I just brought them along in a hurry."

"And you did just right," said the widow. "Come with me, boys."

She took them to a bedchamber, and said :

"Now wash and dress yourselves. Here are two new suits of clothes—shirts, socks, everything com-

plete. They're Huck's—no, no thanks, Huck—
Mr. Jones bought one and I the other. But they'll
fit both of you. Get into them. We'll wait—
come down when you are slicked up enough."

Then she left.

CHAPTER XXXV

Huck said :

"Tom, we can slope if we can find a rope. The window ain't high from the ground."

"Shucks! what do you want to slope for?"

"Well, I ain't used to that kind of a crowd. I can't stand it. I ain't going down there, Tom."

"Oh, bother! It ain't anything. I don't mind it a bit. I'll take care of you."

Sid appeared.

"Tom," said he, "auntie has been waiting for you all the afternoon. Mary got your Sunday clothes ready, and everybody's been fretting about you. Say, ain't this grease and clay on your clothes?"

"Now, Mr. Siddy, you just 'tend to your own business. What's all this blow-out about, anyway?"

"It's one of the widow's parties that she's always having. This time it's for the Welshman and his sons, on account of that scrape they helped her out of the other night. And say—I can tell you something, if you want to know."

"Well, what?"

"Why, old Mr. Jones is going to try to spring something on the people here to-night, but I overheard him tell auntie to-day about it, as a secret, but I reckon it's not much of a secret now. Everybody knows—the widow, too, for all she tries to let on she don't. Oh, Mr. Jones was bound Huck should be here—couldn't get along with his grand secret without Huck, you know ! "

" Secret about what, Sid ? "

" About Huck tracking the robbers to the widow's. I reckon Mr. Jones was going to make a grand time over his surprise, but I bet you it will drop pretty flat."

Sid chuckled in a very contented and satisfied way.

" Sid, was it you that told ? "

" Oh, never mind who it was. Somebody told, that's enough."

" Sid, there's only one person in this town mean enough to do that, and that's you. If you had been in Huck's place you'd a sneaked down the hill and never told anybody on the robbers. You can't do any but mean things, and you can't bear to see anybody praised for doing good ones. There—no thanks, as the widow says." And Tom cuffed Sid's ears and helped him to the door with several kicks. " Now go and tell auntie if you dare, and to-morrow you'll catch it ! "

Some minutes later the widow's guests were at the supper-table, and a dozen children were propped up at little side-tables in the same room, after the fashion of that country and day. At the proper time Mr. Jones made his little speech, in which he thanked the widow for the honour she was doing himself and his sons, but said that there was another person whose modesty—

And so forth and so on. He sprang his secret about Huck's share in the adventure in the finest dramatic manner he was master of, but the surprise it occasioned was largely counterfeit, and not as clamorous and effusive as it might have been under happier circumstances. However, the widow made a pretty fair show of astonishment, and heaped so many compliments and so much gratitude upon Huck, that he almost forgot the nearly intolerable discomfort of his new clothes in the entirely intolerable discomfort of being set up as a target for everybody's gaze and everybody's laudations.

The widow said she meant to give Huck a home under her roof and have him educated; and that when she could spare the money she would start him in business in a modest way. Tom's chance was come. He said:

"Huck don't need it. Huck's rich!"

Nothing but a heavy strain upon the good manners of the company kept back the due and proper complimentary laugh at this pleasant joke. But the silence was a little awkward. Tom broke it.

"Huck's got money. Maybe you don't believe it, but he's got lots of it. Oh, you needn't smile; I reckon I can show you. You just wait a minute."

Tom ran out of doors. The company looked at each other with a perplexed interest, and inquiringly at Huck, who was tongue-tied.

"Sid, what ails Tom?" said Aunt Polly. "He —well, there ain't ever any making of that boy out. I never——"

Tom entered, struggling with the weight of his sacks, and Aunt Polly did not finish her sentence. Tom poured the mass of yellow coin upon the table and said:

"There—what did I tell you? Half of it's Huck's, and half of it's mine!"

The spectacle took the general breath away. All gazed, nobody spoke for a moment. Then there was a unanimous call for an explanation. Tom said he could furnish it, and he did. The tale was long, but brimful of interest. There was scarcely an interruption from any one to break the charm of its flow. When he had finished, Mr. Jones said :

" I thought I had fixed up a little surprise for this occasion, but it don't amount to anything now. This one makes it sing mighty small, I'm willing to allow."

The money was counted. The sum amounted to a little over twelve thousand dollars. It was more than any one present had ever seen at one time before, though several persons were there who were worth considerably more than that in property.

CHAPTER XXXVI

THE reader may rest satisfied that Tom's and Huck's windfall made a mighty stir in the poor little village of St. Petersburg. So vast a sum, all in actual cash, seemed next to incredible. It was talked about, gloated over, glorified, until the reason of many of the citizens tottered under the strain of the unhealthy excitement. Every "haunted" house in St. Petersburg and the neighbouring villages was dissected, plank by plank, and its foundations dug up and ransacked for hidden treasures— and not by boys, but men—pretty grave, unromantic men, too, some of them. Wherever Tom and Huck appeared they were courted, admired, stared at. The boys were not able to remember that their remarks had possessed weight before; but now their sayings were treasured and repeated; everything they did seemed somehow to be regarded as remarkable; they had evidently lost the power of doing and saying commonplace things; moreover, their past history was raked up and discovered to bear marks of conspicuous originality. The village paper published biographical sketches of the boys.

The Widow Douglas put Huck's money out at six per cent., and Judge Thatcher did the same with Tom's at Aunt Polly's request. Each lad had an income now that was simply prodigious—

a dollar for every week-day in the year and half of the Sundays. It was just what the minister got—no, it was what he was promised—he generally couldn't collect it. A dollar and a quarter a week would board, lodge, and school a boy in those old simple days—and clothe him and wash him, too, for that matter.

Judge Thatcher had conceived a great opinion of Tom. He said that no commonplace boy would ever have got his daughter out of the cave. When Becky told her father, in strict confidence, how Tom had taken her whipping at school, the Judge was visibly moved; and when she pleaded grace for the mighty lie which Tom had told in order to shift that whipping from her shoulders to his own, the Judge said with a fine outburst that it was a noble, a generous, a magnanimous lie—a lie that was worthy to hold up its head and march down through history breast to breast with George Washington's lauded Truth about the hatchet! Becky thought her father had never looked so tall and so superb as when he walked the floor and stamped his foot and said that. She went straight off and told Tom about it.

Judge Thatcher hoped to see Tom a great lawyer or a great soldier some day. He said he meant to look to it that Tom should be admitted to the National Military Academy, and afterwards trained in the best law-school in the country, in order that he might be ready for either career, or both.

Huck Finn's wealth, and the fact that he was under the Widow Douglas's protection, introduced him into society—no, dragged him into it, hurled him into it—and his sufferings were almost more than he could bear. The widow's servants kept him clean and neat, combed and brushed, and they bedded him nightly in unsympathetic sheets that had not one little spot or stain which he could press to his heart and know for a friend. He had to eat with knife and fork; he had to use napkin, cup, and plate; he had to learn his book; he had to go to church; he had to talk so properly that speech was become insipid in his mouth; whithersoever he turned, the bars and shackles of civilisation shut him in and bound him hand and foot.

He bravely bore his miseries three weeks, and then one day turned up missing. For forty-eight hours the widow hunted for him everywhere in great distress. The public were profoundly concerned; they searched high and low, they dragged the river for his body. Early the third morning Tom Sawyer wisely went poking among some old empty hogsheads down behind the abandoned slaughterhouse, and in one of them he found the refugee. Huck had slept there; he had just breakfasted upon some stolen odds and ends of food, and was lying oft, now, in comfort with his pipe. He was unkempt, uncombed, and clad in the same old ruin of rags that had made him picturesque in the days when he was free and happy. Tom routed him out, told him the trouble he had been causing, and urged him to go home. Huck's face lost its tranquil content and took a melancholy cast. He said:

"Don't talk about it, Tom. I've tried it, and it don't work; it don't work, Tom. It ain't for me; I ain't used to it. The widder's good to me, and friendly; but I can't stand them ways. She makes me git up just at the same time every morning; she makes me wash, they comb me all to thunder; she won't let me sleep in the wood-shed; I got to wear them blamed clothes that just smothers me, Tom; they don't seem to any air git through 'em, somehow; and they're so rotten nice that I can't set down, nor lay down, nor roll around any-wheres; I hain't slid on a cellar-door for—well, it 'pears to be years; I got to go to church, and sweat and sweat—I hate them ornery sermons! I can't ketch a fly in there, I can't chaw, I got to wear shoes all Sunday. The widder eats by a bell; she goes to bed by a bell; she gits up by a bell— everything's so awful reg'lar a body can't stand it."

"Well, everybody does that way, Huck."

"Tom, it don't make no difference. I ain't every-body, and I can't stand it. It's awful to be tied up so. And grub comes too easy—I don't take no interest in vittles that way. I got to ask to go a fishing; I got to ask to go in a swimming— dern'd if I hain't got to ask to do everything. Well, I'd got to talk so nice it wasn't no comfort; I'd got to go up in the attic and rip out a while every day to git a taste in my mouth, or I'd a died, Tom. The widder wouldn't let me smoke, she wouldn't let me yell, she wouldn't let me gape, nor stretch, nor scratch before folks." Then with a spasm of special irritation and injury: "And dad fetch it, she prayed all the time! I never see such a woman! I had to shove, Tom, I just had to. And besides, that school's going to open, and I'd a had to go to it; well, I wouldn't stand that, Tom. Looky here, Tom, being rich ain't what it's cracked up to be. It's just worry and worry, and sweat and sweat, and a wishing you was dead all the time. Now these clothes suits me and this bar'l suits me, and

I ain't ever going to shake 'em any more. Tom, I wouldn't ever got into all this trouble if it hadn't a ben for that money ; now you just take my sheer of it along with yourn, and gimme a ten-center sometimes—not many times, becuz I don't give a dern for a thing 'thout it's tollable hard to git —and you go and beg off for me with the widder."

"Oh, Huck, you know I can't do that. 'Tain't fair ; and besides, if you'll try this thing just a while longer you'll come to like it."

"Like it ! Yes—the way I'd like a hot stove if I was to set on it long enough. No, Tom, I won't be rich, and I won't live in them cussed smothery houses. I like the woods, and the river, and hogs-heads, and I'll stick to 'em too. Blame it all ! just as we'd got guns, and a cave, and all just fixed to rob, here this dern foolishness has got to come up and spile it all ! "

Tom saw his opportunity :

"Looky here, Huck, being rich ain't going to keep me back from turning robber."

"No ! Oh, good licks, are you in real dead-wood earnest, Tom ? "

"Just as dead earnest as I'm a sitting here. But, Huck, we can't let you into the gang if you ain't respectable, you know."

Huck's joy was quenched.

"Can't let me in, Tom ? Didn't you let me go for a pirate ? "

"Yes, but that's different. A robber is more high-toned than what a pirate is—as a general thing. In most countries they're awful high up in the nobility—dukes and such."

"Now, Tom, hain't you always ben friendly to me ? You wouldn't shet me out, would you,

Tom? You wouldn't do that, now, would you, Tom?"

"Huck, I wouldn't want to and I don't want to, but what would people say? Why, they'd say, 'Mph! Tom Sawyer's Gang! pretty low characters in it!' They'd mean you, Huck. You wouldn't like that, and I wouldn't."

Huck was silent for some time, engaged in a mental struggle. Finally he said:

"Well, I'll go back to the widder for a month and tackle it, and see if I can come to stand it, if you'll let me b'long to the gang, Tom."

"All right, Huck, it's a whiz! Come along, old chap, and I'll ask the widow to let up on you a little, Huck."

"Will you, Tom, now will you? That's good. If she'll let up on some of the roughest things, I'll smoke private and cuss private, and crowd through or bust. When you going to start the gang and turn robbers?"

"Oh, right off. We'll get the boys together, and have the initiation to-night, maybe."

"Have the which?"

"Have the initiation."

"What's that?"

"It's to swear to stand by one another, and never tell the gang's secrets, even if you're chopped all to flinders, and kill anybody and all his family that hurts one of the gang."

"That's gay—that's mighty gay, Tom, I tell you."

"Well, I bet it is. And all that swearing's got to be done at midnight, in the lonesomest, awfulest place you can find—a ha'nted house is the best, but they're all ripped up, now."

"Well, midnight's good, anyway, Tom."

" Yes, so it is. And you've got to swear on a coffin, and sign it with blood."

" Now that's something like! Why, it's a million times bullier than pirating. I'll stick to the widder till I rot, Tom; and if I git to be a reg'lar ripper of a robber, and everybody talking 'bout it, I reckon she'll be proud she snaked me in out of the wet."

CONCLUSION

So endeth this chronicle. It being strictly a history of a boy, it must stop here ; the story could not go much further without becoming the history of a man. When one writes a novel about grown people, he knows exactly where to stop—that is, with a marriage ; but when he writes of juveniles, he must stop where he best can.

Most of the characters that perform in this book still live, and are prosperous and happy. Some day it may seem worth while to take up the story of the younger ones again, and see what sort of men and women they turned out to be ; therefore it will be wisest not to reveal any of that part of their lives at present.

THE END